The Clock Tower Treasure

Victor Hess

*Cheryl,
Be like the community
that helped Jesse
along.
Victor Hess*

BROTHER MOCKINGBIRD • DIAMONDHEAD, MISSISSIPPI

Copyright ©2019 by Victor Hess
All rights reserved
This is a work of fiction. Names, characters, businesses, places, events, locales, and incidents are either the products of the author's imagination or used in a fictitious manner. Any resemblance to actual persons, living or dead, or actual events is purely coincidental.

Library of Congress Control Number: 2019938684

Cover Design by: Janet Dado, iampersevere@gmail.com

No part of this book may be reproduced or transmitted in any form or by any means without written permission from the publisher.

For information please contact:
Brother Mockingbird, LLC
www.brothermockingbird.org
ISBN: 978-1-7322155-8-0
First Edition

Dedicated to Carol Jean, Brian, Stephen, Christina, Tony, Paul, Clark, Cheryl, Debbie, Joyce, Jenny, Jerry, Candie, and all cousins and siblings, brave, loyal, and keepers of secrets.

Chapter One
Advice from a Dead Man

Behind the Bigley Funeral Home was a small brick building that used to store tools until this guy was found dead at the edge of Sabina, Ohio. They cleaned out the shed and laid the corpse out inside, so people could come by to try and identify him. That was twenty-six years ago, 1929, and he's still there. People from everywhere came to see Eugene and write their name in his visitor's book. Tonight, it was locked, so I pulled out my knife to jimmy the latch like my friend Karen showed me. I looked around through the mist to be sure no one could see me. Once in, I closed the door and flipped the light on.

Both of my closest friends were girls. Lynn was almost ten years old, like me and lived downstairs from us. Karen was nineteen and lived across the street. Karen told me she liked to visit Eugene when she had some problem to fix. Eugene was a temporary name they gave to that dead man. Even though he never spoke, she said just talking to him seemed to inspire the right answer in solving her problems, although she was so cool, I never thought she had any problems.

Eugene lay there in his small room, waiting, arms on stomach, and his gold tooth glistening from the bare light bulb.

"Hi, Eugene. It's Jesse." I offered. "Karen, you know, the clerk at Knisely's Five and Dime. She said you helped her think through her problems. Can you help me?" I stepped toward him.

"I have to move, and I'm not happy about it. We're moving in with my brothers and their dad. You know, Gary and Danny. They were here yesterday." I leaned my head against the chicken wire that separated Eugene from the people who came to see him. It was very quiet in the room.

"We've lived here a whole year and now that I have friends and a paper route, Mom wants us to move." I backed away and put my hands in my pockets.

"I don't want to go. I like it here." I turned and glanced up at the wall, covered with news clippings about Eugene.

"By the way, how did you end up in Sabina? You don't know anyone here, cause by now you'd have a real name and a headstone in the cemetery.

"Did someone drive you here and drop you off? Did you stay with someone here? What were you looking for?" The article I was looking at had a photo of Eugene taken before they put up the chicken wire.

"My dad made a mess of it. He hurt Mom and now we're split up. Did you make a mess of it?" I stared at him. His eyes were closed, like he was sleeping or praying. He was wearing a suit, white shirt and tie, ready for burial.

"Did you gamble. Did you get drunk? Is that what you did? That's what my dad did.

"How come you didn't have any identification? Did the guys that found you take your billfold? They said all they found was a piece of paper with an address. Look, it's right here in this article about you." I pointed at the framed article from the Wilmington paper.

"They said they found you lying in a ditch by the Cantrell farm. What happened?

"Were you sick? They said you died of a heart attack.

"Do you have kids? Because, if you do, I wonder why they didn't look for you?"

I waited, staring at the sign on the wall describing Eugene's history. I'd read it a hundred times, and he was still a mystery. I tried to imagine him alive, back in 1929, walking through Sabina. I wondered if he was wearing a suit when he was found.

"Did you have a wife? Did you guys fight a lot?" I waited after each question, like he was really going to answer me.

The pamphlet never said where he was from, only that a Cincinnati address was found in his pocket.

"Where did you sleep the night before you died?" I asked him questions the pamphlet didn't answer, so I waited for a sign or something. Anything. But nothing happened.

"You know. Once you're identified, they're going to bury you. They say you're just good for business. Did you know that? More than a million people have visited you. Did you know that?" I studied the visitor's book counting the different states people came from.

"My dad is supposed to pay us child support, but he's always late or skips a week. Mom says we won't have to worry about that in Xenia. She won't need his money anymore, because Albert's going to take care of us. Albert is Gary and Danny's dad. She divorced him once. I wonder why she would even want to get back with him.

"Mom's been singing a lot since she told me about us moving. You should hear her sing. She's really good. Maybe you remember when she came here. She brought me the first time I met you.

"I guess I'm lucky. It's a new house. She said we have to move on." I was back clinging to the chicken wire.

"It's not fair. Everyone else who comes to Bigley's gets their own grave with their name on it. All you get is this shed and a borrowed name. Once you're identified, maybe then, I bet, you'll have your family."

Suddenly, I heard the doorknob jostle. I reached over and flipped off the light and hid behind the table that held Eugene's visitor book. The door opened.

"Jesse. Are you in here? It's me, Karen." She flipped on the light. I stood up.

"How did you know I was here?" I was glad it was her.

"It's the first place I'd look. There was a light under the door," she said. "Your mom is worried sick. What are you doing in here?"

She quietly closed the door.

"I have a big decision. I thought Eugene could help." I walked toward Eugene.

"Well, Eugene, did you help Jesse?" She turned to Eugene with her hands on her hips. I edged closer to her.

We both stared at him. I was waiting for him to nod or utter some wise words. She reached for my hand. I tingled at her touch. I always did.

"We're moving, but not 'til Christmas. I'll miss you," I said.

"We're gonna miss you, too, Jesse. Right, Eugene?" Then she turned to me. "I think we're the only ones who talk to him." I was still looking at Eugene's face, waiting for some sign but he just lay there, still dead.

"Shh." She flipped off the light. We heard steps. They stopped, then continued down the street.

"Let's go, Jesse. Bye, Eugene." She smiled at him. Her face was beautiful.

She opened the door slowly and peeked outside. "C'mon."

We walked quietly for a few minutes.

"We could always write each other, Jesse. Your mom told me about your new house. I bet Mr. Davis could get you a paper route in Xenia. You'd make a lot more money there. You need to ask him about that. It's a big city. Xenia's a lot bigger than Wilmington. You'd have some keen stories to tell your new friends. Like bustin' up the purse snatching kids."

"Mike Stafford still doesn't talk to me. Do you think he knows I'm the one who took that picture that got him caught?"

"Does that bother you?"

"A little. I wanted to see his dad's car showroom. I've never been in a show room."

"You sure like your cars."

"I want to see the new Ford Thunderbird."

"Me, too. That's one fine car, Jesse," she said.

She held my hand all the way home. She was like a big sister.

Victor Hess

Chapter Two
Wedding Announcement

When Karen and I got home, Joyce, our back-door neighbor, was there with Mom at the kitchen table along with Lynn and her mom, Arlene. Even though Karen said Mom was worried sick for me, once I walked into that room, obviously safe and unharmed, Mom stood up so quickly it was clear she had no further concern for my welfare.

"Where have you been, Jesse Leon Hall?" She had that look. I didn't think I was gone that long. Her look made me glad there were witnesses. Otherwise, she would have probably broken a yardstick paddling my butt. She was a seamstress and had a yardstick in every room of our apartment.

"I had to see Eugene."

"You're lucky you're not laid out on display in that shed with him, young man," she said. The look was still pinned on her face.

Then Arlene started laughing.

"This is serious!" Mom said, still staring at me.

"I know, Vi. I'm sorry. I'm just picturing people lined up to see a dead colored man and white boy on display in that shed."

"Mama! That's terrible," Lynn said.

Then Karen started laughing. "It would be good for business."

"But Viola, who'd you get to baby sit Christina?" Joyce asked. Mom's face melted into a different look. Not quite a smile, but I felt suddenly safe from that paddling.

We gathered around the little kitchen table reliving the story about Eugene being stolen and tied onto Karen's front porch post last Halloween by some college fraternity. Karen opened her purse and pulled out the Polaroid of us kids in Halloween costumes posed next to Eugene with a black hat cocked on his head.

"Now, that's a family picture," Joyce said, holding it out for all to see.

It was true. Our little neighborhood was like a family.

"Well, when's the big day?" Joyce asked, looking directly at Arlene.

To my relief, the subject was changed to Arlene's wedding.

"June 11th. We already met with the pastor of the Methodist Church. It'll be a small wedding. Can you come?"

Brian Baker and Arlene had been dating each other for almost a year and everyone knew they were crazy for each other. A wedding was the next logical step.

I looked over at Lynn and motioned toward my room. We left them talking.

Lynn Ott was my best friend and lived downstairs from us with her mom. When we weren't in school, we spent most of our time together delivering my newspapers, babysitting my little sister, collecting bottles, and scrounging vending machine change slots for forgotten coins. We were a team, one from two parts, not obligated, just connected, inseparable. Ever since she and her mom moved in, we were like brother and sister. Even though we were best friends, I don't remember either one of us ever telling the other that.

We sat on my bed with our backs propped against the wall.

"What were you doing in Eugene's shed?"

"I had to sort things out, you know, like Karen does when she talks to Eugene."

"You're both weird. Have you talked to your mom yet?

When are you moving? "

"Not 'til Christmas. The house has to be built first."

"That's not so bad."

Lynn began checking my paper route book. I handed her $3.45 out of my pocket.

"What's this?"

"Owens and Knisely, plus a quarter tip. I collected it before I went to see Eugene. You're lucky to get Brian as a dad. He's done more for me than my dad ever did. He'll be a good dad," I said, as she recorded the money in my route book.

Brian Baker was a deputy sheriff and the assistant coach of the Little League team. Even though I didn't make the team last year, he worked with me and another boy all summer, so we could improve enough to make the tryout this year. He even got me a Rawlings fielder's glove last year for my birthday.

The bed squeaked as Lynn scooted off.

"We're going to move to a bigger place after the wedding. I wish you could come with us," she said pulling my storage chest out from under the bed, opening the secret compartment and placing the money in my money bag.

"You're gonna stay in Sabina, aren't you?"

"Oh, yeah. We can still see each other until you move." She then latched the secret compartment in my chest.

"I figure we have eight months before I move to Xenia, unless a miracle happens with my dad. Can you still help with the paper route?"

"Sure. What do you mean a miracle?"

"I think he can stop drinking and gambling. If he does, then Mom and him can get back together."

"It doesn't sound like he wants to change." I don't think she meant her words to hurt my feelings, but they did. She started dealing cards on the bed. "I don't think your mom wants that, either," she said.

I laid the nine of clubs on the nine of diamonds in the

discard pile. She played an eight and changed the suit to diamonds. I played an eight and changed it back to clubs.

"Momma said Vi will let me stay here while she works. Is that okay?"

"Swell. I'm going to see if I can get a route in Xenia when we move. Karen says it's a bigger city. Maybe I'll get a bigger route."

"You'll need a bike then."

I always wanted a bike, but every time I would save for one, we'd have an emergency pop up like Dad missing a child support payment or having to pay down one of our charges at the Corner Market or the Five and Dime.

We kept playing Crazy Eights until Mom yelled for me to change Christina's diaper.

"I win. Sixty-three to one-oh-five," Lynn said.

"I'll get you next time," I said and helped her gather up the cards.

When we returned to the living room, Lynn left me with Christina on the couch and joined in the wedding discussion at the kitchen table.

"Oh, Jesse, Brian and I would like you to sing at our wedding. Lynn said you have a beautiful voice," Arlene said.

"Really? I've never sung at a wedding," I said. I sang "God Bless America" once at one of our school assemblies.

"Then it will be the first time for both of us. I've never been married before. Brian thinks it's a great idea."

After I changed Christina's diaper, I held her up, feet on my lap, with her legs straight. Bright-eyed, she squealed with a big smile, while pulling on my ear.

She was not even one year old but could smile, hold, hug and when hungry, demand. The way she demanded was in stages. It began with her smile going away, then an attention getting grunt, accompanied by a clinching of her body, squinting of her eyes and, if by then, you have not figured out what she wanted, she would start crying, which quickly evolved into a scream. But, not tonight. Mom must have fed her.

"You're moving to a new house," I said and then blew raspberries on her bare tummy. She giggled.

From the couch, I could see the four women discussing Arlene's wedding. Lynn stood behind her mom, and all faces were smiling as they talked about the wedding day and how they had to do the reception because hiring someone was too expensive. After all, it was the bride's responsibility. Arlene described the blue suit she would wear and how practical it would be because then she could wear it to work if she got a better job. As the conversation continued, Lynn glowed. Every time Brian's name was mentioned, she smiled, obviously happy to have a father after nine years.

Joyce talked about practical things. What time would the wedding start? How would Andy, her husband, get the reception refreshments to the church in time while picking up Lynn, me and the twins? Who would get the bride? Karen volunteered to take us when she and her parents left. Then everyone wondered how the Corner Market and Knisely's Five and Dime could stay open when everyone who worked there was at the wedding.

"Let's write that down," Joyce offered when they discovered a little dilemma like that. Soon there were pages of notes.

Mom's smile faded, and I was sure she was tired, but she looked sad, too. Arlene and Brian's wedding was moving along a lot faster than our new house in Xenia.

Mom's bedroom and mine were separated by a glass door. I could only get to mine by walking through hers. Actually, my bedroom was more like a big closet with a little bed in it.

I had a window I left open for the evening breeze. I could hear the frogs, the night birds, and smell the farms. Our little town was in the middle of farm country and planting season just started, where the ground was plowed and disked, churning up all sorts of aromas from the earth. There was a newness to it, and each gust of wind brought the fresh reminder a new season had begun. This would be hard to leave. This town had saved us. I couldn't imagine spending time anywhere else.

A year ago, Mom brought me here, the last stop of more than six moves. Sabina magically freed Mom from my dad's abuse.

We were poor in Sabina, but never hungry, cold, or homeless. The years we lived with Dad, a man who couldn't straighten himself out, only brought hardships. Dad got violent with Mom when he was drunk and desperate, and I admired her gumption to leave him, especially when she was pregnant, but that's another story. Mom said it was a miracle to find someone in Sabina to rent to us when we were so poor. Other little miracles happened, and many days, we needed miracles to eat or pay the rent.

I always hoped Grandpa Hall's lessons, like, *first do no harm,* and, *second, do all the good you can,* would work on my dad. Grandpa was my dad's dad and I admired him more than anyone. Every time I saw him, he had some advice usually in the form of a good Bible verse.

Grandpa Hall told me to pray for God to heal my mom and dad. I prayed for my mom to get off the pills she was taking. It worked. I couldn't tell if prayers were helping Dad quit drinking, because he only visited us a couple of times. Grandpa always said, "Don't give up." So, I kept praying.

I pulled the small cedar chest from under my bed. First, I checked the secret compartment where I kept my newspaper money. Only Lynn and I knew how the handles of the chest could trigger the secret panel on the lid. I counted the money to be sure I had enough to pay Mr. Davis, my newspaper route manager. This week I would have at least six dollars left.

I latched the compartment and studied the contents in the chest. Except for my clothes, the chest had everything I owned. There were magazines about cars and some *Archie* comics. There were books I had outgrown, like *Pinocchio* and *Three Little Pigs*, but I couldn't throw them away. My spiral pocket notebook was on top of everything. It had my favorite Bible verses written in it and Bible words I had trouble understanding, like espoused, begat, and virgin. Mom explained espoused and begat, and Lynn explained virgin. The stainless-steel coin changer Lynn got me last Christmas was laying in the pocket of the Rawlings fielders glove Brian Baker, the Sheriff's deputy, gave me my last birthday. It was a great glove with a deep pocket. That was the same day Brian met Lynn's mom. They started dating right away.

My paper route book and canvas newspaper satchel were rolled up neatly on one end. Tinker toys, Lincoln Logs, Tiddlywinks, and a deck of playing cards were under the satchel. A White Owl cigar box held my collection of green army soldiers and a Prince Albert tobacco tin protected my Topp's baseball cards that included Ted Kluszewski, Jackie Robinson, and Yogi Berra. I had plenty more. My baseball rolled around where the comics were stacked. I put the chest full of my possessions back under the bed.

I liked being right where I was, in Sabina. The breeze from outside lulled me to sleep. I had a dream about Eugene, sitting up and starting to speak.

Victor Hess

Chapter Three
Disappointment and the Thunderbird

On his weekly visits, Gary and Danny's dad asked me questions about my grades, my paper route, and baseball. It was the most we ever talked. I talked mostly about Little League.

"Well, Jesse, you know baseball isn't everything," Albert said.

But I knew I would make the team. Brian Baker said I was good enough. It's all I could think about. Gary and Danny started bringing their gloves and a bat, so we went across the street to the ball field to practice.

Recently, Lynn missed a few of the newspaper deliveries because Brian was taking Arlene and her to movies or out to eat in Wilmington.

One Saturday, Lynn was quiet during the whole route until we got to the Bigley Funeral Home.

"We're moving to Wilmington," she finally said. I barely heard her, but her words registered immediately. My best friend was moving away, too.

"When?"

"Right after the wedding." She began to cry.

"Shh. Why are you moving there?"

"Mama and Brian found a house to buy. It's a good deal. They showed me last night."

"Why so soon?"

"He can't pay for both places. I won't be able to help you deliver papers. It's not fair," she said between sobs and grabbed my arm.

All kinds of things went through my mind at once. Who

would help me with my paper route? Who will I talk to and play games with? How could I continue doing the paper route, collecting bottles, and checking candy machines for left-over nickels without Lynn? Then there was Little League.

"Will Brian still coach Little League?" I asked.

"Jesse! Is that all you can think of right now?"

"Well. Will he? Did he say?"

"I don't know. The house needs work, and he said we'll be painting and cleaning all summer." She pulled a hankie out of her halter and blew her nose.

"Guess what?"

"Jesse, stop it. Tell me."

"I bet Mr. Davis would like to have you as a paperboy, I mean, girl. He knows all about you helping me."

"I never thought of that." Her sobbing stopped.

"I'll tell him on Monday," I said and stood up, feeling lost inside, like both of us would have to start all over again, except, she would begin with the dad she wanted.

By the time we finished delivering papers, she was begging me to get Mr. Davis to give her a route in Wilmington.

On Monday, Mr. Davis let me know there weren't any routes open in Wilmington, and I struggled with breaking the news to Lynn.

"He said when school starts in September something would probably be open."

Thursday was Little League tryouts. Brian wasn't there but, even so, this time, with my new glove, I was catching balls as good as most of the other kids. I could hit balls just like them. In the middle of tryouts, a white 1953 Lincoln Capri pulled up, and Mr. Mallard introduced the new assistant coach, Pastor Randy Shepard. He was short and plump with deep set eyes, his forehead thrust forward, shading his empty eyes.

"Well, hi, boys," he said with his big smile. I shuddered.

I wondered if he remembered me or how Mom got him in trouble with the Children's Services Board last year. They removed him from the board after he sent us a fake letter threatening to move me into foster care.

He walked toward me. I gripped my Rawlings glove and walked past him, over to Mr. Mallard.

"Is Pastor Shepard really the assistant coach, Mr. Mallard?" I looked back at the pastor putting his ball cap on.

"He is Jesse. Brian's getting married and moving to Wilmington, so Pastor Shepard is helping us."

"I'm sorry. I can't be on the team this year." I looked over at the short chubby preacher.

"We need you Jesse. You're a good player."

"I can't, Mr. Mallard." I backed away.

"Why did you try out, then?"

"I didn't know Pastor Shepard was coaching. I can't." I turned, half mad and half hurt. I marched past the preacher and wanted to kick him, right there for that bogus letter. He stared at me as I walked by. He called my name, but I ignored him. He was not going to be part of my summer.

After I went home, I watched the other kids practice from my porch across the street, and when Pastor Shepard swung the bat to hit balls, he'd miss half the balls. Even though I was mad at him, I had to laugh when he stumbled after a ball he missed and wondered what possessed Mr. Mallard to make that preacher the assistant coach.

When I got upstairs. Karen was with Mom. I told them about tryouts and why I left.

"Is he the one who wrote that letter?" Karen asked.

Mom handed Karen a pair of black slacks she had just altered.

"Yes. That was not a good time for us. Try these on." Karen went into Mom's bedroom to change.

"They fired him from the church. Did you know that?" Karen yelled from the bedroom.

"They kicked him off the Children's Services Board, too," Mom said.

More and more I was wondering how Mr. Mallard would let the preacher be an assistant coach.

"He's Mrs. Mallard's brother, I think," Karen yelled, like she could read my mind.

Then she walked out of Mom's bedroom completely transformed. Her slacks were tight, she had changed into a red sweater, and was tying a black scarf around her neck.

"Vi, can I have Jesse for a while? We're going to run an errand before his newspapers get here." I would go anywhere with her if Mom would let me.

We walked across the street and got into her father's car. She drove me past the edge of town.

"That was a brave thing you did with that preacher, Jesse. I could tell your mom is proud," she said. She was putting lipstick on while she was driving.

"He's not going to last long. He can't even hit a ball."

"I bet Mrs. Mallard had something to with all this."

"I guess. Where are we going?"

"It's a surprise, you'll see."

She pulled up directly in front of the Stafford Ford dealership show room. When we got out of the car, she grabbed my hand and led me inside and, right there, between the Ford Ranch Wagon and the Ford Fairlane Crown Victoria, was a blue 1955 Ford Thunderbird convertible. We stopped and were greeted by three car salesmen.

"Can you tell my brother and me about this car?" I looked up at her and she winked. All three started explaining the function of the convertible top and the 292 cubic inch V-8 engine. An older man looked at me.

"You want to sit in it?" He opened the driver's door.

I sat behind the steering wheel as he punched seat buttons to move me up and forward and adjusted the steering wheel, so it nearly fit me. I was still just nine and a half.

"How fast will it go?" I asked.

"Oh, one-ten, one-twenty."

I felt so different, so powerful. It was the smell of that new car. New carpet. New upholstery. New paint. New tires. All working to transform all of my feelings. I wanted this car and decided I needed to deserve it first. I resolved I would work hard until I had this car or one better.

While I sat in the driver's seat, imagining myself powering through curves and hills in the countryside, the other two sales guys were competing for Karen's attention, offering to take her for a test drive.

"Here, Karen. You want to sit in it?" I asked.

I moved out of the driver's seat as the two salesmen fumbled with the switches and telescopic steering wheel, so it fit her perfectly.

Karen, in her red sweater, black scarf, sitting in that blue Thunderbird, was beautiful. So beautiful, I felt older, important, of value. Little League was the last thing on my mind.

"Can I take it out?" she looked up and smiled at the young salesman. In ten minutes, the car was moved from the showroom into the parking lot. The salesman opened the door for her.

"Get in Jesse." I climbed in on this hump on the middle of the seat, Karen on my left and the salesman on my right. Once his door was shut, she had the car in first gear heading out on the 3C highway and shifting into second and third, while I tried to keep my knees away from her hand moving the floor shift. I thought there should be more wind with the top down. Then, I raised my arm over the windshield, and it was nearly ripped off my shoulder.

The salesman kept asking questions about her, and if

she had a boyfriend or not. The more personal his questions, the faster she went. When we got back to the dealership, she said, "I don't have a boyfriend. I have a husband." I think this is the first lie I ever heard her tell.

On the way home, she told me she was leaving the next morning with friends to hike through France. She hugged me and kissed me on the forehead. She promised to send me post cards.

"Thanks, Karen. I'll never forget that." I walked across the street to our upstairs apartment.

"Don't you move away before I come back!" she yelled. That made me feel good.

Chapter Four
Preacher's Revenge

Every time the Little League practiced across the street, I'd sit on my porch with my Rawlings glove and watch them until my papers arrived. Sometimes, when you watch people long enough, it's almost like being there. A shrug of a coach's shoulder or kid's sideways glance provides a clue about what might be happening even though you can't hear their words.

Today, what I saw was very mysterious. It started with Tim and two other players waving at me. I stood up and waved back. They practiced a while when Pastor Shepard's white Lincoln pulled up. Before he got out of his car, Coach Mallard was standing by his door and leaning up against the car. Coach Mallard kept shaking his head and in less than one minute, the white Lincoln pulled out of the school yard. Coach Mallard said something to Tim, and Tim ran all the way over to the highway, waving at me and yelling something.

"What?" I yelled back, as I ran through the yard, glove still on my hand.

"C'mon, my dad says he wants you on the team."

I couldn't believe my ears. I checked both ways and then ran across the highway.

"Does your dad want me?"

"Yeah, c'mon."

"What about Pastor Shepard?"

"We were losing players. Dad said he's a pervert. C'mon." He had already turned around and headed to the baseball diamond. "C'mon."

There were only five players there. Tim and I made it

seven.

"Hi, Jesse. Do you still want to be on the team?" Coach Mallard asked.

"Yes sir, I'll try."

"That's all we ask. You line up in the outfield behind Tim. If anything gets through, you run for the ball and throw it to Tim. Okay everyone, let's play ball!"

He hit balls and we all fielded them. This time I was ready. Any ball hit past Tim, I scooped up and threw back to him. When practice was almost over, the coach gathered us together.

"Good practice. We need more players."

"Where's Billy Archer?" I asked. "He practiced all last summer with me and Deputy Baker."

"Who knows Billy?" the coach asked.

"He lives next door to me," one of the kids answered.

"Okay. Invite him to Thursday's practice."

"A new kid just moved next to me. He likes to play catch. He's got a glove," someone else said.

"That's good. Invite whoever you want. I need you guys to stick around for a few minutes, so pair up and throw to each other," he said just as a sheriff's car pulled up. I was encouraged when Brian Baker stepped out of the car.

"Hey, Jesse. Hi, boys," he said walking over to the coach. We kept playing catch, while we watched the two men in deep discussion.

"What's going on?" I asked Tim.

"I'll tell you later."

"Is Brian going to coach?"

"I don't think so. Dad says Pastor Shepard was bad news. He's mad."

"What happened?" Before he answered, Coach Mallard came over to us and told us to keep playing while he and Brian talked to each of us.

When my turn came, Brian asked me, "Did Pastor Shepard ever touch you?"

"No sir. Why, what did he do?"

"We aren't sure, Jesse. That's why I'm asking. Did you or your mother ever hear from him again after he sent that letter?"

"No sir."

Last year, Pastor Shepard sent Mom a fake letter telling her to bring me to a fake hearing to discuss foster care for me. Brian told Mom to call Clinton County Child Services and that's when she found out they didn't know about the hearing or the letter. They would check it out. That's when they kicked Pastor Shepard off the Child Services board. If it wasn't for Brian Baker, no telling who I'd be living with, but that's a whole other story.

Then, Brian and the coach started talking with Mike Stafford. I was back playing catch with the other guys. We'd glance over at Mike and, sometimes, he would start crying. We couldn't hear what was being said, but they talked a long time. He shook his head 'no' a lot. After Brian talked with everyone, he told us we were looking good and he'd see us soon.

The team was full of questions. Some of us were asking the coach if Brian was going to come back and help coach, while a smaller group surrounded Mike Stafford. But he was quiet, and, this once, he was not enjoying the attention he was getting.

"Okay, boys, be here for practice Thursday, the next game is Saturday at 2:00 p.m. here. We play the Wilmington Crawdads. They're two and zero. Let's make them two and one."

Everyone cheered, except Mike, who sat staring. I wondered if he was in trouble again like when he got caught stealing stuff off the tour buses.

I just had a dream come true of playing Little League, so the first thing I did was run upstairs and tell Mom.

"Where have you been, young man?" She got up from her sewing machine.

"Mom, guess what? That preacher quit. I'm on the team. We even have a game Saturday. You can come and watch me play."

She looked pleased and sat back down.

"It's a good thing, Mom. I'm on the team."

"I hope this isn't going to cost us money," she said, as she started pedaling the treadle on the sewing machine.

"Don't worry. But I gotta deliver papers." I grabbed the coin changer and canvas bag from my room.

Lynn was waiting for me, already folding papers.

"I just saw Brian. Guess what?" I said.

"I'm not guessing, Jesse. Don't ask again."

"I'm on the Little League team."

"What about Pastor Shepard? I thought you were mad at him."

"He's not coaching anymore. They want me on the team." I felt so much better now, almost like when I was with Karen riding in that Thunderbird. "We play Saturday. Can you come watch?"

She was quiet.

"We play Wilmington at two o'clock."

"I can't. Brian wants us to help him paint the house. He said you can help if you want. We have a lot to do before the wedding."

"Will you be back in time to deliver papers?"

"Probably not. We might all stay there. He has cots set up. It's fun. You'd like it."

Saturday, the Little League game was called early because of rain, but not before I scored a run and threw a runner out at first.

I was on the porch reading a post card from Karen when my newspapers arrived. The rain was steady, which always added an hour to my delivery time because I had to keep the newspapers dry with the canvas flap. I also had to walk them to the customer's door to be sure they'd stay dry. Today, I didn't have Lynn to help.

The rain was so intense I did not see or hear this car pull up and stop where I was standing. The window rolled down and I heard a voice from the inside.

"Is that you, Jesse? You need a ride?" I edged close to the vehicle and recognized the white Lincoln, and the pudgy red face of Pastor Randy Shepard. "Let's get you out of the rain."

"It's okay. I'm fine," I said and backed away.

"You'll catch cold. Now, get in the car." The preacher was insistent. Not only was I scared, I had to pee so bad it hurt.

"It's okay, Jesse. Don't be chicken," said this voice from the back seat. When I saw Mike Stafford's face, I turned and ran away, making sure I remembered the last house I delivered papers.

I still had to pee, but didn't dare stop with that preacher following me, and I ran, but then I got sloppy and was stepping into ruts and potholes up to my ankles and eventually I was soaked. The pain from having to pee and the chafing of wet jeans defeated me, so I let it all flow out, instantly relieving my pain and just as quickly renewing my strength. My pants were wet and warm.

As I got to my porch, like magic, the rain stopped and by the time I changed into yesterday's jeans, the clouds parted, and the sun shone through.

"Mom, remember about Pastor Shepard? He tried to get me in his car!" As I started my story, the danger seemed more real and I breathed heavily.

"Tell me everything," she said as she motioned me to

the kitchen table.

After I told her about the rain and Pastor Shepard and Mike offering me a ride, we went to the Corner Market public phone and she made a call. I held Christina.

"Abigail. It's Viola. We're worried about your nephew. Should he be riding around with the preacher? Uh . Shepard?"

"Well, he was with him when Shepard tried to offer Jesse a ride a little while ago." I could hear Ms. Stafford's voice get louder on the other end of the call.

"No. Jesse's right here. All right, we will."

Mom hung up the phone and we rushed back to the apartment.

My mind reviewed the earlier events. I tried to remember Mike in the back seat. It was odd. He was telling me it was okay, but I was sure he was shaking his head like he didn't want to be in the car with Pastor Shepard.

"Mom, I've got to finish my route." I still had five houses for delivery. I never missed a delivery.

"I don't want you to go back out there."

"It's okay. It's sunny now. I'll be safe. I'll be walking along Washington Street." Washington Street was the 3C Highway in Sabina and was well traveled, especially in the late afternoon. I was insistent.

"You come straight home."

"I will. I promise."

I ran down the stairs, picked up my canvas bag, and retraced the last few houses on my route. I dropped off the papers, the first to the Knisely's, and on down Washington Street.

At the fifth house, I heard the soft crunch of tires on gravel and looked back to see that white 1953 Lincoln Capri following along behind me. When I turned, the car sped past me and went up Jefferson Street. I had one more paper to deliver and that was to the funeral home, then I would run home.

I kept watch all around me as I walked up the wide

stairs to the wrap around porch. Today, the door to the funeral home was locked. No one answered the bell. Mr. Bigley's car was gone. I dropped the paper by the door and then heard the crunch of gravel again. The white Lincoln stopped in front of the funeral home, but I didn't think the preacher could see me since I was behind a big plant. I crawled behind a wicker chair and peeked through the porch posts. I could still see Mike in the back seat, and the preacher was behind the wheel, wiping his face with a handkerchief.

They were after me and I had to get away somehow. I sneaked along the porch, crawling on my hands and knees until I got to a rear set of stairs that led behind the funeral home where I was out of their view. Now, with the funeral home between me and them, I ran to Eugene's shed and unlocked the door with my knife.

"Eugene. I need your help!" Only I would ask a dead man for help.

I left my canvas bag outside the door, left the door slightly open, turned the light on, went back outside, and hid in the thick shrub behind Eugene's shed.

Again, I heard the crunch of the Lincoln's tire. When it stopped, I could hear the six-cylinder engine hum and then that engine rattle from cheap gas when he turned the key off. I was sure he could hear my heart beat and then there was my heavy breathing.

"Jesse, is that you in there?" The preacher's voice pierced my soul, and right there, I prepared for death while silently imploring God to take the preacher instead. I held my breath.

"Jesse."

I heard the door to the shed squeak open. I waited an instant, then ran around the shed, grabbed the door, slammed it so it locked and leaned against it hoping Pastor Shepard was inside.

Movement to my left got my attention and there I could

see Mike Stafford carrying a baseball bat and running toward me at full speed. In my haste to dodge him, my foot slipped on the wet gravel and I lay there, hands to my face, Mike Stafford still bearing down on me.

"We've got you, jerk," he yelled, eyes bulging out of their sockets. He took the bat and jammed it in the dirt right beside my face and then propped the handle under the door knob. He was trapping the preacher.

Pastor Shepard pounded on the door for a second or two before all became silent.

"We've got you, you pervert!" Mike yelled through the door. "Jesse, you saved my life."

He was gasping for breath. Then, he started crying. We both were crying. My heart was trying to break through my chest. Both our hands were gripping that baseball bat propped under Eugene's door knob, even though there was no resistance on the other side.

"I don't hear anything," I said, sniffling.

"Me either," he said.

He scooted close to the door and put his ear next to it. We heard nothing inside. Then there was the crunch of tires on the gravel from a car, and all we could see was the bright spot light.

Someone came toward us, a gun in his hand.

"You okay, Mike? Your aunt called us."

We both started telling Sheriff Clendenning everything.

"Hold on. One at a time. Where's Shepard."

"In there." We were still clinging to the baseball bat.

"Step aside boys."

We got up quickly and that was when I realized Mike's hands were tied in front of him. I pulled out my knife and cut the rope.

"Why was he after me?" I asked Mike.

"He's weird. He kept talking about you ruining his life."

"Why you?" I cut through the ropes, careful not to cut Mike.

"He was mad at my aunt." His hands broke free. "If you hadn't shut him in there with Eugene, I'd be a goner."

Up until this moment, Mike had been the cocky, rich kid who had caused my concussion last year during an indoor Red Rover game where he purposely let me break through the line too close to a concrete wall. Later he locked Lynn and me in Eugene's shed, but that's another story. Now, he was different. I didn't even notice his bug-eyes. In an instant he had changed.

"You saved my life, Jesse. I'm sorry about all that stuff I did to you and blackballing you from Little League."

"That's okay. My head doesn't hurt anymore, and Eugene and I have become good friends."

He laughed. I think Pastor Shepard scared the bad out of Mike.

"Your wrists are bleeding," I said. He was still breathing hard and just wiped the blood on his jeans.

The Sheriff yelled, "He's locked inside."

I rushed over, jimmied the catch with my knife and ran back to Mike.

"Randy Shepard. This is the sheriff. Come out with your hands over your head." His gun was poised, and we all watched the motionless door for an eternity.

"Randy Shepard! We know you're in there." He then looked at Mike and me and we both nodded. "Does he have a gun?"

"No, but he's in there all right. Don't let him hurt Eugene." I said.

The Sheriff slowly pulled the door open. He edged inside and said, "Stay there, boys."

He was in the shed for a long time and then came out, alone.

"He passed out," he said.

"Is he dead?"

"Nope, but I think Eugene might have scared him." Mike and I looked at each other. I wondered if Eugene sat up or said something to the preacher. The sheriff called in for help saying the suspect needed medical assistance. He put Mike and me in the back seat of the sheriff's car. Other cars started pulling in. Mike's Aunt Abigail was first and then Karen ran over to us. She opened the back door.

"Jesse, what happened?" She grabbed my arm.

Mike answered for me, holding my other arm. He described how Pastor Shepard tried to kidnap both of us and how I saved his life. The way she looked at me, her eyes, her smile, I don't think I'll ever forget that.

"When did you get back?" I asked.

"This morning. I couldn't miss this excitement. Your mom was worried. I told her I'd find you. This is the first place I checked."

"The suspect is in the shed there," the sheriff said to a deputy who had just arrived.

After they put the preacher in the back seat of a deputy's car, Mike and I stood watching the car carry him away.

"I have to check on Eugene," I said. Karen and I went in the shed. The floor was wet, right in front of Eugene. I could tell it was pee.

"We'll check him later, Jesse. I think Pastor Shepard lost more than his freedom tonight."

"We'll get this cleaned up," Mr. Bigley said from behind us. "What on earth went on here?"

"That dumb preacher broke into Eugene's shed," said Sheriff Clendenning.

They went into the shed while Karen and I left. I told her the details. When I described the preacher following me and locking him in the shed, she gripped my hand, tighter and tighter.

"When we get home let's just say the police picked up that preacher. Your mom will get upset if she thought you were in danger," Karen said. While we walked home, she told me all about hiking through France.

Victor Hess

Chapter Five
Lynn Gets a Father

Arlene and Brian's wedding was less than a week away. Mom planned a big surprise for her with the help of Joyce and Karen.

Karen bought white satin and lace material at her store while Joyce learned Arlene's opinions on wedding dress styles from an old June issue of Glamour magazine. Karen then ordered a dress pattern closely matching Arlene's desire. Mom knew Arlene's measurements from doing alterations for her over the past year, so the surprise was well planned.

That's all it took for Mom to make a wedding gown on her treadle Singer sewing machine. She cut, pinned, sewed, and cut again while Lynn and I were in school. She managed to get her other alterations work done by getting up earlier and, even this past week, had me delivering papers while Lynn pushed Christina in the stroller. She said she needed some peace and quiet or she'd lose some customers.

Wednesday, after I dropped the paper off at the funeral home, Lynn and I stopped at the Methodist Church where Brian and Arlene would be married. Arlene asked me to meet with the pianist to learn a song for their wedding. I agreed only because Brian had done so much for me, teaching baseball tips and getting me that Rawlings fielder's glove for my birthday last year. A lot of people at school, specially the teachers, liked my singing. Last year, I sang "God Bless America" at our school's March of Dimes assembly. Lynn must have told her mom. Anyway, Lynn insisted. That was another reason.

"Do you think it's open?" Lynn asked.

"It should be. This is when we're supposed to be here."

We walked up the steps. I pushed down the thumb latch

and the huge door opened, easily and quietly. We both stepped in and heard a beautiful melody. We walked down the aisle into the sanctuary. The pianist had not seen us yet and kept playing. The music was soothing and held our attention. We edged slowly toward the piano.

"Gloria, I think I found two admirers," a man said from behind.

She looked up. "Hi, Lynn. Is this your paperboy?"

"That's Jesse. He's gonna sing in Mama's wedding."

"We see you two delivering papers. You two are hard workers. You are always on time," the man said. I looked back at him and smiled.

"We saw your picture in the paper. They should release that vaccine soon. That was a good thing you did for the March of Dimes," said Gloria.

"Brian will be a wonderful father. He is very proud of you, Lynn," said the pastor. "Do you go to church?"

"Well, not exactly," she said. "We went to the Temple of Jesus to go to Vacation Bible School last year. They wouldn't let us go."

"Why wouldn't they let you go?" Gloria asked.

"They said they were full after I said my dad was in jail, and Lynn told them she didn't know who her father was," I said. Pastor Armey stepped closer.

"The person who told you that was wrong. God's house is big enough for everyone. God loves both of you and would never turn you away from his house." It was comforting to hear another pastor challenge Randy Shepard who was now locked up.

"Okay. Jesse, you come up here and sit with me. I heard that you sang at the March of Dimes assembly. Let me know if you have heard this before." I sat down on the bench and listened.

"No ma'am." It was beautiful.

"It's called Panis Angelicus. The words were written by St. Thomas Aquinas. You'll sing it in Latin. The music is by Cesar Franck. He lived in Belgium, a long time ago."

"It's beautiful." I hummed the tune while she played. Then she started playing the piece all over again, singing the words. Her voice was like an angel's.

"Do you think you can reach the high notes, Jesse?" she handed me a typed page with the words.

"I think so. What are these words?"

"Latin. It's an old language," she said.

"Lynn, Brian and your mother want to have Communion as part of their wedding. Jesse, you'll sing this while that is happening."

We looked puzzled at each other. "What's Communion?" I pulled out my notebook and wrote the word down. Gloria helped me spell it. Ever since we moved to Sabina, I would write stuff in my spiral notebook. It was reserved for things I didn't understand in the New Testament.

"Have you ever heard of the Last Supper? When Jesus and the disciples ate before he was crucified?" Pastor Armey asked.

"I know, like in John and Luke, right?" I said.

"And Mark and Matthew. I thought you never went to church, Jesse."

"I read it in my New Testament. I keep my notes here." I handed him my tattered notebook. He thumbed through the pages.

"Communion is when we celebrate the Last Supper by sipping grape juice and eating bread like Jesus did with the disciples," Gloria said. "Let's see if you can reach these notes. Just sing with me."

She taught me that panis was pronounced pahh nees, and angelicus was pronounced ahhn jell eee koos. I hit all the high notes and was, this once, happy that my soprano voice was still working. Sometimes, at school, a boy like me singing soprano was more of an embarrassment, but not today.

"It would be nice if you could memorize it. Do you think you can learn the words by Friday?"

"Sure, I'll practice."

"Meet me here Friday at the wedding rehearsal, and we'll practice one more time."

As we walked out, Pastor Armey handed me my notebook. "Let's talk sometime, Jesse. Okay?"

"Sure."

"Maybe you two can join us for Sunday School." Gloria said. "9:00 a.m. Sunday."

When we left, Lynn was the first to speak. "That was different."

"What do you mean?"

"They asked us to come back," she said.

"Do you want to go Sunday?"

"Yeah, but we have to get the papers out early."

"Okay."

Thursday night, Mom asked Lynn and me to take Christina out for a walk so she could get some sewing done. First, we sat on the porch and helped each other with the math worksheet we had. I held Christina and Lynn filled out her answers. Then she held Christina while I did mine.

It was still daylight when I pulled Christina's buggy out of the downstairs hallway and onto the porch. The buggy was old and still rusty even though I scoured it down with steel wool and 3-In-One oil. It squeaked with each bounce going on a curb, or crack in the sidewalk, or tree root we crossed. Lynn and I hung round plastic rings from the buggy top, so Christina could grab at them and hit them. Tonight, we went down streets we hadn't been for a while, so we could investigate other vending machines for orphaned nickels and dimes.

"I hope Brian and Mama have a baby." Lynn reached in and flicked a blue ring. Christina laughed and hit it with her fist.

"Do you want a sister or a brother?"

"I'll take both, or either, I guess." She flicked another ring, causing Christina to use both her hands to flail at the moving toys.

"Brian will probably want a boy," I said.

"I just want us to be happy. Mama's happy now. They're in love. Mama's different now."

"What do you mean?" We stopped at the Gulf Oil station and Lynn ran in to check the cigarette machine for coins in the change slot. I could tell by her face that it was empty.

"How's your mom different?" I asked.

"She talks about important things, like getting a better job, going to nursing school, and fixing up the house. She's so happy."

Christina started fussing. Lynn put her finger under Christina's diaper. "She's wet." We stopped, so Lynn could change the diaper.

"What are you wearing for the wedding?" she asked.

"I don't know."

"Do you have a white shirt?"

"I think so. Do you think your mom wants a baby?" I asked.

"She hasn't talked about that. I don't know."

"What if she doesn't?"

"I guess I'll have Brian and Mama all to myself." She rolled up the wet diaper and put it in a paper bag.

"Are you going to keep calling him Brian?"

"What should I call him?"

"Dad, daddy, pop, papa."

"Father, pappy? I'll ask him. I think father would be nice. That's what Betty Anderson calls her father."

"Who's Betty Anderson?"

"You know, *Father Knows Best*. Betty's sister Cathy calls him daddy, but Betty calls him father." She pulled up the pants over Christina's dry diaper as it started raining.

"Oh, yeah. That's right."

"What will you call Albert?" she asked. We started running, and Christina was delighted with the jostling.

"Albert, I guess." It started pouring. By the time we got home we rushed Christina upstairs to get her dry and towel off our wet hair.

It was one more thing we had in common. We were getting new fathers. She was more excited about hers.

Friday, I went to the wedding rehearsal with Lynn. While Pastor Armey gave everyone instructions about the wedding, Gloria took me into a room where there was another piano. We practiced my song. There were only two verses and I had memorized them. After two times through, she was satisfied.

"There are going to be some very surprised people at that wedding tomorrow. I do hope you like our church," she said.

Joyce took us home while Arlene and Brian went to his apartment to get it ready for them to move.

"Is it done?" Joyce asked Mom when we got home. The gown was hanging alone on the dress rack. It was long and white.

"I think it's done," Mom said, reviewing her work. She lifted one of the sleeves.

"Viola, it's beautiful," Joyce said.

"Is that Mama's dress?" Lynn asked. She ran over to the rack.

"Yes, honey, do you like it?" Mom asked.

"I love it. Does Mama know yet?" she asked.

"It's still a surprise," Joyce said. "Unless you told her."

"No ma'am."

"Lynn, your job is to get your mama to come up here after she has her bath in the morning," Joyce said. "I will do her hair up here, then she can get dressed. Andy will take us to the church and then come back and get Viola, Christina and the twins." Joyce had it all planned.

After Joyce left, Lynn and I sat on the porch and waited for her mom to get home.

"I wish you weren't going to move," I said.

"Me, too. It's a nice house though. Oh, Brian's getting us a television," Lynn said enthusiastically. "You can come over and watch sometimes."

I wondered how that could happen with her living ten miles away in Wilmington.

I never even considered us having a television. They cost a lot of money. A Philco TV was $199.95. We never saw that kind of money. I guess deputy sheriffs got paid good.

A car pulled up, a door shut, and then pulled away.

"What are you two doing out here?" asked Arlene.

"What time is it?" I asked.

"It's eleven o'clock. You guys need to be in bed," she said. "Is Viola awake?" she asked.

"I think so," I said. "We were waiting for you."

Lynn and I looked at each other in a panic. We couldn't let her go upstairs and see the surprise dress yet.

"Let me check," I said. I ran upstairs and warned Mom, who rushed the dress into her bedroom.

"She's still awake, Arlene. Come on up," I announced from the landing.

"What's going on up here?" Arlene asked.

"Did you get your packing done?" Mom asked.

"If it wasn't for the packing, I'd be a nervous wreck. Are you staying up?" Arlene asked.

"I have sewing to catch up on," Mom said.

"Can you sew and talk?" Arlene asked.

"Of course. Sometimes I think I can sew and sleep," she said. "Are you okay?"

"Yes." Arlene started crying. "I'm so happy."

"So happy that you have to cry over it?" Mom said.

"I'm so lucky," she continued. "I've worked so hard. I have a wonderful daughter." She hugged Lynn. "I have the best friends." She was bawling now.

"Mama, are you okay?" Lynn started crying. I sat on the couch watching.

"Slow down, Arlene. Have you guys been drinking?" Mom said, laying her sewing aside.

"Viola, I never thought I would get married. Brian has been so good to us. What if he changes his mind?"

"Did you two have words?" Mom looked worried.

"Oh no, nothing like that. I don't deserve him."

"Arlene. I promise that he's thinking that he doesn't deserve you. You're very special. Look how you've handled yourself and Lynn since you've been on your own. That man is not going to change his mind."

"Viola, I need to try on my blue suit. Will you help me make sure it fits good?" Lynn and I looked at each other.

"You get some rest and when you get your bath in the morning, we can try it on. You've been packing. We can't get that suit smudged. I'll make it fit, don't worry. Let's all get some rest." Mom said.

"Okay, I'll miss you living upstairs." They hugged. Mom let out a sigh of relief.

The next morning Joyce and Arlene, on schedule, walked into our apartment. Joyce was carrying the blue suit.

"We have a surprise for you!" Joyce announced.

Arlene walked in the room with just her slip and bra, never mind me sitting at the kitchen table.

Hanging alone on the clothes rack was the simple white, satin and lace wedding gown. Everyone expected an immediate response from Arlene. She turned around to grab the blue suit from Joyce. She hadn't seen the dress.

"Are you sure you want to wear this?" Joyce asked, dancing around the room again with the blue suit until she was directly in front of the rack with the white gown. "Or should you wear this?" She lifted the white satin and lace wedding gown off the rack.

"It's beautiful! Oh, my God. It's beautiful," she said. "Vi, I can't wear this!"

"Of course, you can!"

"It's white. I can't wear white."

"Yes, you can!" Joyce exclaimed. "You are very pure in the sight of God, and don't you make the Lord regret how much he loves you. Viola worked two weeks on this dress, and you deserve to wear it more than any other woman getting married today." Joyce was firm, like when she walked us kids out of Pastor Shepherd's church last year.

"It's so beautiful," Arlene said.

They lowered the dress so she could step in it and then pulled it up. She reached through the sleeves made of lace while Mom lined up the hooks on the back. Once she had all hooks hooked, and snaps snapped, they positioned her in front of the full-length mirror. Mom moved around and inspected her work.

"Okay," Mom said. "I have a little adjustment to make." She strategically placed pins at one side of the dress.

"Take it off. I'll fix this while you get her hair done," Mom said to Joyce and Karen.

They had combs, bobby pins, and makeup poised for action, sweeping Arlene's hair back into a tight bun while Mom started ripping a whole seam open on Arlene's new wedding gown. Everyone gasped.

"Don't worry, this will just take a minute. Jesse, get your bath and get ready," Mom said, waving her hand toward the bathroom.

"Lynn, you need to get ready," Arlene said.

Somehow, we all showed up on time for the wedding of Arlene Ott and Brian Baker. When Gloria started playing "The Bridal Chorus," Brian stared, astonished, as Arlene stood at the back of the church on the arm of Vincent Jefferson, her boss. The veil softened her face as she walked down the aisle in her white satin and lace wedding gown. Lynn followed her in a blue satin dress, another surprise sprung on Arlene before the wedding. Somehow, Mom had found time to make Lynn a beautiful dress.

During the wedding, I sat in a choir pew, wearing a white acolyte robe, close to Gloria. I could see everyone's face, except Pastor Armey.

Mom was holding Christina on her shoulder and Karen sat behind her, leaning forward. Christina was gripping Karen's finger, trying to wave it back and forth. Brian and Arlene looked at Pastor Armey, then glanced at each other. As they exchanged rings, Brian's mother smiled and wiped a tear from her eye with a tissue. I looked around the room and most of the women were doing the same thing, including Joyce. Lynn stared at her mom and new dad with a smile I've never seen before. I felt happy for her. After nine years, she has her own father. Now, I envied her, because she got the father she wanted.

The Pastor came to the part where Arlene and Brian received Communion. Gloria nodded to me. I stepped down by the piano and faced the audience. Lynn sat in a front pew smiling at her mom and Brian as I started.

"Panis Angelicus." I pronounced each word as Gloria instructed.

"Fit panis hominum, dat panis coelicus figuris terminum."

At the rehearsal, the night before, Gloria explained what the words meant. Communion was a sacrament Jesus started the night before he was crucified.

> *The angels' bread becomes the bread of men*
> *The heavenly bread ends all symbols.*
> *Oh, miraculous thing! The body of the Lord will*
> *Nourish the poor humble servant.*

As I finished singing, Communion for Brian and Arlene was completed as if it was timed. The church was silent. My mother was sobbing, and Gloria smiled at me as I went back in the choir pew. Lynn kept staring at Brian and Arlene.

After the wedding, Lynn and I went to the front of the church where Joyce had made a bowl of punch. We poured punch and handed the full Dixie cups to the guests. I felt out of place because I didn't have a tie or a jacket. Just a white shirt with rolled up sleeves and my best blue jeans. But nobody said anything about it. Then we passed out plates with cake.

Brian and Lynn left the church about a half hour after the wedding. Joyce gave us all orders and by noon, we had the church looking like nothing ever happened.

The entire event was an adventure. The dress, the service, the solo. I was relieved.

"Mama was beautiful. Vi made her look like a princess," Lynn said.

"You were beautiful in that blue dress," I said.

By the time we got home and changed, my newspapers were on the front porch ready to be delivered.

"They're early today," I said, and we started folding them.

Victor Hess

Chapter Six
Wesley's Rules

"Have the Brown's paid?" I asked.

Lynn looked at the route book.

"Yes," she said. "I feel different now."

"What's different?" I pitched the paper on their porch.

"Mama and I have always lived alone. Now I have a dad. I don't know what that's like."

"I know. Brian will be a good dad. If I could just change my dad."

"What are you talking about?"

"He drinks. A lot. It made him gamble our money away. I memorized a verse last night. It reminded me of Dad."

"From the Bible?" Lynn asked.

"Yeah. I couldn't sleep. 'For the drunkard and the glutton shall come to poverty.' It's true!" I surprised myself by remembering it. I searched for it in Proverbs after Grandpa Hall quoted it before we moved to Sabina. Proverbs had a lot of verses about drinking. I think Grandpa knew them all.

"Mama drinks beer," Lynn said. "What's wrong with that?"

"Nothing, I guess, unless you get drunk. Dad quit drinking right after Mom tried to kill herself. I think that scared him."

"I forgot about that. Why'd she do it?"

"Dad drank and played cards a lot. He lost our money every time he got paid. We couldn't pay rent. Mom couldn't buy food because we didn't have money. That verse is true! A doctor gave Mom pills to calm her down, but it got so bad, she cut her wrists and had to go to the hospital. I think Grandpa Hall said something to Dad, because after that, we moved, and he quit drinking and spent more time at home." I dropped a paper on the next porch.

"Then Mom got mad when Albert didn't bring Danny and Gary for Christmas and yelled so much, Dad walked out and started drinking again." While I was telling Lynn, I was reliving that Christmas day in my mind. I stopped and leaned against the Jefferson's picket fence.

"Mom said Dad was drunk when he hit her. It's no good. It made him weak. That's why we're split up. It's not fair. I've got to make him quit."

"It sounds like he doesn't want to stop."

"He's got to stop."

"If he didn't do all that, we wouldn't have met. Then what?"

"I know. I didn't mean that."

Mrs. Williams met us at her door and opened it up before I had time to knock.

"That was a beautiful wedding today, Lynn. Jesse, I cried when you sang that beautiful song," she said.

"Sorry, Mrs. Williams."

"No, it was beautiful. Now, I want to remind you two that next Sunday is Father's Day. Here's something extra for each of you. Get something nice for your dads." She handed each of us a quarter.

"Thank you, Mrs. Williams." We said it at the same time and moved on to the next house.

"I think I'll make Brian, uh, Father something. Maybe a card."

"If I get anything for my dad it may as well be a Thanksgiving card. That's the next time I'll see him, I bet."

"Jesse, you can mail him a card."

Often, after we delivered to the funeral home, we would sit down on the bench by Eugene's shed. Today we stepped inside. I still had the canvas newspaper bag and Lynn held the route book and money bag. We said "Hi" to Eugene and then Lynn signed his book and held it up with a big smile on her face.

> Lynn Arlene Baker June 11, 1955

After we finished the route, we went home and tallied the results at the kitchen table.

"Jesse," Lynn said. "I'm hungry."
"Let's go to the Busy Bee?" I said.
"Yeah. That would be fun," Lynn said.
"Don't bother Brian and your mama," Mom said.
"Okay," we both said. I hadn't even considered it.

It was after five o'clock and cloudy. No wonder we were hungry. We had missed breakfast and all we had were those little pimiento cheese sandwiches Mom made for the reception and some cake.

I ordered a grilled cheese and chocolate malt. Lynn ordered the Coney dog with a root beer.

"Are you still hungry?" Lynn asked after we had eaten.
I asked Sally what kind of pie they had.
"Banana cream and apple."
"Banana cream," said Lynn.
"I'll have the apple," I said.
"Did you mean it when you said I was beautiful?"
"That was the first time I ever saw you dressed up. Did I look okay in that robe?"
She just glared at me and didn't answer my question.
The waitress brought the pie, glasses of water and the $1.65 bill. I paid it with two dollars. Lynn reminded me to leave a tip.
"Keep the change," I said.
On our way out, the waitress said, "That boy left me a

thirty-five-cent tip" loud enough for most to hear.

"He's young. He'll learn," said one of the regulars. Everyone laughed.

"Let's go to Knisely's," I said. "Karen will help us find something for Father's Day."

We studied the display windows for new stuff before we walked inside. Karen was just putting a sign beside three pencils: Liquid Pencil - 39c. "Come on," Lynn said and pulled me up the steps.

"What are you two up to?" Karen asked.

"I need a Father's Day card," I said.

"I want to make mine," Lynn said.

"Hmm. Jesse, look on the rack over there. Lynn, I have an idea you might like. Come with me."

While I labored through cards with messages thanking fathers for the ways they love and care for their families, Lynn and Karen went into Mr. Knisely's office with some construction paper, glue and pens. I finally found a card that said "Happy Father's Day" on the outside, and "You Deserve the Best" on the inside. I was studying the model airplane kits, when Lynn came up behind me, announcing her hand made card.

"Voila!"

On the front, she had written, "Thank You," and on the inside left was "For Becoming My Father," and then on the right was a neatly trimmed Polaroid of Brian, Arlene and Lynn that Karen took at the wedding. They made a clever frame of construction paper and drew hearts and flowers all over the rest of the card.

"Wow. He'll like that," I said.

"I hope so. Thanks, Karen."

"How much is this, Karen?" I asked, holding up my simple card.

"Fifteen cents."

"Jesse, don't you need two cards?" Lynn asked.

"What?"

"You know, Albert?"

"Not yet."

I wasn't ready for two fathers.

"Karen, I need a stamp."

I walked across the street and mailed the card at the post office.

On the way home, Lynn described her new house and how close it was to the Kroger's. I could sense her drifting away. She had Brian now, and I was sure any of her plans that had the word "we" in it excluded me. He would be there for her. I wondered if he would still have time for coaching baseball.

"Do you think Mama and Brian ... Mama and Father will be in his apartment when we deliver papers tomorrow?" she asked when we got to our yard.

"Sure. They'll go out tonight and have dinner. Then they'll go to Brian's apartment and have a beer or highball. They'll go to sleep. Maybe they'll watch George Gobel if Brian got the TV," I said.

"They'll sleep in because they'll be tired. Mama will make breakfast. I hope they got groceries," Lynn added, and sat on the edge of the porch. The breeze blew her hair over her eyes and she just let it stay that way.

"We will quietly put the paper on the porch. We won't wake them up," I said.

"We have trash!" Mom yelled from the upstairs window. We took two sacks of trash and dumped them in the burn barrel. The rusty fifty-five-gallon metal drum had holes punched around the side, so air would get into the barrel and feed up to the top, making sure the fire burned the trash quickly. All I had to do was light a kitchen match, then catch a section of newspaper on fire and drop it into the barrel where the paper bags were deposited. It didn't take long for flames and smoke to start reaching to the top. We stood by the barrel and watched.

Soon Joyce's twin girls, Diane and Denise, joined us around the barrel. When someone was burning trash, it would attract others to join the occasion. If the fire died down, I took a stick and jostled it around. The flames shot up above the top of the barrel. We could smell potato peelings, bacon grease, egg shells, bread pieces, and pancakes all being consumed by fire, sending out aromas of meals past. Then the pine cones started burning. The flames seemed to get brighter, and the aroma changed from trash to a sweet campfire.

The sky was so clear we could see the constellations.

"I'll meet you guys by the pine tree," I said while the fire died down. I came back down with the old blanket. I chose a spot beyond the tree and spread the blanket on the ground. We lay down next to each other and stared at the stars.

"Where's the Big Dipper?" Denise asked. Few people could tell the twin girls apart, they were that identical. It was the way they would look at you that was different.

I pointed the Big Dipper out to her like Gary had shown us on one of his visits.

"Where is the Little Dipper?" Diane asked.

Lynn pointed it out to her.

"Mama said you can't count the stars," Denise said.

"Because there are so many," Diane added.

"Look!" Denise yelled. "A falling star."

We all saw the bright light streak across the sky. Then another one.

"Ohhh," we said in unison.

"Where is Virgo?" one of the twins asked. I looked up, getting my bearings. Then I pointed. I'd learned so much from Gary.

"There's Sagittarius." Lynn pointed up in the sky.

"Oh, look, Diane. Lightning bugs." Denise got up and chased after the tiny flashing lights with wings.

"Denise? Diane? Who's hungry for popcorn and cokes?"

Andy, the twins' dad yelled. "George Gobel is on in thirty minutes." He shone his flashlight on us.

"Look Daddy, lightning bugs. Can we catch some?"

"You'll need something to put them in," he said. We were all standing up by now our eyes following each yellow flicker of light.

"Mom's got Mason jars," I said.

We ran around the yard leaping for the blinking lights and carefully putting them in the jar. Even in the jar their bodies glowed bright.

"Yuk," Diane said when she accidentally squeezed one and it got on her fingers, which started glowing for just an instant.

We studied the jar of blinking insects when Andy said, "What should we do with them?"

"Keep them," Denise yelled.

"We have to feed them. What do lightning bugs eat?" he said.

We all looked at each other.

"They light because they are looking for a friend. Look in the yard." We could see little flashes from bugs deep in the grass. "They signal each other. We might be breaking up a lightning bug family if we just take these away from the others."

"Let them loose," Denise yelled. She reached for the jar and uncapped the lid, freeing them.

"Bye bye lightning bug," Diane said.

"What were you guys doing?" Joyce asked as we walked in their house. She was popping some Jiffy Pop popcorn. The twins told her everything about lightning bugs and shooting stars.

The popcorn was divided in bowls, cokes were poured, and *The George Gobel Show* came on.

We laughed at George Gobel's jokes and the commercials, which were almost as entertaining. We had the jingles memorized:

> *The soap that gets you extra clean is Dial, Dial, Dial*
> *The soap with hexachlorophene is Dial, Dial, Dial*

We stayed to watch *Hit Parade*, and then went home. Lynn changed into her pajamas in her apartment and came upstairs. Mom had a sheet for the couch where I would sleep while Lynn slept in my bed.

"Mom, we have to get up early. We have to finish the route in time to go to church."

"Which church?" she asked.

"The one where Arlene and Brian got married," I said.

"That's a Methodist Church. Your dad and I met in a Methodist Church in Xenia," Mom said with a smile.

"Do you want to go?" I asked.

"Maybe. I'll think about it. If you are starting early tomorrow, you need to get some sleep." Lynn hugged Mom and went to bed in my room.

Mom looked over at me on the couch. "I love you, Jesse. I'm very proud of you," she said. "Oh, Jesse, by the way, we're getting a telephone on Monday."

"We can call each other," Lynn yelled from my room.

I smiled. I wondered how we could afford a phone.

The next morning, we were up at 6:30 to deliver the papers. It took one-and-a-half hours to do the route and that got us home in time to change clothes and go to Sunday school. Karen saw us and offered us a ride with her parents. We arrived just in time for Sunday school. Karen guided us to the fourth to sixth grade Sunday school class. We recognized some kids who were in our class at school. We studied John Wesley and learned his three rules:

> First, do no harm.

Second, do all the good you can.
Third, do all you can to be close to God.

It reminded me of Grandpa Hall, and I hoped I could remember the third rule to surprise him the next time I was at the farm. He had already taught me the first two. The first, when I stepped on some of Grandma's baby chicks while exploring the chicken coop, and the second, after Mom tried to commit suicide. I wrote the third rule in my notebook.

After Sunday school, we sat in the sanctuary in the pew with the Knisely's. Before the service began, I nudged Lynn. "Look!" I whispered, motioning two pews up. We both recognized the heads of Brian and Arlene, sitting in the second row. Arlene was in her new blue suit.

"What are they doing here?" Lynn whispered to me.

"Go up there," I said.

"You come with me," she whispered.

"You go. I'll come up later," I said.

"Okay," she said with a smile and stood up. She was wearing the dress Mom made her.

Lynn walked slowly down the aisle, just two pews away, and stopped by Brian. He stood up, smiled broadly, and let her slide by him and Arlene. Arlene looked at her with tears in her eyes. She hugged her as if she hadn't seen her for weeks.

Lynn turned and looked at me, beaming, and mouthed, "Thank you." I smiled back to her. After they sat down, I felt sad and alone.

Victor Hess

Chapter Seven
Can a Book Change My Dad?

After church, Pastor Armey seemed happy to see me.

"We were hoping you would be back. Are you still writing in your notebook?"

"Yes, sir."

"Do you have any questions about what you have written there?"

"Mr. Williams told me this book could change a person's life. How do I get it to change my dad?" I pulled the New Testament out of my back pocket.

"That's a powerful question, Jesse. Tell you what. I'll be here Wednesday night. When you deliver your papers, why don't you come on into the church. I might not have the answer, but we can talk about it."

That was good enough for me. I had given up on Eugene.

"Bring your notebook with you," he said.

Lynn stayed with Brian and Arlene while the Knisely's drove me home.

I ran upstairs and found Mom sitting at the kitchen table drinking coffee and smoking a cigarette. She had that faraway look. I often wondered where her mind was when she had that look.

"Where's Lynn?" she asked.

"Brian and Arlene were at church, so she went home with them."

She smiled a little and then moved her eyes back to the window. Christina was napping on the couch.

"Why did you and Albert split up Mom?"

"If you must know, I fell in love with your father. Albert was always traveling, leaving me alone with Gary and Danny. We met after your dad's first wife died." Dad and his first wife had one daughter, Paula Jean, my half-sister. I thought it was odd we never lived together.

"How come Paula Jean didn't live with us?" My question went unanswered and she continued staring out the window.

"How come Gary and Danny don't live with us?"

"They did, for a while, before the accident."

"What accident?" She really had my interest now.

"Gary fell out of the car and hit his head on the street. He can't hear well out of his left ear. Albert took them both back after that."

"Was it Dad's fault?" Mom never drove a car, so it had to be Dad.

"Your grandpa was driving."

"Grandpa Smith?"

"He has never gotten over it."

"Maybe that's why Gary's so smart," I said. I was serious. She came over to me and gave me a big hug.

"Let's finish that pimiento cheese," she said and pulled out two slices of Wonder sandwich bread. The little bowl of pimiento cheese left over from the wedding was just enough to fit into the slices and then she cut the sandwich diagonal. One side for her, one side for me. She poured us each a glass of cherry Kool-Aid. Christina was still napping.

Wednesday was cold, even though it was the middle of June. I dropped my canvas paper bag by the church door and made sure I had my notebook with me. I hoped Pastor Armey could help me change my dad. Gloria was playing "Panis Angelicus" and that made me think of Lynn and her mom's wedding. She stopped playing when she saw me.

"Hi Jesse, Pastor Armey asked if you could wait here while he finishes a Stewardship meeting."

"Yes, ma'am. Are you playing that this Sunday?"

"We're hoping you could sing it for the church service. What do you think?"

"Really?" For some reason, today, I liked the idea. "Will you be playing it, like at the wedding?"

"Kind of. This time, I will play it on the organ. Come and listen."

The organ sat next to the choir pews and she slid the cover up and flipped a switch. A whooshing sound filled the sanctuary. Then she pulled knobs with names like trumpet, strings, and oboe, adjusting each one, then tapped on wooden slats on the floor with her foot and on three rows of piano keys with her fingers. The room rumbled with the sound.

"Do you remember the words?"

"I think so. This is louder than the piano."

"Go stand over there by that microphone." The microphone was on a pole and looked like the one last January in the March of Dimes assembly.

I tapped it once and a loud thud filled the sanctuary. Then, Gloria started playing the introduction to my solo. I started singing, "Panis Angelicus." It sounded so loud I had to step back from the microphone.

"Do you like it with the organ, Jesse?" she asked when we finished.

"Yes, and the microphone. It sounds nice," I said. My voice filled the sanctuary. Just then, I heard a door open somewhere.

"God has given you a beautiful voice, Jesse. Do you want to share it Sunday during the church service?" Pastor Armey asked as he walked in from a side door carrying a box in his hand.

"Yes sir, sure," I said into the microphone.

"Come on down here and we'll talk," he said, stopping halfway back. "Did you bring your notebook?"

"Yes sir." I pulled it out of my back pocket and sat beside him in one of the pews.

"What's your plan for the summer?" he asked.

"I have my paper route and I babysit my sister," I said. "I'm doing Little League this year."

"Sunday, you asked me how this can change someone." He gripped the box and held it, so I could read it. "Holy Bible" was written in large letters on the front. "That's a tough question." He set the box on the pew right between us.

"Tell me about your dad."

"He works in Dayton for a trucking company, I think. He has a 1950 Buick Special. My mom divorced him last year before my sister was born. I know that if he can quit drinking, he'll be better and not hurt Mom."

"How do you know that, Jesse?"

"He did it once, before we moved here."

"How long did he quit?"

"Three weeks, but then Mom and him got in a fight Christmas and he left us."

"Where did he go?"

"Mom said a poker game."

"Why do you want him to change."

"So he can put our family back together," I said. "It's just Mom and my sister and me here, but I have an older sister and two other brothers. I want us all together."

"Is that what your mom wants?"

"I don't think so. She wants to marry her first husband, my brothers' dad. He's building us a new house in Xenia."

"What's wrong with that?"

"I want my dad doing that. If he could change, he could do that."

"What does your dad want? Does he want your family

back together?"

"I think he does."

"How often does he visit you."

I started breathing hard from a sudden sadness I was feeling.

"It's not fair. Dad has only come to see us three times. I know he can change, if he stops drinking." My lip was quivering.

"Do you know about prayer?"

"I pray for Mom and Dad. It worked for Mom."

"What do you mean?"

"When she was sick, she took pills. She doesn't need them here. I think God heard me about Mom. Why didn't he do the same thing with Dad?" I wiped a tear from my cheek. He handed me a tissue. There was a box in every pew. The tears and the newspaper print on my hands turned the tissue black. Maybe my face, too.

"Sometimes, God is more patient than we are. I think he's waiting on your dad to reach out."

"How do I make him reach out?" I'm not even sure what that meant, but it was not the answer that I wanted.

"Jesse, you asked me how this book can change your dad. It can, if he wants to change, and he's willing to read it. Here, this one's for you." He handed me the red box. Inside was a black leather full size Bible. The first page had a place for my name, and it said, 'To Jesse Hall, our heavenly voice, from David and Gloria Armey.'

"This is mine? I can keep it?"

"Yes. This one has the Old Testament in it. You'll need it for Sunday school. Now, tell me about your new home in Xenia."

I described it, the way Mom told me.

"Maybe that's what God wants for you. A new safe home. Do you like your mom's first husband?"

"He's okay. He doesn't drink or gamble."

"How about your brothers?"

"Gary's cool. They're both cool." This was going in the wrong direction.

"What was that church you and Lynn couldn't go to last year?" he asked.

"Tabernacle of Jesus."

"You'll be fine here, Jesse. We're glad you're here."

When I got home, I went straight to my room and started a letter to my dad. All I could write was "Dear Dad," but nothing else came to me. I knew what I wanted him to do, but I couldn't get it into words. Then there was the smell of grilled cheese sandwiches. I took the Bible into the kitchen to show Mom.

"Pastor Armey gave me this tonight. It's brand new."

"When did you see him?"

"I stopped by the church. They want to me sing Sunday. I'm going to sing that song I sang at the wedding."

She cut the grilled cheese sandwich into three strips and sat it down beside a cup of hot tomato soup.

"That was such a pretty song. Where did you get your talent?"

"From you, Mom. You sing beautifully."

She gave me a hug, sat down at the table, and reached for the Bible. I dipped one of the sandwich strips in the tomato soup and quickly took a bite before the soup dripped on my shirt.

"This is um um good," I said, like the Campbell's soup commercial.

"This has pictures," she said.

"It has maps, too. The words make more sense."

"Hmm. Revised Standard Version." She read from the box.

"Look at the front. They put my name in it."

She studied the simple inscription for a long time, while holding a spoonful of baby food she was feeding to Christina. She finally fed my sister and then took her hankie out of her sleeve and blew her nose.

"We'll have to find a church in Xenia," she said. I dunked the second sandwich strip in the soup and repeated the ritual until my dinner was finished.

After I bathed Christina, I took her into Mom's room, laid her in the crib, and gave her a bottle. I sang, softly, "Panis Angelicus," and she fell asleep halfway through the second verse, but I kept singing. I stared at the ten-month-old infant, so lovely and knew that if Dad could only look at her, right now, he would change. How could he not? He shouldn't need a book.

During recent visits, Albert had shown very little attention to me. I thought maybe he liked me, probably because of the paper route and getting my picture in the paper for getting lots of donations for the March of Dimes. Albert never said an unkind word to me or Mom during his visits. He just read the newspaper and listened to music on the radio. I still wished Mom would change her mind about moving.

"I like it here." I did, because it was Mom and me. We were still making ends meet. I couldn't imagine living a day without Lynn. "Do we have to move?"

"Wouldn't you like to live with your brothers? You've been saying you'd like us all to be together."

"I know. But I want to be with my dad. He'll change, Mom. We just need to give him a chance."

"Jesse! What is wrong with you? After all that man did to me? You weren't there when he beat me. You saw him come home drunk and broke from gambling. He's had plenty of time to change, and he's still the same. Why do you think I divorced him? He's not going to change!"

I stared out the window. My lip was quivering. The anger in her words bit at me.

"Do you know how many times he made us move? When was the last time he came to visit you and your sister? Christmas! That was five months ago!" Her fist hit the table and I jumped.

"Albert hasn't taken you out for a movie or dinner. It just seems weird. If you divorced him once, why would you want to go back with him?"

"We have an understanding now." She was suddenly calm.

"What school would I go to?" I turned and sat down at the table.

"I'm not sure. It's a new school. That could be fun," she said. "You can ask him those questions next weekend."

"I have a job here. Can't Albert build a house in Sabina?"

"Xenia is close to his job. Gary and Danny need us. This is best for us, Jesse. We're not making enough money to stay alive. Your father is way behind on child support. I can't keep up with everything now that we have Christina." She put a plate of hot French fries on the table, and we both reached for them. Her wrist still had the scars from her suicide attempt that landed us here.

"It's going to be so nice. All new kitchen appliances, Jesse. Hardwood floors everywhere. It will have a basement." She deserved a nicer place, like you see in magazine ads. I glanced around our living room, scarred pine floors, ceiling stains where the roof used to leak. Just then, a semi-truck drove by on the highway, drowning out Mom's description. "No more traffic every ten seconds." She yelled at the traffic outside while I dipped my fries, one by one, in ketchup.

"It's like a dream come true. We won't have to worry about money either," she said.

"Maybe you won't. I can't make money without a paper route."

"You can get one there, if you need it. Do chores around Albert's house, and I bet he will give you an allowance."

She made up her mind. I knew about our money and how stressed she got every time Dad missed a support payment. Her sewing money was never enough. But, I didn't want to leave my paper route. It was good money for me, except when Mom needed help with the rent.

After I sang on Sunday, a lot of people stopped me in church to tell me they liked the song I sang. Some of them were my subscribers, and I noticed that the next Saturday I got more tips. The following Sunday, two different people asked me to start delivering the paper to them. Once a month, Gloria had a song picked out that I could sing. A couple times I sang the refrain when Pastor Armey read the Psalms for that week.

The Bible Pastor Armey gave me had colored maps and drawings. It was easier to understand than the New Testament Mrs. Williams gave me. The verse in my notebook, "He that spareth his rod hateth his son; But he that loveth him chasteneth him betimes," made more sense in my new Bible: "He who spares the rod hates his son, but he who loves him is diligent to discipline him." It still reminded me of Grandma Smith. She never spared the rod.

I went straight to Romans 12:9 and read with more interest because these verses made so much more sense. "Hate what is evil, hold fast to what is good; Love one another. Rejoice in your hope, be patient in tribulation, be constant in prayer." I liked those verses.

This was the book Dad needed to read. One Sunday, I mentioned it to Pastor Armey, and he said he had one for him. He said for me to bring Dad to church, and he will give it to him personally. For the moment, it sounded like such a good idea.

Now that I was playing in Little League, I listened to the Redlegs broadcasts on the radio while I babysat Christina. Mom was okay with it, but I knew she would rather listen to a music program. My favorite player was Wally Post, because he played right field, like me.

We played games on Wednesdays and Saturdays. We played against two Wilmington teams, a Bowersville Team, New Vienna, and Leesburg. We had tee shirts with Sabina Hogs written on it.

During one game, it was windy and the farm next door to the school was baling hay, so all the players and their parents started coughing and sneezing from the dust. After I had struck out twice, I was back at bat when something landed in my eye just as the first pitch approached the plate. I turned away so quickly that my bat, still on my shoulder, connected with a high inside ball, sending it down the left field line, and eight other players started yelling, "Run Jesse, run." A hand grabbed my arm, pointing me toward first base and I started running, nearly tripping over the first base. "Keep going. Keep going." The chorus of voices urged me on, and I kept rubbing my eye and the pain teared me up.

"I can't see!" I yelled. A hand grabbed my arm and turned me toward third while voices yelled, "Bring it home, Jesse. Bring it home!" I tripped on third and fell on my stomach.

"Safe," yelled the ump. I still couldn't see and kept wiping my eye with my shirt. My eyes were nearly swollen shut but felt better because whatever was there before, was gone now. Suddenly, I could see, but only out of my left eye. As soon as I focused in on home plate, I saw the ball go past the catcher into the backstop. "Run Jesse." This time the coach said it. I sped off the base watching the catcher chase after the ball, retrieve it, and start back toward home. It looked like he was closer to home than I was, and we both collided at home plate, me sliding on my stomach, eyes shut, and him on top of me.

"Safe!" yelled the ump, as the ball rolled out of the

catcher's glove.

I wished Dad was there for this magical moment when all the players surrounded me, hitting me, and jumping up and down with me, all because I got a piece of dust in my eye. Mom was there, holding Christina. She probably didn't know exactly what happened but was beaming at me, until she saw how dirty the shirt got on that last slide. We beat Bowersville that day, five to four. At that moment, baseball was everything to me. That same day I listened to the Redlegs beat the Milwaukee Braves ten to five. A perfect baseball day.

Mom took Christina to some of my games and sometimes Karen would be there, too. She would yell so loudly that the other players wanted to know if she was my sister. When I said she was just my friend, they thought I meant girlfriend and I didn't bother to say otherwise. Karen talked Joyce into bringing the twins and selling Kool-Aid off an old card table. Mom baked oatmeal raisin cookies and sold them. Nobody seemed to mind.

Chapter Eight
Karen and the Corvette

My birthday wasn't the same without Lynn and Arlene, but I did get a birthday card from Lynn. It was home-made from clipped newspaper headline letters:

Have a Happy Birthday or I will get my revenge. Eugene.
Inside was a dollar.

Karen walked in wearing the same outfit she wore when we went to the Ford dealer to see the Thunderbird.

"You ready for my gift? You want to see a Corvette?" She smiled. I did, too. I looked over at Mom.

"Don't be too long," she said.

She drove us to Wilmington to the Chevrolet dealership.

"You know it's made out of plastic," she said as we stepped in the showroom.

"Fiberglass. It's strong," I said.

I couldn't believe my eyes. There was a bright red 1955 Corvette convertible sitting right next to a red and white 1955 Chevrolet Belair. I was in the same room with both of them.

Karen got even more attention at the Chevrolet dealership. Maybe because her sweater matched the color of the cars. When we got home, we played a game of Scrabble while Mom gave Christina a bath.

"I miss Lynn. Have you talked to her?" Karen said, as she spelled out A-C-C-I-D-E-N-T on the T I just put down. It was a double word and she used all her letters.

"Not fair. How'd you do that?"

"Let's see, thirteen, times two, plus fifty for using all my letters. That's seventy-six."

"We talked today. Her paper route is getting big. She has

more customers than I do already."

"Wilmington is a lot bigger. What do you do now that Lynn is gone?" She was drawing a fresh new batch of letters.

"Sometimes I go to Joyce's to watch TV, but then the twins pull out their dolls and I'm stuck playing house with them." I placed the word M-O-S-T-L-Y next to Karen's.

"Triple letter on the Y, look, twenty-seven points."

"Good for you. Those twins miss Lynn, too. How about Sunday, after church, I'll take us all to Semler's for some really good ice cream."

"I love Semler's," Mom said

"We'll pick up Lynn and take her, too. Why don't you call her and see if she can go."

It was a good reason to call her, even though it broke Albert's rule about calling more than once a week.

At last, September came along with the fifth grade. Tim was in my class, but Mike Stafford was missing.

"He's in boarding school this year," Tim told me and then described what it was like at Olney School. He said it was close to West Virginia. "He might visit for weekends. When are you moving?" he asked.

"I don't know. They just dug the basement last week," I said.

I was still singing soprano in the fifth grade and embarrassed about practicing my part with the girls. My teacher would say, "Girls, let's do this again." When I wouldn't sing, she seemed to get it and would then say, "Sopranos and Jesse," which made me feel a little better.

Times seemed to be better in town, but it didn't help Mom with her sewing.

"People can afford new clothes now," she explained. "They aren't altering their old stuff. We need to cut back."

I was still wearing Levi's Gary and Danny grew out of.

The pants had already faded. At least they were warm, and I could get two years out of a pair. Gary and Danny were taller than me. When I first put a pair on, Mom would fold up the pants' leg half-way to my knee in order for them to fit me.

Dad hadn't changed yet. He missed child support payments, and Mom would send me out to find more bottles and loose change in the vending machines. At least I didn't have to split it with Lynn, but I still missed her. Mr. Williams had to raise our rent five dollars a month, which made life tougher. "Gas and electric keeps going up," he'd say every time he'd come to collect rent. I had forty-five subscribers now and cleared about ten dollars each week with tips, but Mom needed money for rent and food for us, so a lot of it went for that. I still didn't have money for a bike.

I know Mr. Williams liked us, but when Mom didn't have his rent on time, he'd come by the house every day trying to collect what we didn't have. When he'd leave empty-handed, Mom would always say, "See what your father has done to us, Jesse?" Then I'd go in my room, lie on the bed, and quietly sob and pray.

Once Mom called Albert, crying and he drove over that evening and gave Mom some money. Then he drove her to Mr. William's to pay the rent up. Every month or so, she'd comment I was paying more than Dad. I doubted that. I was losing interest in him, especially since he hadn't visited since last Christmas. It was almost like he was ashamed of us or still mad about Mom having him put in jail last year for hitting her.

Victor Hess

Chapter Nine
Dad and the Holidays

In November, it was announced that the Salk vaccine for polio was safe. They had been holding up vaccinations for months while some committee studied tests and reports. Some batch in Utah caused a case of polio, and they had to check out the lab that made it. We hoped they would get to our school soon. So far, Greg Davis was the only one in our area who caught it, and he got the worst end of polio and died in 1954. People commented on how lucky we were to make it through the summer of 1955.

When we finally got the vaccine, they took us in the cafeteria and formed us into two lines to get our shots. They called off our names and told us which line to stand in. That happened twice that year.

November was also the coldest it had been in years. Each day it snowed, I watched out the front window at the school and listened to the radio station, hoping that they would announce our school was closed that day. Since most of our students lived on farms, and the snow made it difficult for the buses, we had snow days a few more times than the big school in Wilmington. On a snow day, though, I still had papers to deliver and it would take twice as long, especially when I got out before my subscribers had a chance to shovel their sidewalk. One house might have a shoveled walk and then the next would have a huge pile of snow. More than once I came home bruised from slipping on the ice with my boots full of water.

Christina was over a year old and entertained us when she would try to walk in the snow, always falling on her butt, sometimes with a cry and other times with a giggle. If Mom was overwhelmed with sewing, she would make me take Christina on my route. It only took once to figure out that a stroller in the snow is dangerous. That was when I was delivering a paper to the Bells' house. As I took the paper up to the porch, Mrs. Bell ran out her door and past me to retrieve the stroller that was sliding down her driveway into the street.

"Jesse, you can't just leave your sister like that!" she scolded.

"I locked the wheels, Mrs. Bell," I explained.

"That does no good in the ice. Be more careful!"

I figured there'd be no tip this week from the Bell's and blamed Mom.

I was running out of time to get Dad and Mom back together. My prayers were intense now, focused on getting Dad just to visit more, so I could tell him about Pastor Armey and the Bible. Albert's house was slowly being built, and now, Mom was saying it wouldn't be done until February. That meant more time to work on Dad.

When Gary and Danny visited, we still did our trips to Eugene's shed and the Busy Bee restaurant. It wasn't the same without Lynn. I think Karen looked forward to our Friday visits at her house and more than once, Albert would have to come over to her house and knock on her door to pick up Gary and Danny to take them home. She became a Scrabble freak and made me stay and play. She always won, but I learned a lot of new words.

I still had not heard from Dad, and when Thanksgiving came, I sat on the porch, praying in the cold for his yellow Buick to show up. That prayer worked.

He arrived at noon and waited in the car, while I ran upstairs to tell Mom. It took forty minutes for Dad to drive to the Hall farm. I would have two chances to make him change. One going and one coming back.

It was sunny, but the roads were still wet with slush and ice. Dad was quiet. I decided to start with reminding him about responsibilities.

"Dad, did you get Christina something for her birthday? It was September 23rd." I didn't mention that he forgot my birthday, too. He lit a cigarette and after a minute replied.

"That's why I pay child support, Jesse. What does your mother do with the money I send?"

I was ten years old and wanted to remind him he was already two months behind, because Mom told me every time she needed an extra five dollars for rent or food. She kept track. Each time was one more reminder Dad wasn't going to change, and we would be living with Albert.

During Thanksgiving dinner, Uncle Virgil told Dad the Eavey plant was looking for good help. The Lions were beating the Packers on TV, and my cousins and I were laid out like spokes of a wheel, playing Tripoley on the floor. Dad said he'd check it out. Uncle Russ asked how long he'd been laid off. Dad said just a week.

"Did your dad lose his job?" Karl asked.

"I don't know," I said.

"If he got laid off, he lost his job."

I wanted to melt into the floor.

Dad and I left early.

On the way back home, he drove through Xenia and by the courthouse clock tower. It was a tall tower you could see for blocks. It was tolling 6 o'clock as we drove by.

"Dad, I sing this Sunday in church. Can you come?"

"Not this Sunday. I have plans." I wondered about his world in Dayton and who was in it, if not Christina, Paula Jean, or me.

"What are you doing?"

"Some buddies and I are getting together."

"Maybe you could bring them, too. My pastor has a

book for you. You'd like it."

"Maybe some other time." For the second time in the same day I felt helpless. We sat silent for a while.

"We're moving to Xenia in February," I finally said.

"Did Viola find a job here? I thought you liked Sabina."

"No. She's marrying Albert."

"That's good, Jesse. I won't have to drive so far to see you."

"Dad, maybe you could get a job in Sabina, and we could all stay there."

"There's no work in Sabina. All they have is that tool mill."

"I'll check if you want. I deliver papers there."

"It's okay, Jesse. I'll find something in Dayton. Tell your mother I'll be holding off on the child support until I get work."

I looked out the window, so he wouldn't see the tears pouring down my cheek.

Last year, Christmas was gift sharing on Christmas eve and then Christmas day on the Hall Farm. This year it was different. It started just after Thanksgiving, where each Sunday at church, we lit an Advent candle and sang carols of hope, love, joy and peace. Advent was every week.

Last year, Joyce and Andy read us the Christmas Story from Andy's Bible on Christmas night. This year, on Christmas eve, we all went to the Methodist Church and I sang, "What Child is This," still in my soprano voice. Even Lynn, Brian and Arlene came.

Christmas used to be gifts, "Jingle Bells", and radio specials. Everything was different to me this year. Because we celebrated Advent, we sang Christmas carols and you can't help but think about the words as you sang the songs. This year it wasn't Rudolf or Frosty, or even Santa Claus. It was the Christ child and how much we adored him. I sang looking straight ahead at a cross and I wasn't alone, because just about everyone was singing, too. The child was sitting on Mary's lap. My heart rejoiced as the words declaring Christ the Lord swarmed out of the mouths of those gathered to celebrate Advent. This was my new Christmas, my Sabina Christmas. As I declared Christ's glory, I prayed for Dad, mostly that he'd change, but I'd be happy if he'd just show up.

The yellow Buick drove in on Christmas day to take me to the Hall Farm where there was always a tree with lights, garland, and tinsel.

Even though it was cold outdoors, the cousins decided to play outside in the yard. Jeffrey had a bow and arrow set he got for Christmas, so we lined up, taking turns firing arrows at the large pole that held the outdoor light.

He had a piece of cardboard with a picture of a rabbit glued on it. No one, but Jeffery, had experience with the bow. First, Kelly's jacket sleeve got ripped by the bow string, and her arrow flew into the chicken coop. Then she nearly got shot by Valerie while she ran to retrieve the chicken coop arrow. But through it all, laughter resulted from each mishap, until it was my turn.

First, I took off my jacket, so it was easier to aim and not get the sleeve caught in the bow string. Then I notched the arrow by a little mark on the string, guided the arrow across my fingers gripping the bow, pulled back, and that's when Karl yelled, "Wait!"

It was too late.

My arrow was splintered from its encounter with the chicken coop, and when I let loose, the narrow splinter drove into my finger going through the full length to the first knuckle before it broke off the arrow ripping my skin. The arrow continued toward the target but had slowed just enough to fall short and embed itself in Bullet, Jeffrey's dog, which reacted slightly, then continued walking, with the arrow still hanging from his side.

"Bullet, come here," Uncle Russ yelled, and the dog obeyed like he was about to be fed. I was still holding the bow, evidence of the near homicide, my left finger bleeding. I ran over to inspect my deed.

"Pull the arrow out, Jesse."

"Will it hurt?" I dropped the bow.

"Only if you don't pull it out." I pulled it out and then Bullet yelped and growled at me.

All the cousins gathered around Bullet, hugging on him.

"What did Jesse do to you?"

"He ran in front of the arrow," I said.

"I told you to stop," Karl said, which I remotely remembered him saying something like that. My finger started smarting from the splinter, so I just turned and went into the kitchen not realizing I was dripping blood on the linoleum.

"Do you have a band aid, Grandma?" I asked

"What have you done to yourself?"

"I shot Bullet with an arrow, and ..."

My audience suddenly went outside to comfort Bullet, while my finger bled. I wrapped a couple paper napkins around it that soon became glued to my finger by the congealed blood.

By the time we had eaten, all was forgiven, and we cousins lay on the floor playing the traditional game of Tripoley.

On the way home, Dad asked for the details about Bullet and me shooting him. He assured me the dog would be fine and by the time we got to downtown Xenia, it was out of my mind. The back seat had gifts and our money envelopes Grandpa gave everyone each Christmas. I knew that Mom would be relieved, like she was every Christmas.

I didn't notice our car veering toward the curb until there was this thud and the car leaped onto the sidewalk, right beside the Greene County Courthouse. Dad fought the wheel and guided the car back onto Main Street, stopped it, put it in park, and then got out. He inspected all around the car. I got out, too. The right front tire was flat.

"Do you have a spare?" I asked.

"I hope so. Have you ever changed a tire?"

"No sir." And then I wondered if he ever changed one.

"Let's check the boot." We went to the back of the car and opened the lid. The spare tire was upright.

"You wanna help?" He took his coat off and rolled up his shirt sleeves.

"Sure, can I?"

He loosened the bolt holding the tire in place and lifted it out with ease. It bounced when he dropped it on the sidewalk.

"Good. It's got air." He even smiled.

The clock in the courthouse struck six times.

He found the parts to the jack, and I could tell he had done this before, like he had practiced it. He jacked it up a little and stopped. He pried the hubcap off and set it beside the tire.

"We'll put the nuts in that. I'm gonna loosen them and then you see if you can turn them off the bolts with your hands."

Once he loosened them, they were easy to turn off. By the time I got two nuts off I learned I could spin them off quicker and then dropped them in the hubcap. I stood back while Dad jacked up the tire, so it cleared the street. By now, my hands were frozen numb. Even the pain from the arrow splinter was gone.

Dad yanked the flat tire off and placed it in the slot for the spare. He rolled the spare to the wheel hub and lined up the holes on the spare with the bolts on the hub. He held the wheel tight against the hub while I screwed each nut back on. I backed away and then Dad used the lug wrench to tighten the nuts. He used his foot to ram the hubcap back on the wheel. A car slowly drove by and pulled in front of us.

"Are you okay, Marshall?" It was Uncle Virgil.

"We're fine. I had a flat. We just fixed it. You got here a little too late." Dad smiled as he put the jack and lug wrench back in the boot.

"Just in time, from my point of view." Uncle Virgil said.

"Is Bullet okay?" I asked.

"He's fine. When I left, he was hunkering on a hambone. Merry Christmas." Uncle Virgil got back in his car and drove off.

Dad slammed the boot lid down, wiped his hands together, and I noticed he had done all this with his gloves on. My hands were filthy. Dad's gloves probably were, too.

"We're a pretty good team, Jesse. That only took us, uhh, under ten minutes." It seemed longer to me, but the clock in the tower showed ten minutes after six.

He pulled onto the street. "I don't know why I didn't turn, I was heading toward Springfield." He made a U-turn and drove south on U.S. 68.

"I sang at church this morning."

"That's nice. We should have had you sing for your grandma like you did last year."

"She's probably mad because I shot Bullet."

"Don't worry about that."

"You should come to church, just once, Dad. My pastor wants to meet you."

"Did you talk to him about me?"

"Yeah, I told him I hoped you and Mom got back together."

"Well, you can forget that. How's your paper route?"

"It's good. I got twenty-six dollars in tips this Christmas."

"That's good, real good. Do they still have that corpse in Sabina?"

"You mean Eugene? He's still there. I'll take you to see him if you want."

"Viola told me about him. Laying in that shed. I never got around to seeing him."

"You want to see him tonight?" I asked.

"He won't be open tonight."

"Let's drive by. I'll check. Sometimes they leave him open. It's only a couple blocks away." Dad was quiet for a minute.

"Show me how to get there," he said.

This was great. If I could get Dad to see Eugene, I knew I could get him to church.

When we arrived, the shed was dark. "Wait here, I'll check."

At Eugene's door, I was in such a hurry I nearly broke my knife jimmying the lock. I ran back.

"It's open, Dad. We're in luck. C'mon." He sat in the car for a moment and then, left the car running and joined me at Eugene's door. I turned on the light, and he walked in with me.

"Well here he is. Dad, meet Eugene." I told him everything I knew about Eugene while he stared at the dead man. I told him about how he died, how they found him, and about them trying to find out who he was.

"He was lost, Dad. I'm sure he got lost and ended up here. Look, here, write your name in his book. A million people have stopped here to see Eugene. He's still lost, Dad. Nobody cared, so he found Sabina. Here he is." He stood by the book, then put his name in it.

"I think I'm his only friend. Me and Karen."

This trip, Dad even came upstairs to see Christina. He helped me with the gifts and when I gave Mom the Christmas envelope, he pulled his out and handed Mom the twenty dollars that was inside. I guess he got his job back. He looked around, picked up Christina and jabbered at her, and said, "Merry Christmas, little girl."

She laughed and smiled.

"Thanks for your help, Jesse." And then he walked out the door.

"Merry Christmas, Dad."

"What was that about?"

"We had a flat. I helped him change it."

She gripped her two twenty-dollar bills. Rent.

Maybe Eugene had something to do with Dad's sudden change of heart.

After the Christmas holidays, my subscribers started asking me about the March of Dimes and if I would have cards this year. Mr. Davis personally brought me 200 cards to distribute to my subscribers and local businesses. Each card held five dimes. These cards were printed up with the *Cincinnati Press* name and, "Our Carriers March for the March of Dimes." Each paperboy was to not only provide a card for the subscriber but also the non-subscriber who lived next door. They doubled our papers and told us to deliver papers to whoever we gave cards to. He told us that we should get an increase in subscribers, which meant more income, and he was right. My route was increased by ten subscribers and netted me two dollars more each week plus tips. It was hard work without Lynn.

Abigail Stafford continued to chair the March of Dimes and smiled when I was again recognized as the top March of Dimes producer for the school. She was a frequent visitor to our apartment, bringing clothes to be altered by Mom. She was also paying Mom fifty cents for each jar of pickled asparagus Grandpa Smith brought to us.

My paper route was taking longer because of the additional customers and now with the snow melted, I was keeping a lookout for empty bottles. If I could get at least five bottles a day, that was seventy cents a week. When I took Christina on my route, I could cinch the canvas newspaper bag on the handle. It was easier that way carrying the papers and the bottles.

Lynn and I were limited to one three-minute call on the phone each weekend. Albert complained when we talked too long, and I realized he was paying for our phone. He and Mom talked a lot, mostly about Danny.

But I wasn't about to give up on Dad. I wrote him.

May 15, 1956

Dear Dad,

Mom said we move to Xenia soon. Before we do, I hope you will come here and watch me sing at church. Pastor Armey wants to meet you and give you a Bible he got for you. He gave me one and I like it. It has maps and photographs of Bible places. I hope you will do that.

I love you.

Your son,
Jesse

Victor Hess

Chapter Ten
Little League in Xenia

Finally, in June, Albert's house was nearly done and, by then, I accepted I would be living with him. Gary told me Albert would be my step-dad, but they were my half-brothers. Paula Jean was my half-sister, but she was their step-sister. I tried to understand it. I was fine with just brother and sister.

Saturday morning Albert, Gary and Danny picked us up for the drive to Xenia.

"Jesse, wait 'til you see the new house," Gary said.

"Where will I sleep?"

"You'll share your room with Christina," Albert said.

"Danny and I will be in the room right next to yours," Gary said.

"I got Gary and Danny bunk beds," Albert said.

"Albert?" I asked.

"Yes, Jesse." I was in the back seat, but we made eye contact through the rear-view mirror.

"Will I call you Albert or Dad? Can I call you Dad?"

"What do you call your father?" Albert asked.

"Dad," I said.

"Then why don't you call me Father, so there's no confusion," he said with a smile. I smiled back.

When we turned onto Marshall Drive there were new houses on each side of the street. Some had people living in them already, some had garages, some had basements, some had fresh new sod grass, and some had dirt with straw to protect the grass seed. There were trucks, tractors, backhoes, and workers everywhere. We pulled up to a house with a dirt yard, no trees, and men in front laying brick. The numbers 7 8 5 were crudely painted on a small piece of board. Behind the house was a field with a fresh crop of corn nearly as tall as my chest. We walked up the front wooden temporary steps to the door that had a rope for a handle and walked in. The odors of paint, spackle, drywall, and freshly sawed wood were combined into a special newness.

We looked at every room. Then we walked down into the full basement. Everything was brand new. The furnace was in the center by the stairs. There were shiny pipes going out of the furnace and new copper water pipes and fresh wood beams held up by metal posts. It was damp, and the drying concrete smelled different from the main level.

"Come on, Jesse, we'll show you your school," Gary said. "Okay, Dad?"

"You guys go. Don't be long. We'll pick you up at the park."

On the way Gary showed me the Field House where they had a gym and played basketball. Then we turned and within a few minutes got to my school.

Shawnee School was brand new, all on one level. The playground had swings and monkey bars and a basketball goal and teeter-totters.

"Why is it called Shawnee School."

"The Shawnee Indians lived all over this place a long time ago," Gary said.

"Really? Real Indians?" I was liking Xenia even more now.

"Yeah. We have Shawnee School, Tecumseh School. Tecumseh was a great Indian leader. We have Simon Kenton School. He was a pioneer," Gary said.

"What grade will you be in?" Danny asked.

"Sixth."

"You'll be here for sixth grade. Then you go to Central.

Come on."

Shawnee School also had a baseball diamond, and this morning there were kids my age with hats and gloves and adults with clipboards.

"It's a tryout!" I yelled and started running toward the players.

I ran past Gary and Danny to one of the men with clipboards.

"Is this a Little League tryout?" I was out of breath but got the words out all right.

"Yes, son," he said. "It is, but you're gonna need a glove."

"I'm new here. We haven't moved in yet. Can I try out?"

"When do you move here?"

"Next week."

"Where will you be moving?"

"Gary, where are we moving to?" I yelled back as he and Danny caught up.

"Marshall Drive, Mr. Arnold," Gary said.

"Hi, Gary. What's your name, son?"

"Jesse, Jesse Hall."

"He's our brother," Gary said.

"You're Gary and Danny Tarrant's brother?" He had a tone of suspicion.

"It's complicated, Mr. Arnold. He's our brother all right. He's our half-brother."

"We just finished tryouts, but I'll give you a shot. There's always room for one more. Neil, can Jesse borrow your glove for a few minutes?" A kid my size ran over to us.

I was exhilarated. Neil handed his glove to me.

"Don't hurt it," he said like he was handing me a new puppy.

"I won't. Thanks. Thanks a lot!"

The inside of his glove was still warm and damp from his tryout, but as quickly as I put it on my left hand, it felt like my own glove.

"Dad probably won't let you play!" Danny said.

"Well, we'll let him try out and deal with that if we have to," said Mr. Arnold.

In fifteen minutes, I hit enough balls, caught enough flies, and fired off enough balls to Mr. Arnold that he smiled and told me I could be on the team.

"Practice starts here in two weeks. Be here a week from next Saturday at 10 a.m. sharp."

The dreaded move to Xenia suddenly was a dream come true. I felt that God was somehow mixed up with this, and I thanked him right there. I was going to be on another Little League team.

We walked completely around Shawnee School and peeked in the classroom windows. These desks weren't bolted to the floors like in Sabina, and the blackboards weren't black, they were green.

While we walked to the park, Gary warned me to not be excited and so happy when I told Albert I had made a Little League team.

"I don't think Dad likes happiness," Gary said, and Danny agreed with him. "I'll start it off, okay?" I agreed and didn't realize how much my own happiness might depend on Gary's skill at communicating with Albert.

When we got to the park, Albert's car was by the pond. Mom and Christina were sitting on the bench watching the ducks.

"Hey, Dad. We saw Mr. Arnold. You remember? My cross country coach. He was at Jesse's school. He said 'Hi.'"

Gary talked like we were at the dinner table in response to "What did you do today?"

"What was he doing at an elementary school? He teaches at the high school," Albert said. I was ready to jump in with my news, but Danny held me back.

"He coaches Little League, and they had tryouts today at Shawnee. I told him about Jesse moving here. He asked about your stereo setup. I told him how good it sounded."

"Does he have a stereo?"

"Oh, yeah. He just has a turntable. He wants to get a tape set up. He asked what kind you had, but I couldn't remember."

"You know I have an Ampex."

"Oh, yeah. I'll tell him."

I moved forward to tell him I had made the team, but Danny squeezed my arm.

"Mr. Arnold offered Jesse to try out."

"I suppose he jumped right in," Albert said with an air of disgust. I stepped back.

"Oh, no. He couldn't, he didn't have a glove."

"Too bad you didn't bring your glove, Jesse," Albert said, like a taunt.

"It's okay, Dad. Mr. Arnold loaned him one of the players' gloves and hit him a few balls. Jesse did okay. It's a new team and Mr. Arnold's in a bind, so we said we'd ask you. Practices are Saturday mornings and that would get us out of the house while you listen to your stereo." Danny held my arm tightly.

"We can't afford to pay for a uniform."

"I could probably make him one, Albert," Mom said.

"I still have paper route money to buy a uniform. I already have a good glove," I finally said, as soon as Danny let go.

"You have to pay for your baseball stuff," Albert said and the conversation was over.

This was amazing. I moved to Xenia and immediately made Little League. I looked over to Mom, who was smiling back. That night, I wrote Lynn.

June 23, 1956

Dear Lynn,

Guess what. We move to our new house next week. Our new address is 785 Marshall Drive, Xenia, Ohio.
Guess what. The blackboards in our school are green. It's called Shawnee School, like the Indian tribe.
How are you? How many subscribers do you have?
Guess what. Billy Archer is going to take over my route. I show him everything this week. Mr. Davis said he doesn't have a route for me in Xenia yet. He might in September, when one of his paper boys goes to college. Tell Brian I got on the Little League team in Xenia. I tried out and made it. You should have seen Gary talk Albert, I call him Father now, into letting me be on the team.
Well, good bye.

Your best friend,
Jesse

The evening of June 29th, 1956, I gathered my belongings in my cedar trunk and helped load it in the back seat. Albert and I maneuvered the sewing machine into the boot of his car and tied the lid down with twine. Mr. and Mrs. Williams said it was to be Mom's wedding gift.

Albert drove Mom, Christina, and me to our brand-new home. All the windows were rolled down in the car and gradually those smells of Sabina and the surrounding farms were replaced with that of fresh lumber, brick, and asphalt.

Chapter Eleven
Fireworks at the Fairgrounds

My first day in Xenia, I sat on the concrete front porch and surveyed the street, dreaming about Little League practice, smelling the fresh asphalt, and studying the maneuvers of the tractor grading the lawn next door. From left to right I studied each house, some occupied, others in various stages of construction, and one lot still vacant, waiting for a new home to be built.

I saw two kids walk into the wooded hillside across the street. I followed them without them seeing me, like I was an Indian scout. I ran over into the wooded area, found a path and followed it into the woods where I heard voices. I moved carefully from one tree to the next. As soon as I made the bend in the path, I saw five kids, all around my age, playing on a hillside that had recently been cut into by a bulldozer or backhoe. It had paths leading to the top of the hill. There was a ledge that was high enough to look dangerous, but at worst, might cause a sprain if you fell from it. They were playing there with some store-bought weaponry that put to shame the sticks we used in Sabina. The kids had strips of white or red cloth tied around their right arms. They didn't see me spying on their maneuvers.

Finally, one of the older ones yelled, "Who is that guy?" They all stopped and stared at me, one aiming his rifle at me.

"Hey," I said. "I just moved here. I live over there." I pointed in the direction of our new house. "What are you playing?"

"Army," said the kid on the hillside. "You're on the Little League team, aren't you? You tried out with Neil's glove."

"Yeah, I'm Jesse. Can I play?"

"Sure, do you have a gun?"

"Not yet. Can I use a stick?" I asked.

"Yeah, but you'll have to be a Jap." Immediately another Jap handed me a stick and a red piece of cloth.

I felt officially part of the neighborhood. Today I was a Jap with boys my age. No girls.

One boy had a complete army outfit like in the Sears catalog, including a helmet. He said he had a BAR, Browning Automatic Rifle, which I learned meant he could kill more people. If we got shot, we had to stay dead until we counted to 100 before we could come back as a reinforcement.

At 9:30 one of the kids reminded everyone about Little League practice and three of us scattered to our houses to get our gloves and get to Shawnee School by 10 a.m.

Practice was not like tryouts. There were three adults, each working with a different group of us. What I learned most at our first practice was what position I wouldn't play. I wasn't good enough to be in the infield. I could throw the ball all right, but I couldn't make it go into the catcher's mitt, so I wasn't going to be a pitcher. I was too new at the game, so I wouldn't be a catcher. That made me an outfielder. Probably right field, Mr. Arnold had said. They worked us hard at practice and I slowly walked home covered with dust and sweat.

Albert was sitting in the living room, drinking coffee, and reading a magazine. I had cleaned up after practice and lay on the rug listening to the music.

"Who is that?" I asked.

"Ella Fitzgerald." She was singing "Just One of Those Things."

There was a shelf full of records and another one with tapes.

"Who do you like most?" I asked. I don't think he heard me.

"I like Patti Page. Mom sings like Patti Page. Have you heard her sing?" I looked up from the floor, but he stared at his magazine and said, "Hmm," but not to me. It was like he was talking to his magazine.

"Little League practice was fun today. I'm a right fielder."

Ella Fitzgerald started singing "Begin the Beguine." I looked up again, but Albert was gone. Then Mom called me into the kitchen.

"You need to leave Albert alone when he's reading. Let's take Christina to the park," she said.

"Where's Danny and Gary?"

"In the basement."

When we got back to the house from the park, we went in through the back door.

"Now, be quiet and let Albert listen to his music. Stay out of the living room."

Monday, the mailman delivered our mail at ten in the morning and one of the envelopes was addressed to me. It was from Lynn.

June 28, 1956

Dear Jesse,

Your school sounds neat. I haven't looked at my new school yet. I have thirty-eight subscribers. I hope you get a route in Xenia soon. Father got me a changer, like I gave you last Christmas. I like my route, but it's lonely without you. Father made a rule. Don't ever go inside anyone's house or in anyone's car. He made me take him around my route with me and he wore his deputy uniform. We went up to every house and he introduced himself. He set up a savings

account. Half my money goes in it. I have $10 so far. You need to do that when you get your route.
Well, call me sometime.

Your best friend
Lynn
P. S. Father says bully for you for Little League.

Wednesday was July 4th. Mom was readjusting her sewing machine, which was set up in the small family room adjacent to the kitchen. Christina was teething and was crying. Albert checked the connection to the reel-to-reel tape machine and turned the music loud enough to cover Christina's cries.

"Dad, can we take Jesse to the fairgrounds for fireworks tonight?" Gary asked over the recorded organ music.

Albert was adjusting knobs and finally responded, "Check with Jesse's mother. You two can go if you want and come straight back." I was learning Albert might agree to anything that got us out of the house while he was home.

"I'll go with you. Christina has never seen fireworks," Mom said after Gary gave her the details.

Christina was almost two years old and loved to go anywhere in her stroller.

We weren't the only ones walking on Fairground Road to see the July 4th fireworks. Cars and people were creeping along the narrow road. I was pushing Christina on the gravelly shoulder that shook the stroller and she'd say "Ahhh," while the vibration made her voice sound like she was speaking through a fan. To her it was entertainment, and by the time we reached the fairground, she was giggling.

Just as we arrived, the sky started exploding with color.

"How about that?" Gary pointed up as simultaneous

red, white, and blue bursts filled the sky.

"Wow, how do they get all the colors?" I asked, still gazing into the sky. I held Christina as her eyes responded to each burst and boom.

BOOM, BOOM, went more fireworks. The ground shook! It went on for fifteen minutes. The air was filled with the smell like a million striking matches. Mom kept her eyes on the sky like the rest of us. There were fizzle sounds and crackle sounds and then another boom followed momentarily by another display of color. Suddenly Christina started crying, but when I pointed at the next display of color, she would giggle.

"Where's Danny?" Mom asked.

"He was just here." I said. "Wow, look at that!" There was a green burst just above us.

"Danny!" Gary yelled as another volley of fireworks exploded overhead.

"Put Christina in the stroller and look for Danny," Mom said.

"Stay here, Mom. We'll find him," Gary said.

In just a few minutes the fireworks stopped and instantly, people started pouring out of the fairground.

Gary took me up in the grandstand. "Look around, Jesse. Let me know if you see Danny."

From the grandstand I could see Mom standing next to the stroller. She was holding Christina in her arms and talking frantically to a policeman.

"I see him," Gary said, pointing to a white building. "Let's go. Danny's in for it."

"Where do you think he went?" I asked.

"I saw Bart Neal here. Dad won't let Danny be with the Neal kid. It ends bad, every time. Let's go."

Mom was still talking to the policeman.

"Mom, he left with Bart Neal. I saw him on the back of Bart's bike. We may as well go home."

When we got home, Albert was listening to "How High the Moon" by Les Paul and Mary Ford on the stereo. The music was like something I had never heard before. I heard the song before, but not like this, blaring different sounds out of two wonderful speakers.

"Is Danny here, Dad?" Gary asked when we got his attention.

"No. Isn't he with you?"

"He snuck away with Bart Neal while we were watching the fireworks. I'll call over at their house."

"How could you let this happen?" Albert said directly to Mom.

"I'm sorry. We were all watching fireworks." She retreated out of the room. I stood quietly in the corner, listening to the music. Then Gary came back in.

"He isn't there, Dad. Bart's missing too. They want us to call them if they come back here."

I went back with Mom in the TV room, as Gary paced from the living room where Albert was to the TV room where we were.

"How could he wander away like that?" she asked.

"He does this all the time," Gary said.

In the meantime, Albert went from Les Paul and Mary Ford, to Errol Garner and then to playing organ music. I really wanted to go in and listen, but Mom wouldn't let me.

At midnight, we were all still awake when a knock on the door presented a police officer escorting Danny.

"Are you Mr. Tarrant?" the officer asked.

"Yes. Danny, where have you been?" Danny was nearly in tears.

"Sir, Danny and his friend were discovered exploding cherry bombs in trash cans. They did some damage, Mr. Tarrant. Trash can lids were blown everywhere."

"I'm sorry, officer."

"We're leaving him with you, but charges are being filed. You know this is his second run-in with us."

"I know. How serious is this?"

"We've had multiple complaints this time. He may have to go to juvenile court this time. It's up to them."

"He's not a bad boy," Mom said. "We'll watch him."

"They'll send you a letter about his appearance in court. I'm going to leave him with you." He got our address and phone number and left.

"Who were you with, Danny?" I asked.

"None of your business." He glared at me.

I stayed out of Danny's way during the week. Instead, I spent time walking Christina to the park or playing war on the hillside or watching Gary build planes and boats out of balsa wood in the basement. I was supposed to let Mom know whenever Danny left the house without telling her. It was easier watching Christina. If part of Mom's purpose there was to keep Danny out of trouble, she had failed her first test.

Chapter Twelve
Frisch's and the Drive-In Theater

Thursday, Paula Jean came by and took me to the Frisch's Drive-In. She was driving a new 1956 Hudson Hornet. It was a surprise to see her in it and more of a surprise when she said it was Grandpa Hall's. It was red and brown with lots of chrome on it.

"Uncle Harold gave Grandpa a good deal," she said.

"It's kind of fancy for Grandpa." It smelled new, like the Thunderbird did last year.

"I know. Grandma loves it."

It was just Paula Jean and me in the car. We parked by a post with a metal box and Paula Jean pressed a button and this voice came over it. "Welcome to Frisch's. How can I help you?"

"I'll have a Big Boy, fries and a medium Coke," Paula Jean said and turned to me. "What do you want, Jesse?"

"Can I have a grilled cheese and chocolate shake?"

"And a grilled cheese and chocolate shake," she yelled in the speaker.

The voice repeated what we had ordered and then asked, "Does that complete your order?"

"Yes."

"Is this for here or to go?"

"For here."

It was my first time ever ordering food from the car.

"I'm getting married," she said. "I want you to meet Charlie. He's from Massachusetts. Wait 'til you hear his accent!"

"Are you moving?" I asked.

"We're going to Boston. You'll meet him Sunday."

"Have you seen Dad?" I asked.

"No."

"Do you think he's still drinking?"

"Well, he still lives over that bar. I know that."

"I wrote him, but he doesn't write back."

"Don't worry, Jesse. You're doing fine. Your new house is beautiful, and you are living with your brothers. Don't worry about Daddy. Don't you like your new house?" she asked.

"It's okay. I don't think Mom's happy. She stays in the TV room all the time."

"She watches TV?"

"No, her sewing machine is in there. She makes clothes for her and Christina. She's always sewing."

"What about Albert?"

"He's always in the living room listening to his Hi Fi."

"They just need to get used to each other."

"Mom even sleeps in the TV room," I said. "Danny got in trouble with the police last night."

"He's not in jail, is he?"

"No, but Albert blamed Mom."

"Do you and Albert do stuff together?"

"No. Gary and him do stuff together. They do hobbies in the basement."

"Well, it's just been a week."

"I know. Are all dads like that?"

"I don't know," she said. I guess neither of us knew.

"He won't even hold Christina."

"That reminds me. Aunt Becky gave me some books to give you, so you can read to Christina."

She reached on the floor for a bag. In it were *Bambi*, *Snow White*, the *Book of Words*, *Nursery Rhymes*, and *Pinocchio*. Christina was almost two and had already learned my name, Mom, and no.

"I already have *Pinocchio*," I said.

A girl, maybe Paula Jean's age, walked to the car and asked us to roll the window partly up, so she could fasten the tray of food to the side of the car. I studied the bracket that fit the edge of the window and the slanted post that fit against the car door, so the tray was level.

"One twenty-five," she said. Paula Jean gave her the exact amount plus a dime tip.

"Open the glove box. You can put your drink there." When I opened it, the inside of the door was like a little tray.

"Charlie and I are going to take you, Viola, Gary, and Danny to Waynesville and go swimming."

I took a bite out of my grilled cheese. It was so good, especially with the shake.

"I can't swim," I said. I had never been swimming.

"You don't have to know how to swim at Waynesville to have a good time. But you know what? Charlie is an expert swimmer. You watch. He'll have you swimming before we leave there."

"I don't have a swimsuit."

"Don't worry. I'll take care of that."

I had never seen a swimming pool except in newspaper ads. The more I thought about it, the more the idea seemed swell, and then, my grilled cheese slipped off my lap. I reached down to catch it before it hit the floor, moving my leg, and that lifted the glove compartment lid, so that the half cup of milk shake fell to the floor directly on the carpet of Grandpa's new car.

"Holy Jesus," I said for the second time in my life, moved my foot, but lost balance, planting my shoe in the middle of the chocolate mess.

"Oh God," Paula Jean said. "Not good."

She pressed the call button on the speaker and requested napkins and a wet rag. Almost immediately, a young boy came over to the car, asked us to get out, and systematically scraped and rubbed until all that was left was a wet stain on the brown carpet.

When we got to Albert's house, she borrowed a bowl, filled it with hot water, Wisk cleanser, and scrubbed the floor while I brought towels in the house and rinsed them out until she got it clean. Through all of this, I'm not even sure Albert knew what we were doing.

As soon as Paula Jean left, I wrote a letter to Lynn.

July 5, 1956

Dear Lynn,

>*How are you? Guess what?*
>
>*We already moved. The house is swell. I share my room with Christina. Tell Brian I already had one practice and they put me in right field.*
>
>*My sister, Paula Jean, is taking us swimming this Sunday to Waynesville Pool. Have you ever been there? I hope this letter gets to you in time so you could come, too. Ask Brian. She said her boyfriend can teach me to swim.*
>
>*Yesterday we went to a big fireworks show at the fairground. It was loud. Then Danny got in trouble with the police. He might have to go to court.*

Write back.

Your best friend,
Jesse
P. S. Don't call here after 5. That's when Albert gets home.

Before supper, I wandered around the house. Albert was sitting on the couch. He called it a davenport. Across from him were two speakers, two amplifiers, a turn table, a reel-to-reel tape deck, and a tuner. I quickly learned that all of that was off limits. The coffee table had an ashtray and two issues of *High Fidelity* magazine and a copy of the Xenia newspaper. There were two chairs by the front picture window with a floor lamp between them. In between songs, I could hear hammers pounding and backhoes moving dirt around outside. Every week a new house was finished and another one was started.

I walked through the dining room, set up with five chairs and Christina's high chair. A doorway opened into the kitchen with a gas range and the new refrigerator, toaster, and AM-FM radio. This was the radio I could tune in for music as long as Albert wasn't playing his stereo outfit. Dishes and food were in the cabinets which lined each wall. The sink had a window over it with a view of the nearly finished house next door. The floor in the kitchen was a checkerboard of black and white tile while the rest of the house had shiny hardwood floors. At the end of the kitchen was a small breakfast room but Mom furnished it with a couch (Mom called it a daybed), her sewing machine, and a small TV. She spent most of her time in there. There was a door that led into the backyard. Straw covered the yard, so the grass seed could take root without washing away in the rain.

Then, there was this hallway full of doors. There was a door to the basement, a door to the bathroom, a door to a closet, and three other doors to each of our bedrooms. My bedroom had Christina's crib in it with Danny's old bed. There were stairs to the basement where Mom had a wringer washer. Clothes lines ran where she'd hang clothes to dry. She had her ironing board in the basement, too. At the other end, Albert had a long table with electronic dials and bunches of transistors and other components. In the middle was the hobby table filled with balsa wood, plastic parts to models, and every color of Testor's model paint ever made. Gary was there cutting out the parts to a riverboat with his Xacto knife. Even downstairs you could hear Albert's music. I finally went outside, into the cornfield. Corn grows fast. It was up to my neck.

Friday night, Paula Jean took Gary, Danny and me to the drive-in theater. I had never been to one where you drive up and stay in your car to see a movie. We had to try out a couple parking spots before we found one with a speaker that worked. They were playing *Square Jungle*, about a boxer and *Silver Lode*, a western. The four of us in the car was so special, except when we had to search for Danny.

He got out to go to the bathroom and when he was gone for a while, Paula Jean got worried and sent Gary to find him. At the end of the first movie, Paula Jean wanted to go home, but Danny was still missing, so she went to the concession stand to report Danny missing. They made an announcement and eventually, just as the second movie was starting, Danny came to the car.

"I couldn't find the car. I forgot what color it was?" He smelled like cigarettes.

Now that we lived in the same town, Paula Jean could visit more often and became the big sister I had yearned for. She paid for the tickets, the popcorn, and drinks. We drove out during the second movie. I'm sure she was disappointed in Danny's antics.

Maybe it would be better when we went to Waynesville on Sunday. That is, if Albert let us go.

Chapter Thirteen
Waynesville Pool

By Sunday morning, Albert agreed we could all go to Waynesville with Charlie and Paula Jean. Albert spent the day at the house, probably happy to be alone listening to his music. Mom fried up two chickens and made potato salad.

"I left you some chicken in the refrigerator," she told Albert as we left.

Charlie's Buick was just large enough for everyone. The plan was to get there by 11, find a picnic table, and eat first. The afternoon would be spent in the pool.

There was just enough room at the table for all seven of us. Paula Jean held Christina, while Mom organized paper plates and the food. Tennessee Ernie Ford was singing "Sixteen Tons" over the pool's loud speaker.

"Vi, you have a good group of kids here," Charlie said. He talked funny. Paula Jean called it a Boston accent. But he was describing an unusual moment. For the first time ever, all of my brothers and sisters were in one place at the same time.

"Mom is not Paula Jean's mom, but her dad is my dad," I said.

"My dad is not Jesse's dad, but we have the same mom," Gary added.

"This is the first time Jesse ever lived with his brothers under the same roof," Mom said.

"I lived half my life with Grandma and Grandpa," Paula Jean said.

"More than half," Mom said.

"Why?" I asked.

"Mom left us and married Jesse's dad, and he left Paula Jean," Danny said.

"Danny, you were only three years old," Paula Jean said.

"That was before I was born," I said.

"Why'd you leave, Mom?" Danny asked. He looked directly at her, no smile, just hurt.

"We're together now," Paula Jean said tenderly.

"But you're moving," I said.

"I'll come back. Maybe you can visit me."

"Who wants chicken?" Mom asked.

"I do," nearly everyone said at once.

As Mom passed out plates with food, her hands were shaking.

"I've made a mess of things. But one thing I am proud of is all of you. Each one of you needs to be a brother or sister to each other. This is the first time you have ever been at the same table together." She had to use one of the paper napkins to wipe tears from her cheeks. "I can't change what has happened in the past, but when I look at you, I don't need to change anything. You are all good."

I hadn't seen Mom this way ever, except maybe when we sat together at the player piano that night she tried to kill herself or at Grandpa Smith's creek.

We looked around the table at each other with curious looks. Danny was already gnawing on his chicken leg.

"Charlie, can you teach me to swim?" I asked.

"You bet. You'll be swimming in just a few minutes once we get in that pool."

"Really?"

"We have to wait thirty minutes after we eat, so we don't get cramped up."

"Yeah, we learned that in Scouts," Gary said.

We followed Charlie to the pool while the Diamonds were singing "Why Do Fools Fall in Love."

I had never seen such a large swimming pool. It had three diving boards, including a high dive. There were two lifeguards. Charlie treated us to the thirty-cent entry fee. As we walked in, we were stamped on our hand. That way we could go back out to the picnic area and then come back in to the pool without paying again. Before we got into the pool, we each went under shower heads to shower off dirty feet and perspiration.

"You guys get in the water, and we'll watch Charlie for a few minutes," Paula Jean said.

Charlie dove in the water from the small board and swam across the pool with little effort. I hoped I could swim like that. Then Charlie dove off the high dive. By now, most of the swimmers had their eye on Charlie, because he was such a good swimmer and diver.

He finally came over to the edge of the pool where we were wading and asked me if I was ready to learn to swim.

"Let me see you duck under the water," Charlie said.

I could do that. I had done it hundreds of times in the bathtub. I ducked under, holding my nose.

"Now do it again but lift your feet off the bottom of the pool. Hold your breath and see what happens."

I ducked down under the water and lifted my feet up, so I was like a human ball. I gradually sank and started running out of breath, I came back up for air.

"That was good. You floated there for a while. Did you know that?" Charlie asked.

"Yeah, that was easy," I said, breathing heavily. Other swimmers were still watching Charlie.

"Okay, now do the same thing, only this time, don't hold your nose. You'll be fine as long as you don't breathe. Hold your breath. When you get under the water, twirl your arms around and see what your body does."

This time twirling my arms caused me to do a quick somersault. I twirled them the other way and did a reverse somersault. I came up for air. "That was fun," I said between breaths. The water went up my nose and burned. I coughed and coughed, and Charlie waited.

"Now, hold your breath and lay down on top of the water with your hands on my hands. Just let your feet float up to be with the rest of your body." In a few seconds, I was floating with Charlie's help, holding my hands above water.

"Don't be afraid to get your face wet. Just don't breathe."

I put my face in the water, and this time opened my eyes. I could see Charlie's legs and feet underwater. I could see kids moving their feet around while they were floating. Water clogged my ears, and everything sounded far away.

"Stand up, Jesse," Charlie said.

I obeyed, wiping my eyes. After a few seconds, my ears popped, and I could hear.

"I'm going to stand over here," Charlie said, moving just a couple feet away from me. "I want you to fall forward, lay full length on the water and start kicking your feet. Just don't bend your knees, keep your legs straight. I'll be right here."

I started to obey, but my feet didn't want to leave the bottom of the pool. Charlie stepped back and encouraged me to try it again.

This time, as my body fell forward toward Charlie, my feet came up and I started kicking, straight-legged. As I kicked, Charlie moved backwards and after about ten seconds of kicking, Charlie reached for my hands and told me to stand up.

"Look, Jesse. You were over there by Paula Jean and ended up here," Charlie said.

"Wow!" I said with a huge smile and wide eyes. I was on the other side of the pool.

"You can swim, Jesse!" Charlie announced.

Paula Jean applauded, along with some parents and

kids watching the five-minute swim lesson.

"You wanna do it again?" Charlie said.

"Yes!"

When I got to him, I stood up but was so excited that I breathed in the water and started coughing again.

"Swim to your sister."

I headed to Paula Jean. I repeated the exercise a few more times and then got out and went over to the fence between the pool and the picnic area.

"Mom, Mom, I can swim! Charlie showed me how to swim."

Gary and Danny joined me in the announcement, and Charlie went back to the high dive. All eyes were back on him.

Gary and I turned around to head back to the pool but stopped in our tracks.

"Lynn?" I yelled.

Brian, Arlene, and Lynn were walking through the entrance.

"Jesse, I got your letter!" Lynn yelled. Lynn was wearing a swim suit. The first thing I noticed were breasts that were never there before. I tried not to stare.

We hugged instantly. She held tightly to me until Brian and Arlene came over to join us. Somehow, during the past year, we became the same height.

"Where's your mama?" asked Arlene.

"Over there." I pointed to the picnic table on the other side of the fence. "Mom! It's Lynn." I grabbed her hand.

"I just learned to swim," I told Lynn, and we both headed to the pool while Brian and Arlene went to visit Mom.

Lynn and I were in the pool, me swimming to Lynn, and her backing up until it looked like I was struggling. Then she would come over to me and stretch like she was trying to pop out of her swim suit. I tickled her ribs each time she did it. Paula Jean, Charlie, Brian and Arlene introduced themselves. Gary and Danny were diving off the diving board.

"How's your new house?" Lynn asked.

"It's fun. There must be ten kids on our block. We're always outside when it isn't raining. My school is brand-new. How's your paper route?"

"Forty subscribers."

"That's eight dollars a week," I said. I was already jealous.

"Plus tips," she said, throwing her butt out of joint to make her point. "I wrote you back."

"Good. You want to see Christina?" I asked.

"Yes! Where is she? Father, we're going to go see Christina."

"Brian, I made Little League in Xenia!" I yelled back to Brian.

"Lynn told me. I knew you would."

"Have you been here before?" I asked Lynn.

"Yep. We love it here. Sometimes Mama brings me when Father's on duty."

We carried Christina to the wading pool.

"Albert won't ever bring us. I'll have to get Paula Jean to do it. When are you coming again?"

"I thought you called him Father."

"He told me I could call him Father, but it doesn't come out."

"I'll call you in a week, when I know. Okay?"

I blew raspberries on Christina's tummy and her laugh became contagious to everyone around the small pool.

Arlene came over and picked up Christina. "You guys go have fun. I'll take care of this one."

When we got to the big pool, Lynn said, "Guess what?" Then she clammed up.

"What?"

She backed away from me. "Swim to me and I'll tell you. Guess what?"

I leaned forward and kicked my way to her.

"What."

When I got to her, she said, "Mama's pregnant."

"Wow."

I looked over to the wading pool where she and Brian were playing with Christina.

"She doesn't look pregnant."

"It's due Christmas."

"Wow."

"Yeah. That means gifts just once a year," she said

"That's no good."

"Yeah."

Before we left, Brian asked me to sit with him and Mom at the picnic table.

"Viola, we finally got the full story about Randy Shepard. First, he wasn't really a pastor. He lied to his congregation for two years. He and his wife couldn't have children, but he didn't want to adopt because he wanted a boy, someone special, like Jesse. That's why he made up that letter. It backfired so much that he lost his church and his wife."

"What was he doing with Mike?" I asked.

"Mike admired the guy. Tim's dad did, too. He was family. That's why he became an assistant coach. When he started acting weird with a couple of the boys, Tim's dad got rid of him, and it just broke him. That day, he kidnapped Mike and thought he could take both of you and start a new life. They're treating him at a hospital." His story was so much different from what Mike told me.

"How could Mr. Mallard let that man get close to our kids like that?" Mom asked.

"Remember, Mom. Mrs. Mallard was the preacher's sister," I said.

"Sister-in-law," Brian said. "He was married to Mrs. Mallard's sister. He conned them all. Shepard made Mr. Mallard feel important and controlled a few other people the same way. Mike's mom was the first to complain, but Mike wouldn't believe it until it was too late."

"Is that why they put Mike in boarding school?" I asked.

"Probably. That and the embarrassment of getting caught stealing stuff off buses. Anyway, you're safe and very brave. Everyone thinks so."

I looked at Mom and she smiled back at me.

The day we spent at Waynesville pool was one of the best days I ever had. Even Danny stayed out of trouble. Gary wouldn't let him out of his sight.

Lynn was so different. I found myself staring at her a lot. I couldn't take my eyes off her.

Chapter Fourteen
"How Brave are You?"

From the very first week we moved in Albert set rules. We weren't supposed to talk in the living room while he was listening to music or reading. Christina and I were not allowed in the living room. It wasn't a rule, but Mom never went into the living room, except to clean. He wanted a home cooked meal by 6 p.m., and it was to be eaten at the dining room table. We were a family of six, sitting around the table, two-year-old Christina in her high chair, just like the ads in the paper that showed happy families. Mom did all she could to make the meals taste good, but often Albert would complain about a minor detail - too much salt, too dry, potatoes undercooked.

"I like it Mom," I said. Mom was a good cook.

One day Mom put the chuck roast on the table in the same bowl mixed in with carrots, celery, and potatoes, straight out of the roaster. That's how Mom made it. You could pass the bowl around, pick out your meat, pick out your potatoes, and pick out the carrots, celery, and onion. The flavor was awesome.

"I can't eat it this way," Albert said. "It's mixed up."

Then, Albert left the table, went to the kitchen and fixed himself a peanut butter sandwich. When he came back to the table, Mom started breathing heavy and left the room.

"Viola, we all need to be at the table," he said. She returned and could only eat a small part of her meal. Danny, Gary and I sat there and looked down, eating quietly. Mom's hand was shaking under the table while she ate with her other hand.

She was cooking food in the most modern kitchen she

had ever had, but no matter how hard she tried, Albert was hard to please. He liked to control, and the way he did it was to criticize and belittle with his subtle methods. Silence, shaking of the head, heavy sighing. He used all those methods to make sure that everyone in the house depended only on him for acceptance and approval. Danny was always nervous at the table because Albert would bring up his school failure, his sneaking off, and his sloppiness. I was new to this and became more and more uncomfortable.

Albert did like some food, like ham, Lima beans, and bread. I hated Lima beans. I was fine with the ham and buttered bread, but I wouldn't touch the Lima beans.

The next day, Albert made me sit alone at the table until I ate all those beans. I didn't understand it and started bawling at the table.

"You don't eat Mom's chuck roast," I said between sobs. "It's not fair." He glared at me.

"Jesse, finish your beans and be quiet. Here, take a bite." Mom reached over to my plate and spooned up two pale green Lima beans to my face. She looked at me, her eyes pleading me to take those beans and swallow them.

The night of the Lima bean affair, my head ached, so Mom sent me to bed early. The next day was Little League practice and even though I had a sore neck, I went anyway. While I was hitting at balls, the bat flew out of my hands and then I stumbled. Mr. Arnold looked at my face and put his hand on my head.

"Jesse, you have a fever. I'm sending you home. Can you make it?"

"Yes, coach."

I felt terrible. I was weak. My head ached worse than that time when I ran into the block wall in Sabina.

"When's the next practice?"

"Saturday at 10. You get well. We need you."

It was four long blocks from Shawnee School to our house. Once, I had to stop and throw up. I felt a little better until, a few doors from our house, I stumbled and collapsed on the sidewalk. I couldn't get back up. One of the neighbors saw me and carried me to our house. I protested, thinking I could make it on my own, but, as hard as I tried, I couldn't stand.

"You need to get this boy to a doctor," the neighbor insisted so convincingly that Mom called Dr. Thompson, who came to our house late. As hard as I tried, I couldn't move my legs to get out of bed.

Dr. Thompson looked at my eyes, in my mouth, and then used our phone to call the hospital just as Albert got home.

"We're going to need a spinal tap, and I want to do it as soon as possible. Meet me at Greene County Hospital. They'll be waiting for us." He was speaking directly to Albert.

"How much is this going to cost?" Albert asked.

"It could cost Jesse his life if we don't act quick. Take him in your car, and I'll be there shortly."

I started throwing up all over my clothes and bed again.

"You shouldn't have made him eat those Lima beans," Mom said to Albert.

Albert put an old blanket in the back seat of the car, grabbed a bucket and made Mom sit with me while he drove us the five blocks to the hospital.

"Make sure he throws up in the bucket," he said.

A nurse was waiting for us. They lifted me into a wheelchair and rolled me through a dark corridor. It seemed like we were going the whole length of the hospital, and finally we came to a large room with four empty beds. The nurse helped me into one of the beds. She had a mask on, and Mom was wearing a similar white mask. They helped me get out of my clothes and into a gown that didn't fit. When I got into bed, another masked nurse entered with a tray of instruments. My eyes focused on a shiny cylinder with a long needle on the end of it. Dr. Thompson appeared and asked me how I felt. He asked about my headaches. He asked if I had trouble swallowing, and I told him about the Lima beans. He said he understood while I stared at the needle.

"Jesse, how brave are you?" he asked.

"I don't know," I said. I was sweating. I felt so bad I wanted to die.

"I have to take some fluid out of your spine, so we can figure out what's happening to your body. It's going to hurt, but it'll all be over by the time I count to ten. Will you be brave for me?"

"To ten?" I asked.

"Yes," he said and then counted to ten, too slow, as far as I was concerned.

"I'll try," I said.

"Roll over on your side. I'm going to clean the spot where I get the fluid."

The nurse helped me roll on my side facing a window. I hurt all over. I could smell the alcohol, and it must have been a lot because even the smell burned in my nose. It was cold where he rubbed it on my back, and I moved quickly from his touch.

"Jesse, this time, you can't move, okay? We'll help." One nurse held my shoulder and arm. The other held my leg, like it was going to move anyway. They assured me that it wouldn't be long, and at "One," I felt the prick of cold steel on my back. I felt it go deeper at "two" and "three," and then a sensation on my spine that I can't explain. He was at number six when I realized how much it hurt. At "seven," I felt sick, and at "nine," he said, "Okay, Jesse. You're a champ."

Then I threw up.

Chapter Fifteen
Polio and Me

I must have slept through the night because sunlight was filling the hospital room when I woke up. I was on my back and immediately felt the pain from the spinal. My head was throbbing, and when I reached up to scratch my eye, nothing happened. My hand and arm would not move.

"Help!" I yelled. Instantly, a nurse came in the room.

"I can't move my arm." As I said it, I could tell my other arm was also limp. "What's wrong with me?"

I was in pain, but my only thoughts were Little League and how I was going to play in Saturday's game when I couldn't lift either arm, let alone walk.

"Jesse, we'll figure this out," she said while pressing the red call button.

I heard a buzzer sound outside the room, and another masked nurse came in.

"Get Dr. Grant." she said, raising the bed, so my head was higher.

"Jesse, my name is Annie. I'm going to take care of you. You're going to get well and I'm going to help."

She poured water from a pitcher into a Dixie cup. "Here, see if you can drink this."

I was thirsty and moved my head toward the cup she brought to my lips. I gulped the water down and drank the entire cup of water.

"That's good," I said. The sick feeling was going away.

"I'll get you a cup with a straw. Give me a few minutes."

I could see by her eyes that she was smiling at me. I was still thirsty.

Annie left the bed up, and I looked around the room. The other three beds had sheets snugly tucked around the mattresses. I could still smell the alcohol and iodine. There was a picture taped on the wall of a house and a stick family holding hands. It was drawn in colored crayons, probably by a child. A bright yellow sun took up the entire left side of the drawing.

Some of the wall behind the beds had medical stuff on them with cords and tubes coiled and ready for some important task, but they were now motionless like they, too, were drawn on the wall.

"Jesse Hall!" A deep voice came from a man wearing a robe and a mask. He rushed to the window and opened the blinds and turned back toward me, a shadow now with the glare of the sun behind him.

"Annie says you drank an entire cup of water!"

I wondered how drinking a cup of water was so special since I couldn't move either of my arms.

"My name is Dr. Guy Grant. You can call me Guy."

His eyes looked young, but he had white hair, cut in a flat top, like mine.

Annie walked in with another cup of water and a straw.

"Show me!" he said.

He bent over close to me as Annie positioned the straw at my mouth. I moved my head forward, took the straw between my lips and sucked in the cool water.

"That is good! Very good!" he declared. "If you couldn't swallow that water, we would be very worried."

Annie wrapped a cloth around my arm and inflated the cloth with a rubber bulb. She squeezed and then let the air out slowly while she listened to my arm through a stethoscope. Dr. Grant was holding my other hand, scraping a metal instrument over the back of it.

"Do you feel this?" he asked.

"No." My answer to his question confirmed to me how

serious my sickness must be and eliminated any expectation of playing ball on Saturday. Annie removed the cloth from my arm.

"One-oh-five over fifty-five," she said.

"What's wrong with me, Guy?" I asked. "Why can't I move my arm?"

"Do you feel this?" He scraped my other hand.

"No. What's happened to me?"

He moved to my feet and scraped the bottom of each one.

"What do you feel, Jesse?"

"Nothing." I started breathing hard. It didn't make any difference what he said. I already knew something terrible was wrong with me.

"Annie, stay with Jesse while I go talk with his mother."

Annie put a thermometer in my mouth and told me that she was sure I would get better, but it might take a while. She put a pill in my mouth, and I swallowed it with more gulps of water.

"What radio station do you like, Jesse?" Annie asked.

"WHIO-FM. Can you get that?"

"That's my favorite. We're going to get along really good."

After a moment, Doris Day was singing "Que Sera, Sera" on the radio.

"Where's my mom?"

"She's in the waiting room with Dr. Grant. We're keeping you isolated until we figure all this out. You won't be allowed visitors for a while."

"Even Mom?"

"We'll see."

"What day is it?" I asked.

"What day do you think it is?"

"I was at practice yesterday, I think. That was Wednesday. Is it Thursday?"

"Yep. See? You're doing better already. Who's your coach, Jesse?"

"Mr. Arnold."

I kept wondering if the Lima beans Albert made me eat made me end up in a hospital bed, not able to move, and probably never able to play ball again. I felt so much like crying, but I wasn't going to do it in front of Annie. That didn't stop tears from forming and slowly running down my cheek, like a fly walking on my face. I instinctively reached to scratch it but nothing happened. My arms were still motionless.

Annie gently wiped the tear away with a tissue. It was such a relief.

"How long will I be here?"

My question was interrupted by Guy escorting Mom into the room. She was masked and wearing a long gown and cap, but I still knew it was Mom.

"Oh, honey, I'm so sorry," she cried as she reached for my hand.

She was wearing rubber gloves. I could see her blue eyes well up with tears. I knew I was going to die.

"Jesse, you remember the spinal tap Dr. Thompson did?" Dr. Grant said.

"Yes, sir. What's wrong with me?"

"Do you know about polio?" he asked.

"Yes, sir. You die from it."

My immediate thought was the image of six-year-old Greg Davis who died of polio in Sabina. He was laid out at the Bigley Funeral Home last year. Lynn and I were so sad when we saw him.

"Jesse, very few people die of polio, and I'm sure you're not one of them. But, to be sure of that, we need to move you to another hospital."

I looked at Mom, feeling guilty for catching polio, being

sick, and causing so much trouble for her and Albert. Oh, Albert was going to be mad.

"I don't know how we can afford a hospital stay. How long will he have to stay?" Mom asked.

"Three months maybe."

The words shocked both of us. Mom started breathing hard. Then Guy and Annie explained how Greene County Hospital had called them in from Miami Valley Hospital because my doctor suspected I had polio.

Guy and Annie were from the polio unit at Miami Valley. They came here to determine whether I had just the spinal kind of polio, or if it would get worse where I would need help breathing or couldn't swallow anymore. He called that Bulbar polio. I immediately swallowed to check. I breathed in deep. Then I swallowed again, suddenly grateful.

"I can't afford this," Mom said softly.

"Mrs. Tarrant, every polio patient we have is taken care of by the National Foundation for Infantile Paralysis. Have you heard of the March of Dimes? That money is used to find a cure and pay the expenses of polio cases. Don't you worry about costs," said Annie.

Annie's words were comforting, like every worry I would ever have was erased from my life. Except playing Little League again. Mom's eyes reacted in such a way that I could sense the worry leaving her masked face. By now, I knew how she felt not having to ask Albert for money for expensive hospital treatment.

"When does he go?" Mom asked. "This needs to go with him." She handed Annie the box with my Bible and an envelope.

"It's a letter from Lynn," Mom said to me. I wanted to open it.

"We're ready now. It'll be a few days before he can receive visitors, and that includes parents, until we know what we are dealing with. I have papers ready for you to sign, and then we'll get him in the ambulance to take him to Dayton," Guy explained.

"Will you go with me?" I looked up at Annie.

"Yes, I will," Annie said, her eyes smiling. "Dr. Grant and I just came over to make sure that you had polio. I'm sorry about that part, Jesse."

"Me, too." I said.

"Jesse, I'll see you in Dayton," Guy said. "Annie will stay and travel with you." Then he turned to her. "Hold off on food until we get him in his new bed. Be sure to mask him up. Give this to him a few minutes before you leave." He handed her a small pill.

Annie started asking me questions about when I realized I was becoming paralyzed and what I ate and drank the day I came to the hospital. When did the headaches start? Was I short of breath during baseball practice? Who had I been very close to over the past few weeks? She wanted names. Was I sure I had received the Salk vaccine?

We were interrupted by two men in masks and coveralls who moved me onto a gurney and wheeled me back through the long hallway to the place Albert had dropped us off the day before. I was feeling drowsy from the pill but not so drowsy that I didn't notice the gleaming red 1956 Cadillac Meteor ambulance. They slid me in from the back, and Annie got in from a side door and sat beside me. It was raining.

Chapter Sixteen
Hospital and Indian Stories

I woke up to Annie and Guy standing beside me in a bright room.

"Are you hungry, Jesse? We are," Guy said.

I remember we had left the hospital in Xenia at 11 a.m., and the clock on the wall here said 12:15. I heard his words, but I was so ill, all I could do was stare at the ceiling.

I was lying on my back looking at a fan turning and turning. I could hear a whooshing sound, but the whooshing didn't match the rotation of the fan. I tried to move my head to see where it was coming from. Next to me was a long silver tube like you might see in a Flash Gordon comic. I could barely see the reflection of a head through a mirror.

"Jesse, meet your roommate, Scott," said Annie.

"Hi, Jesse." Scott turned his head just enough that I could see his face through his mirror. I could just barely make out his words over the whoosh, whoosh of the machine.

"Hey, Scott." I wanted to wave. "What's that?"

"It's an iron lung," she said

"Do I get one of those?" I asked Annie.

"Let's hope not. We'll know soon enough."

I imagined such a machine surrounding Greg Davis, the boy from Sabina. I felt a dread because of his lost battle with the disease that now held me motionless and Scott trapped until who knows when. Mostly, I felt sorry for Scott.

"Oh, here's food! Who's ready to eat?" Annie asked.

"I am," Scott said.

Two masked nurses wearing gowns carried in the trays of food. They put a napkin up to our chins and let us know that this was a bite of mashed potato or roast beef. The smell of food woke up my hunger.

"Do you like gravy, Jesse?" asked my nurse.

"I don't feel good," I said.

"Try a bite. Food will help."

"Hi, Scott. Who's your friend?" came an older male voice behind us.

"That's Jesse. He's new."

"Hi, Jesse, I'm Jim. I'm going to read to you two," he said. "Where are you from?"

"Xenia." I swallowed the bite of mashed potatoes and gravy. I smiled for another bite.

He pulled out a book from his bag.

"I have *Tecumseh*. Is that okay?" he asked. "Have you ever heard of him?"

"We have a school named that," I said after swallowing another bite of mashed potatoes and gravy.

Jim had pale eyes and a gray beard sticking out of the bottom of his mask. "Can you two hear me okay?" he asked, and he started reading right away.

"Chapter One, Tecumseh's Nation. Since the savages on this continent were known to civilized men, the Indian race has produced no more splendid genius than Tecumseh. Now, this book was written in 1878 and there was a perception of Indians that has been worn away by empathy and understanding. Anyway, there was just as much savagery on the pioneer side. To put it in perspective, the Indians had the land and the pioneers wanted the same land."

He sounded like a professor, but I still understood him. With each bite, I was feeling a little better.

"Whenever we played cowboys and Indians, I always wanted to be an Indian," I said.

"It might be the water. The Shawnee Indians camped around a lot of areas near Xenia. They even buried some treasure there that's never been found," he said as I gulped my water through a straw. It was like the nurse could read my mind when she tilted the glass toward my mouth.

"You can hunt for that treasure, Jesse," Scott said.

For one hour Jim read the first six chapters that was more like a history lesson than an adventure story. He even had a map showing the many places the Shawnees traveled. He said they moved and split up a lot. I knew how that was. I could tell that he would skip sections and learned later from him that the author considered Indians as savages, but then he said, "What would you do if someone tried to steal your land?"

Jim's reading was an escape from the dreadful disease we had. The book he was reading had boring sentences until he would stop, sit back in his chair, and then say, "Let me tell you something interesting." He had our attention.

"Jesse, when Tecumseh was six years old, his father was killed in a skirmish against British forces at Point Pleasant. With the aid of tribal elders and family, Tecumseh grew up to be a great Indian leader, even though his father was long gone."

I thought about my dad, and even though he wasn't killed or anything, he was just as gone. Then, like it was timed, Scott burped, then I burped. I felt a whole lot better, and it started a little burping contest.

Scott was a year older than me and lived with his parents in Troy, Ohio. I thought it was interesting that I had lived on Troy Street when we were in Dayton, and he said that the street went straight to Troy from Dayton. He had respiratory polio and needed the "lung," or iron lung, to help him breathe.

Someone was constantly coming into our room to give us a sip of water, massage legs, wash our faces, or test my breathing. Scott asked a nurse how Stella was doing, and we learned she stood on her own today. Stella was from Wilmington. I wondered if I knew her.

Whoosh, whoosh, went Scott's iron lung machine, and

its steady rhythm put me to sleep. Whoosh, whoosh.

When I woke up Friday morning, Guy and Annie were at Scott's lung machine, and I realized it was no longer running. The whoosh was gone.

"You undo the collar; I've got this end," said Guy.

"What happened! What's wrong with Scott?" I asked. I could see the iron lung coming apart and kept listening for the whoosh.

"It's okay, Jesse!" Annie said. "We're going to let Scott out for a while."

They placed him in a wheelchair and gave him a pair of gloves, and in seconds, he wheeled beside me.

"Hey, Jesse. Now I can see you without a mirror."

"Wow, how long can you stay out?" I asked.

"He'll be out a long time today. You help us watch him," said Guy. "If he gets to breathing too heavily, just yell for us. We'll come running," Guy said with a smile.

"Scott, show Jesse how you get when we need to get you back in the lung," Annie said.

Scott drooped his head down and started doing quick breaths.

"You guys watch out for each other," Guy said as they walked out the door.

Scott needed the lung to breathe. His legs were paralyzed like mine, but his arms worked.

"It sure feels good to be out of there," he said. "I hope you don't get respiratory." He deliberately took in a deep breath, a sign that his stomach muscles were working again.

"How long have you been here?" I asked. By now, a nurse was changing Scott's sheets in the lung.

"Two weeks. I'm one of the lucky ones. Some kids have been here for months. They think I only have one more week in the Silver Bullet."

"Silver Bullet?"

"Yeah, I named my lung the Silver Bullet. You know, like in the Lone Ranger."

"That's cool. I hope I don't have to name one."

"Me too, Jesse. You want some water?" He reached over for my cup with the straw and held it close to my lips. I sipped and swallowed. So far, so good on the swallowing. Scott took another deep breath.

"What's this?" He held up the letter next to my water. I had forgotten about it. The Bible was there, too.

"It's a letter from my friend, Lynn. Can you open it and hold it so I can read it?"

"Sure."

He opened it and pulled out a single page written on both sides along with a Polaroid. He held the picture for me to see. It was Lynn, Arlene, and Brian dressed like they were going to church. On the back, it said April 1956.

I wondered who took their picture.

"Okay. You ready for the letter?" Scott asked.

He held it in front of my face.

July 7, 1956

Dear Jesse,

You Guess What? Ha Ha. I got your letter. This is a picture of us Easter at the Methodist Church in Wilmington. I told Father about you playing right field. Good for him he said. Be sure to run fast. We might go to Waynesville, too. I hope we do.

I miss you, but I am happy here. I wish you were walking my route with me.

"Okay, you can turn it over," I said to Scott.

> *Mama got a job at the hospital. She said she might go to school to be a nurse.*
> *I will see you Sunday (I hope). I've changed. You'll see.*
>
> *Your best friend,*
> *Lynn*

"Do you want me to write her a letter for you?" Scott asked.

"Not right now. I have to think about it. Anyway, I saw her right after she wrote it."

So much had happened in between our two letters. A tear rolled down my cheek.

"I got it," Scott said and wiped it with a cloth. "I know the feeling." I still tried to move my arm.

Scott told me about the other kids who were on the polio ward. He talked a lot about Stella. I'm pretty sure he liked her. He wanted to be out of the hospital by September. It was still July.

"I have to stand all by myself. That's when it all gets better. Kids stand and then they can leave."

The two days since I got polio had gone by so fast. A lot of it I slept. When Scott told me about standing by September, I realized I'd be here a long time. My leg and arm muscles did not work, so I depended on people to hold napkins while I blew my nose and sit me on the commode, but they were all nice about it. Doing this for weeks and weeks frightened me. I swallowed. I was vaccinated against polio and got all those donations for the March of Dimes. It wasn't fair.

Our room had a radio on a table by Scott's bed. The room was big enough for four beds, but Scott's lung took up the space where the other two beds would be. A window was on the east wall and the sun filled the entire room in the morning. There was a clock above the doorway to the hall. It was two o'clock.

"Scott! It's your best friend," said a large nurse rolling in a table with a steaming pot on it.

"Bertha, this is Jesse," Scott said as he wheeled his chair around to face this huge woman whose mere presence demanded respect.

"Hi Jesse. Okay Scott, hop in the bed," said the lady.

She stood close to his chair as Scott locked the wheels and leaned forward, nearly thrusting himself on the bed with his arms. Bertha moved his legs onto the bed and extended them out after moving the chair out of the way. She lifted the lid from the large pot, and the steam billowed out, filling the already warm room. There were rollers like on our washing machine in Sabina. She ran some very smelly towels through and then jostled one from hand to hand, and then folded it and placed it on Scott's leg.

"Ouch. Ooh. Oooh!" he cried out. It frightened me.

"You're doing good, Scott. I'll be back. I'm going to work on Jesse now."

In between all of that, she cracked open the windows, immediately moving air through the room and forcing the smelly steam out.

I expected her to roll me over and lay hot towels on me, but she just lifted the sheet and started massaging my legs, one at a time. I couldn't feel it. I could see her hands moving on my legs but couldn't really feel it. I sensed it; I just couldn't feel it. I tried closing my eyes to see if that made a difference. I imagined having to live like this the next few months, or longer, and was sobbing. When I opened them again, she was gone. I turned my head and could see her pull another hot towel through the ringer. The smell was like when Mom washed our old wool blanket. It wasn't pleasant.

"Ouch. Ooh. Ooooh!" Scott said as she worked on his

other leg.

Back and forth, Bertha worked alternately on Scott and me. Towels on his legs and massaging my legs and then my arms. It seemed like an hour, but she still wasn't finished.

"You ready, Scott?" she asked. Before he could answer, she started bending one of his legs back. By his reaction, it must have really hurt. I could tell he was holding back tears.

"It has to hurt, Scott, or it doesn't work," she said. His head was now buried in his pillow.

"I know. It still hurts like hell," he said.

I expected a retort from Bertha about Scott's language, but she just repeated, "I know. We're going to get you out of here. No pain, no gain."

Between Scott's cries of pain and my questions about the towels and hot water, Bertha let us know about Stella and her standing up by herself, and the new Jewish girl who had arrived this morning from Tipp City.

"Jim told me he's going to read more about Tecumseh tomorrow morning after breakfast."

Jim made an otherwise boring story of Tecumseh interesting by explaining what he read. We wanted to learn what was going to happen after Tecumseh grew up. Maybe Jim had a clue about that Indian treasure. It lifted my spirits.

That night we listened to the Redlegs beat the Pirates on the radio as the night nurse helped Scott back in the Silver Bullet. The game went twelve innings.

"Scott, you did ten hours out this time. Dr. Grant is going to be very happy," the night nurse said.

Even though Scott had been at Miami Valley for only a few weeks, he was already getting better. The nurses were encouraging and congratulating him on the slightest improvements. If he could improve and get out of the bed awhile, I hoped I could too. Scott was smiling in the mirror. No wonder the kids in the iron lungs were always smiling in those *Life* magazine pictures. I guess they knew they were getting better. I swallowed and smiled. It was only my second day at Miami Valley Hospital. Behind my smile, I was afraid.

Whoosh, whoosh.

Victor Hess

Chapter Seventeen
Leaving Isolation

"How about those Redlegs last night!" Guy's voice woke us up. "How about Kluszewski's home run!"

"We heard it on the radio," Scott said.

"Yeah, it took us a while to get the right pitcher in there," I said with a yawn. "What's that?" I asked. Guy was at the foot of my bed.

"What's what?" he responded with a grin.

"My foot, did you touch my foot?"

"Which foot, Jesse. Which foot?"

"The right one. Yeah, the right foot."

"Try to move a toe for me, okay?"

I thought I moved a toe or maybe my foot. There was a tingle. I couldn't be sure. I smiled.

"We're on the mend, Jesse! You are going to break records here."

He moved around to my hands. "Grab my finger!"

I could move my fingers. I felt a tingling in my hand, but I couldn't do anything else. He moved to the other hand with the same results.

"I see them move. Jesse, we do miracles here at Miami Valley. Ask anyone."

"Way to go, Jesse. Let's see who walks first." Scott said, and the contest was on.

Then Jim read five more Chapters where we learned about Tecumseh's first battle, while nurses fed us a breakfast of eggs, bacon, and pancakes.

Tecumseh was with a group of Indians on the Ohio River seeking revenge for a raid by some pioneers on an Indian village. They spied a flatboat being oared down the Ohio and fired on it, killing all the men but one. They took him captive along with the cargo on the boat. At camp that evening, they brutally killed their captive by burning him alive. That act disgusted young Tecumseh so much that he made an eloquent plea to his older companions that turned them away from such viciousness. In future encounters, they would just shoot and kill the enemy.

I respected Tecumseh for that, but I was still sad the boatmen had to die.

A nurse was standing by the Silver Bullet to let Scott out, while an aide washed my face. I tried to make my fingers grip the sheet and then I just fell asleep. Sometime later, I'm not sure how long, I woke up inside a plastic enclosure.

"Jesse, wake up," a voice from faraway said. It was a woman's voice. "Jesse, can you hear me?" It was closer now.

"Where am I?" I asked.

"Jesse, you're in an oxygen tent. Can you count for me?" the voice asked.

"What?"

"Count for me, Jesse." I finally understood she just wanted me to count.

"One, two, three, four, five..." She stopped me at five.

"Jesse, I'm Doris. I'll be taking care of you the next few days. You're an odd one, young man."

"What?"

"Hi, Doctor," she said, and I could barely make out Guy through the plastic cover over my bed.

"Jesse." Before he finished, I was laughing. "Do you feel this?"

"Stop it!" I yelled. I could not stand my feet being tickled. Danny used to break into my room and hold my arms down while Gary would sit on my legs and tickle the bottom of my feet. I would laugh until I cried.

"HA!" Yelled Guy. "You want to tickle him, Doris?"

"No, no, please," I implored.

I was trying to reach to stop them. It felt like my arms were moving, and I was sure my fingers were grasping, but nothing really moved. He stopped, and I stopped laughing. I was breathing heavily.

"One step at a time, Jesse. It looks like the polio is attacking your respiratory system, but I think yours is fast moving."

"Where am I?"

"You're still here," Scott said. I looked around, and he was sitting in his wheelchair. "You're in our room. You passed out when Jim finished *Tecumseh*."

"Well, Jesse, we see some progress, but this respiratory thing is a set-back."

He described that respiratory was what Scott had, and that's why I needed the oxygen tent, because now I had it.

"Did I get it from Scott?"

"Oh, no, can't blame Scott. You had it the day that baseball bat flew out of your hands. It waited until today to present itself."

How did he know about the baseball bat?

"Do I get a Silver Bullet?" I asked, like it was a trophy.

"Not yet," he said.

I was slightly disappointed. He said that my polio was moving quickly and that as long as I was doing good under the tent and swallowing my food, the tent should do the job for now.

"But I need to do a test. I need to get more fluid out of your spine. Can you handle that?"

My back still hurt from the spinal I had gotten three days before, and no one said I would ever have to do it again.

"Here's my plan. We do a set of exercises since you are getting feeling back in your limbs. Right after the exercises, we'll do the spinal, and then we'll get a phone in here, so you can talk to your mom."

I liked the part where I could talk to Mom, but after watching Scott go through the exercises with Bertha, I wasn't sure I could do it. But I knew I would have to. Scott could do it.

"We'll do it," Scott said, on my behalf, so I was committed.

It was like a conspiracy because as Scott said his words, I heard, "Hi, Jesse, I hear you're ready for Bertha and the Kenny treatment." Even in the oxygen tent, I could smell the odor of Bertha's towels. I finally learned how Scott felt. She cranked open the windows.

"Ouuch. Ooh. Ooooh!" It was my turn.

Then Doris and another nurse arrived with a familiar looking tray. Even through the plastic I recognized the needle.

"Do you know what to do?" Doris asked.

"I know. Roll over. I'll need help." Bertha and the nurse positioned me on my side.

"Get ready. Here we go," Doris said.

"You're doin' good, Jesse," Bertha said and suddenly that cold steel was in my spine and I started breathing hard trying to get more air. And then, it was over. I was on my back, the plastic was back over my head and minute by minute, I felt relief.

Doris set the phone by my bed.

Even though I had feeling back in my hands and feet, Scott still had to hold the phone to my head so I could talk to Mom.

"Hi, Mom."

"Jesse! How are you? Tell me everything."

She started crying when I told her that I could feel my arms and feet. She said she would visit next weekend. She said Gary, Danny, and Christina were vaccinated with the Salk vaccine the day I left the hospital. She said Mr. Arnold called and said he would pray for me. I didn't tell her about the oxygen tent, but I did tell her about my second spinal.

"Mom, I had that vaccine. It doesn't work!"

"They told me you were in the trial group that got the salt water. Yours wasn't supposed to work."

"That's not fair. Can I come home?"

"When you're better, Jesse. It's not fair, but we'll fix it."

Doris took the phone when we hung up, wiped it with gauze and alcohol, unplugged it, and took it to another ward, so some other kid could talk to his parents.

Scott and I were alone in the room. He turned the radio on to a station that talked about weather, corn prices, and pork bellies. Then he found one playing Perry Como singing "Hot Diggity Dog Diggity."

"Is Lynn your girlfriend?" Scott asked.

"We're just friends." I told him about her helping me on the paper route and living downstairs from me in Sabina.

"Is Stella your girlfriend?" I asked.

"I don't know. She hasn't said anything yet."

"Girls are funny, I guess. One day, I turned my head around, and Lynn just kissed me on the lips. It was weird."

"What was weird."

"She wouldn't move away. She just stayed there moving her lips on mine. She never did it again."

When I told him that happened in Eugene's shed and he learned that Eugene was a corpse, he got real interested. We talked a long time.

"Scott, can you help me write to her?"

"Sure. I'll get the pen and paper."

He wheeled around the room, opened a drawer, and came back beside me.

I dictated my letter to Lynn.

July 14, 1956

Dear Lynn,

You'll never guess what. I have polio. I am at Miami Valley Hospital. I'll be here for a while. My friend Scott is writing this for me because my feet and hands don't work right now. They will later because Guy, my doctor, said so. I hope you don't get it. Please write me and let me know.

"How will she know the address?" I asked Scott.
"They'll send it in a Miami Valley envelope," Scott said. I kept dictating.

Except for the polio, it's nice here. The food is good. Every day they put hot cloths on me and bend my legs. It hurts and the cloths stink, but it has to hurt for it all to work.
Tell Brian, I didn't even get to play in the first game. I guess I have to wait one more year.

Please write.

"Sign my name, J E S S E." I wanted Scott to spell it right.
"I'll take it to the nurse. They'll mail it," Scott said. He picked up Lynn's envelope and my letter to her.

"How about those Redlegs? Where are their bats? They better win today!" Guy said. "Both you guys will be out there playing ball by next spring. You mark my words!"
"Did you know I didn't get the real vaccine?" I said.

"I know. We found out after we brought you here. You were dealt a bad hand. If it wasn't for that test, they couldn't be sure the vaccine worked. We'll get you through this. You're kind of a hero. Like when you made all that money for March of Dimes."

"How'd you know about that?"

"I know everything. Jesse, you did fine. You're on Bertha's list for another Kenny treatment today. I'll see you two tomorrow."

He left the room as nurses brought in our lunch. After we ate, a masked nurse came in with good news for Scott.

"Scott, wear this mask. We're going for a walk. Jesse, try to get some rest while I take Scott outside."

Watching Scott leave the room in his wheelchair was promising, but I was still stewing about the vaccine. It wasn't fair.

I remembered us lining up for those shots. There were two lines. I figured they were going by the alphabet or something. The shots hurt and some kids broke out of line, afraid to have that needle stuck in their arm. Why did I get chosen for the fake vaccine?

The oxygen tent was circulating oxygen infused air into my plastic canopy and had a cooling affect. Even better was the occasional visit by a nurse or intern who would wipe my face, arms, and legs with wet rags to cool me down. Scott was back just in time to hear the Redlegs lose to the Phil's, two to nothing.

"Dr. Grant isn't gonna be happy about that," Scott said.

Sunday morning, they took the oxygen tent away. Scott's parents visited us, donning gowns and masks. By watching them with Scott, I knew this was the kind of family that I yearned for. They talked about good times before Scott got polio and their plan to handle Scott's school this fall if he was still in the hospital. These were things I imagined Albert and Mom discussing. I was anxious to get back to our new house.

"Look what I got, Jesse, an *Archie* comic. I'll read this to us later," Scott said.

The Redlegs were winning the first game of a double-header in the background, and then we listened and cheered when the game went into extra innings.

Monday started with Annie waking us up with good news.

"We're moving you guys today. How would you like to get out of isolation?"

"No more masks?" Scott asked.

"Yep, one step at a time."

"What about the Silver Bullet?"

"Silver Bullet stays here. You'll have to fend for yourself, kemo sabe! You guys will have to name your chairs."

They moved both of us to the same room. One oxygen tent was available for us, but I didn't need it anymore. Scott used it a couple times, but only for a brief period. Bertha saw us twice a day. Unfortunately, we were told the hot towels and stretching therapy were a daily routine until we went home and even after that.

After dinner, Annie wheeled me into the TV room with Scott following us under his own power. I counted nine kids in the room in various stages of treatment. It was good knowing we were not alone. Kids were in wheelchairs, braces, and crutches, gathered around the eighteen-inch TV to watch "The Little Rascals." At another end of the room were shelves with games and books.

"I see you finally got out," said a black-haired girl about my age. She was wearing braces on both legs.

"Hi, Stella," Scott said. "How come you're not watching TV?"

"I'd rather read." She had thick pink glasses on. Underneath them she was a very pretty girl.

"I'm Stella," she said directly to me. Her glasses magnified her eyes and I felt small.

"This is Jesse," Scott said, rolling his wheelchair close to Stella.

Suddenly, I realized my hands could move. I grasped the wheel. One step at a time.

"Are you from Wilmington?" I asked.

"Yep, how about you?"

"I lived in Sabina before we moved to Xenia."

"I've been there to church camp. We went to see the dead guy they have in that little building."

"Yeah, Eugene. Did you write your name in the book?"

"Twice. Is he still there? They should bury him."

"He was when we moved away. We went to a Halloween party and some college guys stole Eugene and put him on the porch at our party. When we got outside on that porch, he scared the dickens out of us. They put this hat on him and tied him to a post." Suddenly we were surrounded by other kids wanting more details about my friend Eugene. I wished I had Karen's picture of us on that porch.

Thursday, I received a letter from Lynn, and I could actually hold it in my hand and read it on my own.

July 17, 1956

Dear Jesse,

> *Oh, no! I cried when I got your letter. Father thinks you got polio from the swimming pool. Mama took me to the doctor, and they don't think I got it. Let me know everything. How long will you be there? Can you have visitors? I want to see you. I told Mr. Davis and he said he'd look into it.*

> *Love,*
> *Lynn*
> *P.S. Eugene says get well!*

"That's weird," I said.

"What," Scott said.

"She signed it 'Love,' The last letter was 'your best friend,'"

"Isn't she your girlfriend?"

"No, but she's my best friend."

"Maybe she thinks you're her boyfriend."

"Wait a minute. How'd you sign that letter you wrote for me?"

"I forget. Whatever you told me, I guess." He wheeled out of the room.

"I miss her," I said to myself.

She included a picture of her on a bicycle with two bags of papers, like saddle bags, on the back of the bike. I was more determined to get a paper route as soon as I could ride a bike.

Bertha walked in and started on me first while Annie tracked down Scott for our Kenny treatment.

"He's probably with Stella," I yelled.

Thursday night we watched "Our Miss Brooks," and I hoped my high school teacher might be like her, and I could be like Walter Denton and Lynn Baker could be like Harriet Conklin. That could be fun.

On Saturday, July 21, Mom finally visited me. This was the longest I had ever been away from her. Before now, we were apart twice, once when she had a nervous breakdown, and then, again when she tried to commit suicide.

"Dr. Grant said you're improving."

"Yeah, but I can't leave until I walk."

"He thinks yours is fast moving." She looked out the window onto the street.

"Who brought you, Mom?"

"Paula Jean. She's downstairs with Christina. Are they taking good care of you?"

"It's nice here, but I want to go home. I want to play baseball. I want a paper route, and a bike, but I can barely move my arms. Can you take me downstairs?" I was already sitting in my wheel chair.

"Here, hold this. Where do we go?" She laid her purse in my lap and started to roll me out of the room, hitting the wall, the bed, and the door on the way out, nearly stubbing my toe.

"Can I help?" A volunteer rescued Mom and me and took us down to the lobby.

After only ten days, it seemed Christina had grown, but she didn't forget me.

"Jesse, you look good," Paula Jean said. I knew I had dark circles under my eyes and had lost weight, but it was nice of her to say that. I smiled.

"Where's Gary and Danny?"

"Albert took them to their aunt and uncle," Mom said. What a family. My brother had aunts and uncles of their own and I had some of my own.

"I thought you were moving?" I looked at Paula Jean. She picked up Christina.

"Very soon," she said.

"They say I'll be able to walk and swim, and even play baseball when I get out of here."

"Dr. Grant said you're almost ready for a rehabilitation center. That's good progress," Mom said. "Then you can come home."

"Does Dad know I'm here?"

"I haven't talked to him. I'll let him know," Paula Jean said. She was holding Christina on her lap.

"I wrote him a letter. He hasn't moved, has he?"

"I don't think so. Do you like *Superman* and *Batman*? I brought a couple comics for you," she said.

"Swell. My friend Scott and I both love these." The cover showed Superman slugging it out with a space robot.

"Good."

"Mom. Is everything okay? Is Albert mad at me? Did you tell him that March of Dimes is paying for this?"

"Right now, he's dealing with Danny. I need you home to help me with Christina. She's a handful." Christina was trying to squirm out of Paula Jean's lap.

A year ago, Mom was jealous of Paula Jean, but now it was different. Dad had hurt them both.

"What's Gary doing?"

"Albert sent him to Philmont Scout Camp," Mom said.

"Where is that?"

"New Mexico. His troop just left."

In just a few weeks, that could be me. At eleven, I can be a Boy Scout, like Gary and Danny. Maybe next year Albert would let me go. I just need to get well.

"How come Danny didn't go?"

"He was supposed to but ran off the night before and missed the trip. He's home now, but Albert's mad at him for wasting the camp money."

Chapter Eighteen
Barney Convalescent Center

Every day Scott and I improved. I could grip the wheel chair wheels and move myself around the hospital. I didn't ever use the oxygen tent after we got out of isolation and the feeling in my legs had returned. It was just that my leg muscles were still messed up. Kenny treatments were designed to fix that. Even though we were improving, the staff was worried though, because there were more cases of polio. The isolation unit was full of new patients and they were running out of space. Some cases were so severe, patients were staying longer.

"We got two more lung cases today," Bertha said. That meant two new patients needed an iron lung to survive their fight with polio.

A few days later, Annie gathered Scott, Stella, another kid, and me in one corner of the TV room.

"I have good news for you. It's your lucky day. You are improving so well, we have decided to promote you four to Barney Convalescent Hospital. After a while, you'll go home from there. Your parents agree with us that this is the next step of your recovery."

I was glad Scott was going with me. I'm pretty sure he was happy Stella was going with us. She grabbed his arm and smiled.

"You leave in the morning, so put your things together. We bus you over tomorrow morning."

The next morning, after breakfast, each of us was wheeled outdoors and helped to a seat on a 1952 Chevrolet bus. Stella and I wore our hospital gowns and Scott and the other boy had street clothes. It took fifteen minutes to get us to Barney.

Scott, Sam, the other boy, and I were taken into a four-patient ward and assigned beds. A boy named David was already a patient and dressed in his street clothes. He had crutches and braces.

"My name is Louise, and I'm your nurse today. First, David and I will give you a tour of Barney Hospital."

Volunteers wheeled each of us to various rooms. My volunteer took me to the "Big Closet," a full-size room with racks of clothes, shelves of socks, underwear and rows of shoes. She helped me find my sizes and right there, changed me out of my gown and into jeans and a yellow plaid button up shirt. Then, we found shoes to fit. I felt so much better, getting out of that hospital gown.

The building was like a big ranch house, all on one floor. No elevators, no stairs. It was more like a school, and the beds were different, depending on the patient. Some had apparatus to suspend legs higher and others were like my bed at home. It was like the place changed a little depending on what the next patient needed.

That night, we had lots of questions for David. We learned he had been at Barney for one month. He could walk with the help of braces and crutches. There was a small building called the brace shop and two men made all the crutches and braces for the patients. He said they would measure you one day and the next day you had your braces and crutches. The braces were made of strong stainless steel and leather. Most of the kids with braces also needed crutches. Not everyone needed braces.

"How long have you had polio, David?" Sam asked.

"Since Easter. One day I was climbing the stairs at school and my legs quit working."

"I woke up one morning and couldn't get out of bed,"

said Sam. "Dad said it was because I had sinned. He kept asking me questions about what I did and all the while I'm lying in my bed waiting for the doctor."

"Everyone sins," I said, remembering the Road to Romans verses. "The Bible says so."

"We're Baptist and Dad is sure I did something bad. He doesn't even visit me. He said I have to confess, but I don't know what to say."

"If everyone sins, then why are we the only ones with polio?" Scott asked. "I don't think God gave me polio as some punishment." Scott was the oldest boy in the room and his words made sense.

"Why are you boys still up?" The night nurse came in our room.

"This is Georgia," David said.

"Hi Georgia," we said, not quite in unison.

"What are you boys talkin' about?"

"My dad said I sinned and that's why I have polio."

"My goodness, Sam. We've all sinned. Is there a Bible in this room?"

I grabbed my Bible and held it up.

"You open that Bible up to John, chapter nine, and start reading while I check your temperatures and blood pressure."

> *"As he passed by, he saw a man blind from his birth. And his disciples asked him, 'Rabbi, who sinned, this man or his parents, that he was born blind?' Jesus answered, 'It was not that this man sinned, or his parents, but that the works of God might be made manifest in him. We must work the works of him who sent me.'"*

This was the story about Jesus healing a blind man by

spitting on dirt and rubbing the mud in the man's eyes to heal his blindness.

"God's got things planned for you, boys. Wait and see. Just keep working. Don't give up. You'll survive this dreadful disease and be better because of it. God's gonna heal that body of yours."

"Can I read it?" Sam asked.

"Sure," I said and handed the Bible to Georgia. "Be careful, it has other stuff in it." She gave it to Sam.

"You show that verse to your dad," Scott said.

"You boys get some sleep. God's plan for you won't be easy."

"Goodnight, Georgia."

The next morning, my Bible was back on the table by my bed.

I hoped the verse helped Sam. I never thought about polio as some punishment God would use. It didn't make sense. The newspaper was full of stories of little babies across the country who died from polio. What sin would they ever be able to do?

We went outdoors a lot. There was a courtyard with sidewalks and shrubs and a flag pole. Every kid at Barney was just one more step away from going home.

That next week, Mom called to see how I was and said she would come visit me on the following Sunday, which was also my eleventh birthday. During that week, we either listened to the Redlegs play on the radio or watched TV. Wednesday, everyone watched "The Millionaire," where this Tipton guy would give away one million dollars to someone who he thought needed it, and then we would watch how the person who got all that money handled it. It got our imaginations going. If I got a million dollars, I would buy a big house for Mom, me, and my brothers and sisters, and then tell them to be nice or I'd take their money away. Maybe, all Dad needed was money.

The half hour show made me wonder if that would do it.

At Barney, if we were going to be out of our room, we wore street clothes. They were clean every day and ironed. If anyone was to visit a Barney patient, they would see the best dressed patient. We felt good each day because it was like we were always ready to go home.

Monday, I was wearing shorts, a button-down short-sleeved shirt and leather shoes, when Louise announced I had company. She made sure my shirt was buttoned and tucked and then handed me a mirror.

"You want to look good, Jesse."

I wheeled over to my drawer and pulled out a jar of butch wax to straighten the front of my flat top haircut and then I followed her to the TV room in my wheelchair.

"Who's here? Is it my dad?"

"No, we're still working on him, but it is someone you know."

As we entered the room, a familiar voice greeted me.

"Hi Jesse. This is the last place I expected to see you."

It was Mr. Davis. Scott and some other kids were already in the room along with a photographer.

Mr. Davis was my newspaper manager in Sabina. His nephew was Greg Davis who died of polio in Sabina a year ago Christmas.

"When Lynn told me you had polio, I had to come see you and make sure they're taking good care of you."

"This is swell, Mr. Davis. They say I'm doing better. Right Louise?"

I glanced up to her. She stayed by my side.

"Jesse's is fast moving. We think we have it under control."

"Thank God!" he said. He rubbed his hand on my head. I should have warned him about the butch wax.

"Mr. Davis, can we show you what we do at Barney? Jesse, let's give him a tour."

"Sure, well, first, this is where we watch TV and play games."

I introduced him to Scott, Stella, and the others and then led him to the cafeteria after the photographer got some pictures.

"That food smells good," he said. They were frying chicken.

"Let's take them to the brace shop," Louise said, so I wheeled outside and across the parking lot to the little building where two guys were busy custom building leg braces and crutches for us.

"Someday, they'll make me braces," I said.

"Jesse may not need them. His polio has moved faster than most we've seen."

That was the first I knew that. I smiled at the prospect.

"Show them the school, Jesse," Louise said.

I wheeled back to the main building and into the school wing.

"Barney has a fully accredited school, so while kids are convalescing, they do not sacrifice their education if we can help it," Louise said.

The photographer took pictures of the classrooms and the books on shelves.

"Are you doing a story on Barney, Mr. Davis?"

"We are, Jesse, and we plan on it bringing in some more money for the school."

"Like we did for March of Dimes last year?"

"Yep. Probably more. This story will run in two papers. This photographer is from the Dayton paper. Were you in an iron lung, Jesse?"

"No, sir. Just an oxygen tent. My roommate, Scott, was in a lung for a month. You need to talk to him. We're the lucky ones."

"Jesse gets the Kenny treatment, and we encourage each patient to work hard to go home," Louise said.

"One step at a time," I said. Louise squeezed my hand. It felt good.

"Bill, get a picture of that sign." He pointed to the sign in the Entry Hall.

'No man stands so tall as when he stoops to help a child.'

Louise and the staff were excited when Mr. Davis and the photographer left. "Jesse, I think we made a difference today."

Victor Hess

Chapter Nineteen
Lynn and Karen Visit

Sunday, the Dayton paper had a full-page article about Barney Hospital and how it and so many other hospitals were still fighting polio. There were pictures of kids in the classroom, including Stella, Gwen, and Scott and one of Louise pushing me in my wheelchair. There was a large print headline, 'Newsboy Contracts Disease He Raised Money to fight.' I hoped Dad read the Dayton paper. I wrote him a letter to remind him I was now at Barney.

Stella poked her head in our room.

"You have a surprise in the TV room."

"What is it?"

"It's two girls. Come see. C'mon, Scott, wait 'til you see them."

I rolled off the bed, into the wheelchair, a move Scott taught me. Once in, Stella grabbed the grips and wheeled me into the parlor where most kids meet visitors.

When I saw Lynn and Karen standing with big smiles on their faces, old feelings welled up and tears came to my eyes. I could wipe them away myself this time. Both of them leaned down and hugged me and kissed me on the cheek. Whistles and whoops followed from the other kids.

"You're famous again, Jesse Hall," Lynn said, handing me a copy of today's paper. "Keep it. It's an extra."

"I couldn't believe it when Daddy showed me your article, Jesse." Karen was wearing her black slacks and red sweater.

"Thanks for the letters," I said to Lynn.

"I had to find out from the newspaper. Here's my address in case you've forgotten about your old girlfriend," said

Karen. I blushed. Scott's eyes got big.

"This is Scott, that's Sam. We share a room. And this is Stella, Scott's girlfriend." They both seemed surprised that I said it. Now they were staring at each other, Stella with a smile, Scott with that speechless look.

"Take Jesse for a walk, Lynn while I show these kids the legend of Eugene," Karen said, pulling her picture out of her purse.

"Follow me," I said and started rolling toward the outdoor courtyard. Lynn took over pushing me.

"We race out here. In our wheelchairs," I said once we were out by the flag pole. She parked me next to a bench and sat down, holding my hand, and sobbing.

"Mama was afraid to bring me here and then Karen called about the article and, well, you know Karen, she said she'd pick me up if I wanted to see you. Are you okay?" She pulled a hankie out of her slacks pocket and wiped her eyes and blew her nose, then grabbed my hand again.

"Mine is fast moving. I might not need braces, but my leg muscles are messed up." I told her about Little League and the bat flying out of my hand, and the two spinal taps. She squeezed my hand with every description.

She pulled a folded-up paper out of her pocket and showed it to me. "See my tears?" There were spots on the letter Scott wrote for me, and then there it was, Love, JESSE at the bottom. Scott wrote *Love* and that's why Lynn's last letter said Love.

"This letter said Love and the rest of your letters said, 'Your Best Friend.' Which is it?"

"Uhh .. Both. Yeah, both."

"I don't want to lose you," she said. "You need to write more often. I will too."

While she wheeled me around the flagpole, she told me her mom was showing now, and then she explained what that meant. When we got inside, Stella and Karen were discussing Sabina Church Camp, while other kids were still looking at the photo of Eugene and us. I looked sternly at Scott, and he immediately joined Stella and Karen's conversation.

"Mr. Davis told me to give you this if I ever see you." Lynn handed me a box. Inside was a canvas bag for newspapers. "He said to get well, so you can use this."

"Would you like to stay and eat with us?" a volunteer asked Karen and Lynn.

"We can't," said Karen. "But we'll be back."

"Come back for Jesse's birthday," said the volunteer. "We'll have a big party for him."

They hugged and kissed me again. I sat in the wheelchair, smiling at them. Lynn looked so much older now. I clutched the new canvas newspaper bag breathing in the newness and the promise of delivering papers again. Maybe Gary could help me get Albert's permission.

I locked my wheels and tried to stand up.

Saturday, we watched "Gunsmoke." Matt Dillon was a brave U.S Marshall stuck with trying to get law and order in Dodge City, but there was always someone coming into town to mess things up. Unfortunately, it made me think a lot about Dad. Maybe it was because of the drinking everyone did in the Long Branch Saloon. Guys would get drunk, pull a gun on the Marshall, and he'd shoot them. When guys got drunk, it never ended up good.

Motoring my wheelchair on my own was tiring, so Stella would have me hold her crutches, she called them *sticks*, in my lap and she would push me around like my wheelchair was a walker for her. Scott followed us. More than once our races would end up with me tumbling out of the wheelchair. We were like the three musketeers, one of the nurses said. Stella messed up her braces once, and they made a rule about unsupervised wheelchair races around the flag pole.

Jim, we learned, volunteered on all the polio wards in Dayton and surprised us by walking in our room with his *Tecumseh* book. He read us more from Tecumseh, which inspired the names of our wheelchairs. Scott called his Cornstalk after one of the Indian chiefs and I named mine after Tecumseh's brother, Blue Jacket. I liked that name because it sounded like an Indian name. One of the volunteers found feathers and brought them in, so we could tape them to our chairs.

"Jesse, you're from Xenia, aren't you?" Jim asked.

"Yes, sir."

"Do you know where the drive-in theater is north of town?"

"Yeah, I've been there. It was fun."

"Well, believe it or not, there is a legend about the Shawnees burying that treasure in a hillside near the drive-in."

"No kidding? Did they ever find it?"

"Not that I know. There are houses on that hillside now, and the owners have to drive out trespassers who sneak in looking for the treasure. It's probably just a legend."

I imagined searching for treasure and finding it and giving enough money to Mom, so she could get a car and learn to drive.

Scott and I weren't always together, just most of the time. When I was alone in our room, I would either write a letter to Lynn, Dad, or someone, or just pull the *Bible* out that Pastor Armey gave me last year. I was remembering the three rules of John Wesley.

First, do no harm.

Second, do all the good you can.

Third, do all you can to be close to God.

The third one, I learned at Sunday School last year. The first two, Grandpa Hall taught me. I searched the Bible for the verse they used to teach us. Finally, I found one I underlined in the sixth Chapter of Matthew. 6:33. "But seek first his kingdom and his righteousness." I guess by seeking God's kingdom, you'll get close to him. Maybe, the closer you get, the closer he'll watch over you. I wondered when that would be.

Then, in Luke, I found another verse I underlined. 6:37 "Judge not, and you will not be judged; condemn not, and you will not be condemned; forgive and you will be forgiven; give and it will be given to you.'

Then, above that one was another verse I underlined, "And as you wish that men would do to you, do so to them."

The *Bible* was full of pages. My *Bible* had 843 pages in the Old Testament and 242 pages in the New Testament. That was 1,085 pages. Each page has about 664 words, because, I counted some pages, just to be sure.

That's 720,440 words. And so, I wondered, why it took so many words to get to John Wesley's three rules, nineteen words. Then, I fell asleep. When I woke up, my Bible was back on the table and Louise was measuring my blood pressure.

"Are your girlfriends coming to your birthday?" she asked.

"I don't know."

"Here's a letter from Lynn. It was in your canvas bag. How'd you miss this?"

I grabbed it and ripped it open. Louise took her blood pressure kit and left me alone.

July 29, 1956

Dear Jesse,

> *I am writing this while Karen is driving us to visit you. First, Mr. Davis gave me this bag a few weeks ago. He asked me to give it*

to you if I see you. When Karen called to say she would bring me, I had to bring it, too.

You need to write more often. I check the mail every day hoping for a letter from you. If you write me, I'll write you. Well, we're almost there, so I'll say bye. I have the newspaper article about you. You are famous. I can't wait to see you.

Love,
Lynn

Chapter Twenty
Uncle Jesse, the Hero

Birthdays are a huge event at Barney. Cake, ice cream, gifts, and party hats. All fifteen kids staying at Barney participated in my party. A committee of volunteers existed strictly for birthdays and holidays. If we had gone too long without a party, they would make up an occasion to have one. Barney had lots of volunteers. There was that sign posted on all the bulletin boards: "No man stands so tall as when he stoops to help a child." I guess that meant women, too, because most of the volunteers were women.

Paula Jean drove Mom again and brought me an *Archie Joke Book* and two pairs of leather gloves I could use to wheel the wheelchair without getting blisters.

"Where's Gary and Danny?" I asked.

"They're watching Christina," Paula Jean said. "But I had to come and say goodbye. Charlie and I got married. We're moving to Boston. The next time I see you, you'll be swimming and playing baseball!"

"Have you seen Dad? I wonder if he knows I'm even here." I asked Paula Jean this while Mom was helping serve cake.

"That's Daddy. Jesse, he probably knows and cares. He just doesn't show it. He's always broke and probably ignores things that remind him of responsibility." I guess Paula Jean would know.

"I'll write him again. My words don't look that good yet. It's still hard to push the pencil around the paper. I hope he read the article in the paper."

"Jesse, once you get out of here, you're going to be so

happy to be back there in that nice new home. Daddy will see you Thanksgiving. Grandpa Hall will make sure. Here's a couple pictures Charlie took of us at the swimming pool." She handed them to me.

"It's okay here, but I'm ready to be home." One day at a time, I thought. I stared at the first picture of us around the picnic table. My family picture - Dad was still missing. The second made me smile. It was Lynn and me in our swimming suits. I wondered when he took that one.

"You have company, Jesse." Louise escorted Karen, Lynn, and Arlene into the party. Stella came directly to Karen and Lynn who were stooping to hug me.

"Did you read my letter?" Lynn said. Stella and Karen walked out of the room.

"It was hidden in that bag. I just found it yesterday. I'll write more, I promise."

"Good. I brought you a gift. It was Father's idea." She handed me a brand-new Louisville Slugger bat.

"What's Karen doing with Stella?"

"You'll see." Mom and Arlene were handing out plates with cake and ice cream.

"Here, look." I handed Lynn the picture of us by the pool.

"Who took this?"

"Charlie, I think."

"Charlie took these, too." Paula Jean said, and handed other pictures of the pool day. "Here, you can have the one of your family."

"Ladies and Gentlemen, meet the new Stella and Eleanor," Louise announced. Stella wheeled Eleanor in, both smiling, and both beautiful. I was sure Karen had something to do with it. Stella was beaming. She wasn't wearing her glasses, so she let Louise help guide Eleanor to the table with ice cream and cake.

"Karen brought her make up kit. You should see it. It has everything."

I looked at Lynn, whose eyes had become appealing somehow and her cheeks had fewer freckles and more color. Her hair was different. I guess it was cut even or something.

"Who's doing this?" Paula Jean asked. "Look how happy the girls are."

"That's Karen. She's my neighbor from Sabina."

"She talks to Eugene," Lynn said. "They both talk to Eugene."

"That dead man? That's weird."

"I know."

"Did you know there is Indian treasure by the drive-in movie?" I changed the subject

"Don't believe those tales. That treasure is buried by John Bryan Park. No one's found it yet."

"Really?"

"We hunted all over that drive-in two years ago and didn't find a thing. Forget the drive-in. It's at John Bryan."

She told us how she and her friends would follow the Old Town Creek looking for the treasure. There was supposed to be silver from some mine. We told her how Jim read to us about Tecumseh and Blue Jacket and then she described how some old lady ran her and some friends off and called the police on them.

"Did you get caught?" Scott asked.

"We ran through the woods and ended up in Amlin Heights." While she described their getaway, I got a tap on my shoulder and looked up at an image that is hard to describe. It was Lynn all right, but, older, smarter, friendlier, warmer and she was beaming. I was speechless.

"Well?"

I maneuvered my wheelchair around, and just then Karen stepped beside her. "How do you like your girlfriend, Jesse."

Scott was the first to speak.

"You're beautiful," he said directly to Lynn.

"Yeah, you look swell," I finally said.

Stella hit Scott, and Lynn hit me. They both walked away. Karen looked at both of us.

"Someday, you'll get it. But right now, you have a lot to learn." She walked away.

The next two weeks were twice-a-day Kenny treatments, evening TV shows, and Redlegs baseball on the radio. I would fall asleep praying for Dad to change, thinking about the Indian treasure or imagining me playing Little League again.

One morning, Louise asked Scott, "What are you waiting on?"

"What do you mean?" he asked.

"You need to practice your standing! I bet you could push Jesse around in his wheelchair by now if you put your mind to it."

"Can you stand already?" I asked.

"Uh, a little," he said sheepishly.

He locked his wheels, reached down to flip up his footrests, leaned forward and pushed up from the chair. Louise moved close to him, and he grasped her hand.

"I was going to wait 'til you could stand," he finally said.

He took small steps, and I started clapping.

"Take one more! Go, Scott!" I yelled like he was racing to first base. Stella must have heard us and showed up at our door.

"You're ready for sticks, Scott!"

Monday, Scott was on crutches.

Mom could only visit when she had transportation. Albert never brought her. Grandpa Smith brought her once, along with jars of grape jelly. He must have sneaked them out. An hour later there was toast and jelly for everyone! Grandpa told Scott about the farm and me helping with chores.

"You can milk a cow?" Scott asked with surprise.

"Sure, can't everyone?" I said.

"Jesse, I brought something for you to see." Grandpa Smith handed me a yellowed envelope. "It's about your Uncle Jesse."

In the envelope was an official letter from some colonel in the Marines. It said that PFC Jesse Smith was instrumental in defeating the enemy in the final battle at Kunishi Ridge to win Okinawa. I read about him and two other soldiers systematically advancing on a machine gun nest until finally getting close enough to toss their grenades in the cave protecting the machine gun position. I imagined how afraid he must have been. It said that later that day he was killed by enemy fire. The U.S. Government thanked them for the supreme sacrifice of their son.

I handed the paper back to Grandpa. "He was a hero, Grandpa."

"He's a dead hero." Grandpa was silent after that.

He gave me the letter and told me to keep it. I looked at it and wondered if this wasn't why Grandma Smith was so angry at everyone all the time. I put it in my *Bible*. I felt sad watching Grandpa leave the hospital.

I found the pad we used to write letters and started a letter to Dad.

August 26, 1956

Dear Dad,

> *I hope you are okay. I am not. I still have polio. Barney Hospital is in Dayton, so maybe it would be easy for you to come and visit me. Did you read about me in the Dayton*

paper?

Mom says Christina is talking now. She is almost two years old.

Paula Jean got married to Charlie. They are moving to Boston.

I made the Little League team in Xenia but could not play in a game because of polio.

I am in a wheelchair now. If you come and visit, you can push me around in it. I named it Blue Jacket, like the Indian.

I have to take my medicine now, so I'll say good bye.

I love you Dad.

Your son,
JESSE

Each day, I got better at maneuvering around in my wheelchair. My arms were getting stronger. During the week after Scott stood up for me, I worked out on the bars we used to help us learn to walk again. It was like our muscles got sick and by the time they got better, they forgot what they were supposed to do, so we had to retrain them. If the muscles didn't get totally well, then the patient was stuck with braces or a wheel chair. We cheered each other on because when someone got well and left, it meant we were close to leaving, too. I hoped that would be soon.

By Wednesday, they were making new sticks for me in the brace shop. By the Labor Day celebration, Scott, Stella, and I were parading around the flagpole on our crutches.

The day after Labor Day, Louise handed me a large brown envelope addressed to me. It contained five copies of the Dayton news article and five copies of the article they printed in the *Cincinnati Press* plus a note from Mr. Davis saying that when I got well to let him know, so he could set me up with a route. That note convinced me that once I got well, I could get back to normal and get to use my newspaper bag. I hoped Albert would let me have a paper route. Gary could help me ask.

I gave articles to Stella and Scott and to Louise. It was our first day of classes, so I took one article to class with me.

Victor Hess

Chapter Twenty-One
School at Barney

Barney had a school wing with desks, blackboard, and a teacher. Our desks were not in a row as you would expect because some kids needed more space and others were in wheelchairs. Polio attacked each of us in a slightly different way. Scott, Stella, and I had trouble with our legs. Stella had her braces and sat in a chair, but her legs stuck out straight because she would lock them in a comfortable position. Gwen Dougherty was a colored girl whose right hand was misshapen from cerebral palsy. The other hand was limp. She wrote with her foot. We were amazed at how she could make her foot do what some of our hands couldn't.

Our teacher was Mrs. Hawk. She was small like my mom. She wore thick glasses and a long skirt with a white long-sleeved blouse with a lace collar and a brooch with lots of pearls pinned to her collar.

Our first day of class, she took the article I brought from the newspaper and passed it around, asking each student to read a paragraph. She took notes as each person read. Then, she started asking questions about geography, arithmetic, and history. She addressed each of us by our name and praised each correct answer and used hints to help us get the correct response. She asked us to tell what books we read. My answer was the *Bible*. Scott's was *Tom Swift and His Motorcycle*.

The next day she organized us differently, so we could help each other. I was positioned between Gwen Dougherty and William Kuntz, so I could help them with their numbers. Stella helped a first grader with his ABCs and Scott helped a third grader with her reading. There were assignments and lessons each day, and when we weren't helping other kids, Mrs. Hawk was giving us a lesson. We took tests and Mrs. Hawk recorded the results on a card for each one of us.

"You don't want to be behind your friends when you get back to your school, do you?" she reminded us.

That night, I took one of the Cincinnati articles and wrote a letter to Dad.

> September 4, 1956
>
> Dear Dad,
>
> I am getting better now. I can walk with the help of crutches. Read this article about Barney Hospital. It has my picture in it and the story about me and the March of Dimes in Sabina. It was in the paper on my birthday.
> I learned in school that it was IRONIC that I raised money to cure polio and then caught it.
> I wish you could visit me because we are in the same city.
> Mom says Christina is a handful. Soon I will be home to help her.
>
> I miss you.
>
> Your son,
> JESSE

Mom's next visit was with a neighbor, Mrs. Grooms. It was her husband who carried me to the house when I collapsed after that baseball practice. Mom said Danny was getting into trouble but that going to school should solve that. She told me about new words Christina was saying.

"I think Scott gets to go home soon. Stella does, too. Have they said anything about me going home?"

"They said you are doing well. Maybe October."

I told her about our teacher, Mrs. Hawk, and how I was helping kids with their arithmetic.

Mom was talkative this visit.

"Do you like it here?" she asked.

"It's okay, but I want to go home."

"Has Karen or Lynn come back to visit you?"

"Yeah, once after the birthday party. Karen did the girls makeup again when they came. She really made them all feel good."

"I miss Arlene and Joyce. They were always there for us," she said.

"Me, too. Lynn and I write. She has a paper route."

"I know, I bet you miss that."

"Mr. Davis told me I could get a route when I get well. Oh, here, look. Here's that article about me." I pulled a clipping out of the big envelope he sent. She studied it for a few minutes.

"I'm so proud of you," she said. "We had a good life in Sabina."

"I miss the church. Pastor Armey taught me a lot." I fingered the *Bible* on my table.

"It was pretty tough there."

"I know, but we had good friends there. Is Mrs. Grooms your friend now?" I asked.

"Not really. She came by and asked about you because her husband was worried. After I told her everything about your polio, she offered to drive me anytime I needed to come."

"How come Albert doesn't bring you?"

"He's busy, Jesse. Gary is learning to drive now. He has his learner's permit."

"That's swell. I'm working hard to get out of here."

"You just take your time and get well, first. I have to get things ready to bring you home."

"Do you think Albert misses me?"

"Don't you worry about Albert. We'll be fine," she said.

It was a good visit. She wasn't as nervous.

Scott was working hard to get the strength to carry his full weight again. It wasn't just that. It was teaching the nerves to keep the legs moving at the right time and in the right direction.

"My dad bought me a Schwinn, Jesse. It's got a generator light." I knew what he was talking about. The comic books we read at Barney were full of Schwinn ads. The generator light was the best light, because you didn't have to mess with batteries for it. His plans to move from crutches to a bike inspired me. That night I cut out a Schwinn ad and put it in my *Bible*.

The following Friday, I watched Stella's and Scott's parents drive them out of Barney's parking lot, but not before I could stand on my own and walk across the TV room. That week there were five new patients arriving to claim Cornstalk and Blue Jacket.

Louise and I worked hard to improve my strength and coordination.

"You're gonna be out of here soon, Jesse," she said while pressing the board against my feet. That stretched my leg muscles and didn't hurt as bad as it used to.

"Do you think I'll be able to ride a bike?"

"Why not. That would be good exercise. What kind of bike do you have?"

"I don't. I've never had a bike. I want a Schwinn. A Schwinn Corvette."

"That sounds fancy."

"It is. It has white walls and a luggage carrier where I can put my paper bag."

"You have a paper route?"

"I will. Ouch! You remember Mr. Davis? He was my manager last year. He visited us with that photographer. Ouch. Will I be able to play Little League?" She was working my legs hard today.

"Oh my. Bicycle, paper route, and Little League. We have to get you out of here. You have too much to live for! I don't think anything is going to keep you from doing what you want."

It was like watching Christina learn to walk. I could move my legs and balance myself, but it was hard work. My legs were slow, so it took me a long time to move from one end of the room to another. My left foot dragged, which meant one leg was sicker than the other.

"Why don't you take Eleanor for a walk," Louise said after a session on the bars. "Is your girlfriend coming back?"

"Lynn? Not for a while, I guess."

"No, the other one, with the makeup."

"Oh, Karen. She's just a friend."

"She's fun. I hope she comes back."

I opened the door to the courtyard and pulled Eleanor through, falling down half way through the process. Then her chair started rolling toward the parking lot.

"Jesse!"

"I'm coming." But my legs weren't operating quick enough. I was back up on my feet, but, without crutches, or something like her chair to hold onto, she was moving farther away from me. The fear that she could topple and get hurt kicked in and, step by step, I closed the gap between us. When I was just a step away, her chair stopped. A second later, I was holding the handles of the chair and latched the lock on the right wheel.

"Look," she said. She was gripping a wheel with each hand. "I stopped it. I stopped it." She was crying.

"You stopped it!"

"Unlock it!"

I obeyed. She was still gripping the wheels. A slight jerk of her right hand twisted the chair away from the parking lot. They weren't working together, but in a haphazard series of yanks and pulls, she pointed the chair back toward the flag pole and zig zagged her way to the bench, where I had talked with Lynn just a few weeks before.

"Let's show Louise," I said, and we fought our way back to the building, her guiding the chair one way while I was moving it another.

It was a simple event. Her chair ran away, she stopped it, and then wheeled herself to the flagpole. When Louise heard it, she leaned over, hugged us both and started crying, and then we started crying, because we knew exactly what one small simple little step meant to each of us at Barney.

I was ready to get back home to Xenia with my brothers and sister. Little League was over without me playing a single game in Xenia. I opened my *Bible* and the picture of all of us Charlie took at the pool fell out. We were all around the picnic table, Mom in the center. He must have taken it before we ate because there was a full plate of fried chicken on the table. It was a new life I was going back to, new house, new school, and new friends. I hoped the hillside across the street was still there. I would work hard on getting that bike. I still had seven dollars in my chest.

Chapter Twenty-Two
Home and Bad News

On Friday, September 28, 1956, I walked out of Barney Convalescent Hospital on crutches and into Grandpa Smith's old 1946 Plymouth. I sat in the back seat with Christina. There were boxes and two pillowcases full of clothes.

Mom and Grandpa were quiet during the drive. It was so good seeing the farms and houses. I hadn't been in the country for over three months. When we got to Xenia, Grandpa turned right instead of left. Two blocks later, he turned left and then after a few blocks, stopped in front of an old house.

"Jesse, we don't live with Albert and your brothers anymore."

Just those few words, and I suddenly felt achy and started breathing hard.

"I found a little place for us here, and I start a job on Monday. It will be just like Sabina."

"What happened? Why can't we live with Gary and Danny?" I held onto two-year-old Christina while Mom opened the car door.

"Just never you mind. This is best."

"Is Danny and Gary going to live with us?" I asked. Grandpa reached for Christina.

"No, they stay with their father," she said.

"What about Dad?" I don't know why I asked. He never visited me at Barney.

"I haven't seen your dad."

"Me neither. Do I go to Shawnee School?" I maneuvered my body out of the back seat and onto my crutches.

"I don't think so. We'll find out."

171

I stood in front of a house that had three doors and three mailboxes. She unlocked the far-right door. Grandpa was still holding Christina.

This place was nothing like Sabina. I wondered how desperate she must have gotten while I was at Barney Hospital. The wooden porch had holes in the floor, so I was careful that each crutch landed on solid flooring. Half the screen was missing from the screen door, and there was no spring to keep the door shut.

We went directly into a living room with an over-sized chair and couch covered with an often-mended throw cover. The wood floor had been painted brown a long time ago and now was scarred where furniture had scuffed it, and maybe even knives had been thrown into the soft pine boards. It smelled musty and unsafe, like the air was not pure, like I remember Christina's diapers.

A small gas heater was centered on the inside wall. Grandpa held Christina as I moved from the living room to the bedroom on my crutches. There was only one bedroom for the three of us. The bed sagged. I wondered how we all were to sleep but was slightly reassured when I saw Christina's crib still folded up, leaning against the wall.

"I'll put the crib together, Vi. Where do you want it?" Grandpa said. He handed Christina to Mom.

"Leave it in the bedroom."

"You want to help, Jesse?" he asked.

"Okay." I was still shocked at leaving the clean, happy Barney Hospital and entering the three-room apartment. It was a big step backward. What could have possibly happened to drive Mom out of a brand-new home to this dreary place? The few visits Mom made to Barney during the last few months had given me no clue of the things she must have gone through.

"Where's my chest?"

Mom was quiet for a moment. "I didn't see it."

"It was under my bed. I always put it under my bed. It had my money in it."

"We'll have to get it later." She wouldn't look at me.

"Mom, it has all my stuff. My baseball glove was in there."

"I got your glove all right. It's in one of those bags. I had to clean it up."

"Can we go to the house and get my chest?" I looked over to Grandpa.

"Jesse, I can't drive at night, and I have to leave now before it gets dark."

The chest also had my notebook, a car encyclopedia, and old letters from Lynn and Karen which I stored in the secret compartment.

"Give me a couple days. We'll get your chest. Nobody will bother it," Mom said. I didn't believe her.

Saturday, Mom and I took Christina the six blocks to Shawnee park. One block, I would push the stroller while Mom held the crutches. The stroller was like a walker until I got tired. Then, the front wheels would raise up because my weight was pushing down on the handle.

At the park, next to the pond, was a large square pavilion with a stage on it. It had a roof held up by columns like a picture of Rome. It sat beside the pond. We sat on a bench next to it.

As soon as we got there, ducks started swimming toward us, and Mom pulled out a single slice of bread, broke it into pieces, and threw it into the water. What the ducks had not eaten was swallowed up by bass and catfish. Christina laughed in amazement.

"You can bring her here on your walks," she said. "It will help you build your strength."

We left Barney too early. I was just now realizing that,

and the fear of staying on crutches forever smothered the joy of being out of the hospital. I had been lucky, not needing braces on my legs, but knew I might need them if my strength and coordination didn't get better, and it wasn't.

"What happened, Mom? Why did we have to move?" Ducks waddled and quacked around us, wanting more bread.

"He hadn't changed. It was worse than living with your grandmother." I knew she meant Grandma Smith who was always mean to both of us, maybe, to everyone.

"What did he do?"

"It was a lot of things, Jesse, but when he couldn't stand your baby sister, I decided we weren't welcome there. I had to wait until they would let you leave the hospital."

"Why don't we just go back to Sabina?"

"Not now. I got a job and our place. We'll be here for a while."

"We need a bigger place."

Just then Christina started screaming, which frightened two curious ducks nudging her for more food. Mom shooed them a way. On the way back, I made it a block and a half before Mom handed me my crutches and she took over pushing Christina.

Our apartment was in a different school district, so I wasn't allowed to continue at Shawnee School. Instead, I walked the seven blocks to McKinley school, the oldest school in the city. The school had stairs everywhere. I was slow with stairs. I had to carry my books and crutches and hold the stair rail. Some kids treated me like I was in their way, but not all of them.

Wally, a lanky guy with black hair stopped and picked up books that I had dropped. Each day from then on, he was waiting for me at school and carried my books.

"You need a backpack for your books," he said. I tried to picture me wearing a brown pack Uncle Jesse Smith would have worn before he was killed in the war.

Mom had found a real job at a drug store, and, after school, I walked to where she worked. I picked up Christina and her stroller there and walked her home. Every two blocks, I would stop and sit on a step while my strength returned. Sometimes I would get home and have to remove a stroller wheel, oil it and put it back on, often creating a cotter pin out of a safety pin I would borrow from Mom's sewing kit. The walking was good exercise for me, and I considered it therapy instead of a consequence of the cruel condition we were in. Louise said a volunteer would contact us to arrange a time to continue physical therapy. That didn't happen, probably because we didn't have a phone.

Tuesday, Christina and I stopped by the Army Surplus store and I asked about backpacks. I showed the man my books and crutches and hoped they had one cheap, since I didn't have any money. He found one for fifty cents and when I asked him to hold it for me, he was okay with that until I knocked over a stack of ammo cases with the stroller. I guess I looked so pitiful, he stopped me and gave me the pack.

"Pay me when you can, son," he said. We went home.

Wednesday evening Mom gave me a *Hit Parade* magazine to study. I brought Christina home as usual, turned the radio to WHIO, and listened to a song, then tried to find it in the magazine so I could follow the words. I started studying the words to "True Love" while Bing Crosby and Grace Kelly sang in harmony. Then Gogi Grant and I were singing "The Wayward Wind." I was still singing in a high soprano voice and, it seemed to entertain Christina. She would even join in with "la la" or "dee dee."

"You're a little singer," I said, and she started dancing. Then she crouched. Then I changed her diaper.

At 6:30, Albert's blue Plymouth Belvedere pulled up in front of the house. I was worried because Christina and I were alone. From the window, I watched Gary get out of the passenger seat and come to our door.

"What are you doing here?" I asked.

"Come on, you have to help me," Gary said. He looked surprised when I grabbed my crutches.

I followed him to the car and saw Albert staring ahead on the driver's side.

Sticking out of the boot of the car was Mom's sewing machine, much like I remembered seeing it the first time John Williams brought it to us in Sabina. Albert finally got out and helped Gary take it in the apartment, probably because he saw me on crutches. He looked around our apartment, shook his head and went back outside to the car. He never said a word.

"Why did Mom move?" Gary asked. Then he opened the car door and pulled out my chest.

"You tell me. She must have been pretty unhappy," I said.

Gary carried my chest into the apartment. I was so happy to see it.

"It got bad when she started taking those pills," he said.

"She didn't need them in Sabina," I said.

"But look at this place," he said. "Dad wants her to come back."

I didn't want to consider moving back into a house with Albert, not if that's why she started taking those pills again.

"Are you sure? Thanks for bringing the chest. I thought it was long gone."

"That's okay. Where's Mom?" he asked.

"She works at Doug's Drugs. Go see her. She'll make you a milk shake."

"How are you doing?"

"I still need crutches, but I was one of the lucky ones."

The car horn sounded twice.

"I have to go," Gary said.

"Where's Danny?" I asked.

"We don't know. We're looking for him."

"What a mess," I said.

"Got that right," Gary agreed.

After they left, I opened the secret compartment and my seven dollars was still there. I found my letters from Lynn and slid them in with the money and closed it up. I kept one dollar out, so I could pay for my backpack. Christina and I played on the floor with one of the picture books Paula Jean gave her.

"What's this?" I asked.

"Cat," she said.

"What color is it?" I asked.

"Lellow," she replied.

"What's this?" I asked.

"Car," she replied.

"What color is it?" I asked.

"Bwue," she replied.

"Yay," I said and applauded her.

"Yay. Let's eat," said the beautiful, brown haired, blue-eyed girl.

"Come on, let's fix another sandwich."

"Okay, peanut butter and jelly." Somehow, I understood her language. She was happy, no matter where we lived.

Maybe, right then and there, I felt that we could make this work. We had to.

Mom walked in at 7:30. Christina ran to her, reaching up for a hug.

"How did that get here?" Mom motioned at the sewing machine.

"Albert and Gary brought it. They brought my chest, too."

"Did Albert say anything?"

"He just looked around. Gary said that Danny was missing again, and Albert wants you to come home."

"Oh, no. Really?"

She went in the kitchen.

"Mom, he runs away whether we're there or not."

"I know. I think that's the only reason Albert wanted to try the marriage again."

She opened the brown paper bag she had brought from work, two pair of trousers the drug store owner gave her to alter. At least now she wouldn't have to do her sewing by hand.

"What did you eat?" she asked. I told her.

"Okay, I'll heat us some soup. Would you fix me one of your peanut butter and jelly sandwiches?"

"Sure. Come on Christina, you can help," I said.

"Saturday, I have to work from 9 to 5. I'll fix us cereal and then I have to go. You need to watch Christina," she yelled from the living room.

"I'll take her to the park. I'll keep her away from the ducks."

"Don't take all the bread," Mom said. "Bring her to the store, and I'll fix you a milk shake," she said. Then I heard the sewing machine running.

My chest had to be stored in the living room, like it was a coffee table, because the bed was too low for it to slide under. That meant there was an ash tray, an empty coffee cup, and magazines on top of it all the time. They all had to be moved if I wanted to get anything out of it. I put the coffee cup and ash tray onto the floor and pulled off the lid. Everything inside was familiar and comforting, like my notebook, *New Testament*, and my comic books, all from our life in Sabina. I put my baseball glove and my Redlegs hat in the chest but decided to keep the *Bible* out. Christina helped by leaning into the chest and banging on the side while I reread all of Lynn's letters.

Chapter Twenty-Three
The Skillmans

I helped out by doing dishes, making our bed, and even washing my clothes. This place did not have a washing machine, so we had to wash our clothes by hand in the kitchen sink. We didn't have an iron, so I went to school in wrinkled shirts.

Each day, I went as quickly as I could from school to Doug's Drugs, where Mom worked. She took Christina to work with her, parked her in the stroller in a back room and then started waiting on the kids who swarmed in after school, looking for *Hit Parade* and movie magazines, comic books, sundaes, ice cream cones, milk shakes, and candy bars. I would get there by 3:30 and Doug, who owned the drug store, was happy when I would roll Christina out, leaving Mom, surrounded by teenagers, digging into tubs of ice cream and topping sundaes with sweet red cherries. Then it was six blocks to our apartment.

Thursday, I paid for my backpack and, while pushing Christina across Detroit Street, I saw a small building surrounded by all sorts of bicycles: Huffy, Schwinn, Hawthorn, J.C. Higgins, and some with no names on them. I locked the wheels on the stroller and let Christina walk around with me, while I checked out each boy's bicycle.

"Can I help you find something, son?"

The gravelly voice belonged to a short bald man with a white beard. Christina grabbed my leg. He bent down, pulled out a handkerchief and wiped Christina's hands which, in less than a minute, had become covered in bicycle chain oil. She fought his efforts for an instant and then let him finish. It wouldn't come off her face.

"There, you need to wash that with soap and water

when you get her home," he said.

"Yes, sir. I'm looking for a bike for my paper route, like a Schwinn Corvette," I said.

He stared at my crutches.

"As soon as I get off these crutches, I'll need a bike."

"You have a paper route?"

"As soon as I get off these crutches, I'll have a paper route."

"That's a positive attitude, boy."

"Jesse, my name is Jesse. That's Christina, my sister."

"I have a couple Schwinn's, but not a Corvette. What size? Twenty-four inch or twenty-six inch?"

"I don't know what size," I said. He stepped back, sizing me up with his eyes, hands on his hips.

"Well, let's try one out. Let's start with a twenty-four inch. He pulled out a red Huffy, with a chain guard, fender and front luggage carrier. He stood there beside it ready for me to mount it. I eased up close to it.

"I've never ridden a bike before. What do I do?"

He walked to the shop entry and yelled, "Della, I need your help."

A chubby, short lady came out. "You don't have to yell. I can hear you!" She was wiping her hands on her apron.

"This young man needs to learn how to ride a bike, and I thought you could watch his sister while I teach him." She looked down to Christina and gave her a big smile.

"What's your name, dearie?" she asked.

I answered for her. "Christina."

"I really have to get home," I said.

"Nonsense, this will only take a few minutes, if you do all I say."

"Snuffy, I'm gonna clean her up. What did you boys do to this girl?" Della asked.

The man got on the bicycle and rode it around the parking lot, describing the brakes, how the chain and pedals and sprocket make it go.

"It's a matter of balance," he said. "If you can stand without falling down, you can ride a bike."

I wondered if I was ready for this, polio and all. But, Snuffy was like Charlie, Paula Jean's husband, urging me to keep my feet on the pedals while he pushed me around the lot, almost like the swimming lesson in July. We both fell down when I turned the wheel too sharp.

"That's okay, that's why I chose this bike. It's already been dinged up. Are you okay?"

"Yes, sir. I guess I'm a little dinged up, too."

"Ha, you're all right, young fella."

He helped me up and dusted himself off.

After we made it around the parking lot a few times, Della was back outside, standing by Snuffy with Christina and clean hands. I don't know what thrilled me most - sitting on that bike or suddenly realizing that I had another reason to lick polio.

"I can't afford a bike right now. I don't have my paper route yet. But I'll get one."

"You come back when you have that route. I'll get you into a bike at $5.00 down and $1.00 a week. You'll have it paid off in six months or so. We'll start with a twenty-four-inch bike and trade you up to twenty-six inches when you get older. Get rid of those crutches, get that paper route, and come back to see me." He took Christina from Della and put her in the stroller.

All night I focused on the picture of that Schwinn Corvette, never once regretting Mom leaving Albert. I knew I could get rid of my crutches.

I found my tablet and envelopes and while Christina was nursing on her bottle, I started my letter to Lynn.

October 4, 1956

Dear Lynn

I got out of Barney last week and got bad news. Mom and Albert split up, again. We are in a three-room apartment. It's like Sabina, except smaller and worse. Mom got a job at the drug store. I watch Christina. I think I left Barney too soon, because I still have to use crutches.

I looked at bikes and decided on a Schwinn Corvette like Scott got. I'll get one as soon as I get off these crutches. Here is my address: 503A East Third Street Xenia, Ohio.

Please write me.

Love, your best friend,
JESSE

I wrote a similar letter to Karen, except for the 'Love' part. Right now, I missed both of them a whole lot.

Friday afternoon, Christina and I faced a torrential rainstorm on our way home from the drugstore. The heavens opened up with rain so heavy that, by the time I was a block from home, the streets were flooded, and we were soaked.

"Come up here on the porch," a voice commanded me with authority that I instinctively obeyed.

"Where are you going in this rain?" she asked.

I wheeled the stroller toward the porch and her hand reached down to lift the front of the stroller onto the covered porch to get us out of the rain.

"I live down there one more block. This is my sister

Christina. I'm Jesse." I yelled over the loud rain.

"My name is Kathy. You stay here on the porch till this rain stops. It's flooding in the streets."

"Yes, ma'am."

She had brown hair partially covered by a large scarf tied behind her neck. She wore a house dress buttoned up the front. I noticed a slight body odor.

"Where's your mother?" she asked.

"She works at Doug's Drugs. I take care of my sister till Mom gets off work."

"How old are you?" she asked.

"I'm eleven. We just moved here."

"Who's this, Mama?" asked a tall blond girl, probably in high school, as she opened the door.

"Jesse, this is my daughter Penny. I have two other girls. Bonnie is your age, and Ellen is going to nursing school. It's still raining hard. You better bring your sister inside."

When I untied the crutches from the stroller, Penny instinctively grabbed Christina and Kathy moved the stroller to the protection of the porch roof. I laid my backpack in the stroller. When we walked inside, my senses were overwhelmed from the aroma of onions, tomatoes, and noodles. Kathy was preparing their Friday evening ritual of spaghetti. The living room was warm and had enough room for their entire family to watch TV.

"Jesse, you and your sister stay here and watch TV until this rain dies down."

Penny was already wrapping a warm blanket around Christina, who was grabbing back at Penny's eye glasses. Bonnie was sitting on the couch and reminded me of Lynn. Her hair was the same color with bangs that covered her eyebrows, but Bonnie didn't have Lynn's freckles. She smiled but didn't say anything. She was watching the "Mickey Mouse Club."

Penny told me to follow her to see the rest of their house.

She and her two sisters shared two rooms on the left side. "Love Me Tender" by Elvis Presley was playing on a record player when I walked into their room.

"Ellen sleeps here." She pointed to a bed by a small desk and portable typewriter. "Bonnie and I sleep here," continued Penny. There were beds and tables everywhere, and I could barely move around with my crutches.

"Who sleeps upstairs?" I asked. It was a two-story house, and all she had shown me was downstairs. "Do your folks sleep upstairs?"

"Oh, no. They have a big room with their own bath at the back of the house. Daddy just turned the upstairs into an apartment. It's for rent."

At that moment, the back door opened, and a man walked in, stomping off the rain. "This one is going to last a while. The radio said at least another hour," he said.

"Henry, we have company. This is Jesse and his sister, Christina," Kathy said, and then motioned him into their bedroom. "Bonnie, stir the sauce. Penny, put the bread in the oven." It reminded me of holidays on the Hall Farm when all the aunts and Grandma got the meal ready. In a few minutes, Henry and Kathy came out of the bedroom.

"Jesse, my name is Henry Skillman. Did you meet all the women of this house?"

"Not all of them. I haven't met Ellen."

"This rain has the streets flooded, so if you want, you and your sister can stay here until there is a break. We eat early here, and we have plenty for two more. Do you like spaghetti?" Henry asked.

Smelling the sauce made me hungry. "Yes, sir. We don't want to be a bother."

"Then it's settled. As soon as Ellen gets here, we'll eat." Henry went into the living room and sat down with the paper in front of the TV. I followed him and sat down.

"Where do you live, Jesse?" Henry asked.

"503A East Third Street, sir."

"You can call me Henry," he said. He learned from me when we moved in, how many rooms we had, why we moved, and how much our place was costing Mom.

"Ellen is here. Let's eat," Kathy said just as the "Mickey Mouse Club" ended.

The table was set for the Skillmans and us, they even had a high chair for Christina. Before they passed the food around, Kathy Skillman said, "Let us pray." And the entire family recited, "Bless us, O Lord, and these Thy gifts, which we are about to receive from Thy bounty, through Christ our Lord, in the name of the Father, the Son, and the Holy Ghost, Amen." They made the sign of the cross and immediately started passing around the food. Ellen took charge of feeding Christina.

"What is the Holy Ghost?" I asked, wishing I had my notebook.

"We are Catholic and believe God has three divine ways to be with us. We pray to him like a father. He provides for us like a father. He is always there for us. His son is Jesus, who came to earth to be with us. He healed and still heals us. He died for our sins, so we could live without shame. When Jesus died, he promised us we would have part of him to live in us and guide us. That is the Holy Ghost or the Holy Spirit," she said.

"I have a ghost?" I asked.

"You have a spirit that guides you to do the right thing."

"Very nice, Kathy," Henry said smiling.

I was hoping I could remember everything she said, so I could put it in my notebook. During supper, I told them about polio and Barney Hospital. Ellen asked a lot of questions. She had already studied the Kenny treatment in nursing school and wanted to know more. Once you have polio, you pretty much become an expert.

The rain cleared away in time for Christina and me to get home before Mom did. When she walked in the apartment, she looked surprised.

"What do I smell? Jesse, what are you up to?"

"Look, Mom," I said from the kitchen. "The Skillmans made you a plate of spaghetti and garlic bread. It's good."

"Who are the Skillmans?" she asked.

"They stopped me and Christina when we walked home during that heavy storm. They even invited us in. We ate with them. Wait 'til you taste the spaghetti!"

"Jesse, you can't just go into someone's home like that. It's dangerous."

She uncovered the plate of spaghetti. "Oh, this smells good."

"It is."

"They live just one block up toward Detroit Street, Mom. They have a two-bedroom apartment upstairs, and they want you to rent it."

"We can't move again," Mom said.

"We have to, Mom. This place is too small. You can't keep sleeping on the couch."

"This is good," Mom said as she twirled spaghetti on the fork with the help of her spoon. "It's the garlic."

"Henry said we could see it tonight if you want. They'll be up late watching TV."

"We don't know these people."

"Mom, you don't know this landlord here. The Skillmans pray at their meal. Together."

"She uses real garlic. Are they Italian?"

"No, Mom, they're Catholic."

"Okay. Put Christina in the stroller while I clean the dish."

"Sorry, Mom, the rain messed it up. I'll fix it tomorrow."

We walked the one block, Mom carrying the washed dish and me herding Christina with my crutches.

Henry and Kathy showed us the upstairs apartment. It had a living room with a coat closet, a kitchen with a table and three chairs, a bathroom with a washer, just like the one in Sabina, two bedrooms, and then back into the living room. It was much larger than the place we were renting.

"Mrs. Tarrant, this is $50 a month and I pay the utilities," said Henry.

"I am here all day and will keep my eye on Jesse and Christina," said Kathy.

"It would be swell to have one more man in the house," Henry quipped.

"I'm on week to week." Mom said and walked around the apartment again.

"You move in anytime; we'll start your rent on the fifteenth of the month," Henry said. "Do you need furniture?"

"All I have is a sewing machine," she said.

"Give me a day or two and you will have some furniture."

"It's a deal, Mr. Skillman," she said. "I do alterations. Will that be a problem?"

"Not if it keeps the rent coming in. You can pay the rent next week."

After a quick repair, I used the stroller to haul our boxes to the new apartment. Henry moved the sewing machine in his car. He and Penny carried it upstairs for Mom.

Victor Hess

Chapter Twenty-Four
Columbus Day Letters

Our new routine was that I came straight home from school to pick up Christina from Kathy Skillman. I usually got home by 3:45 p.m. Sometimes I would stay and watch the "Micky Mouse Club" with Bonnie.

Mom worked from 3 p.m. to 7 p.m. and was home by 7:30. That's when we ate.

October 12th was Columbus Day and a Friday, and I decided to take Christina upstairs into our apartment and write letters.

October 12, 1956

Dear Dad,

I'm out of Barney Hospital. I still use crutches, but I'm getting better. I miss you. Why didn't you visit me? Paula Jean visited me. She and Charlie moved to Boston.
We don't live with Albert anymore.
Can you visit us? Here is my new address. 197 1/2 E Third Street, Xenia, Ohio

Your son,
JESSE
P.S. Happy Columbus Day

October 12, 1956

Dear Lynn,

Guess what? We moved again.

My new address is 197 1/2 E Third Street, Xenia, Ohio. We live upstairs, of course. I still need crutches. If Mr. Davis gives me a paper route, I will buy a bike after I get off the crutches.

Christina talks a lot. She walks better now. Better than me. I go to McKinley School. Most of the schools are named after pioneers or Indians, except mine. He was a president. I think McKinley is the oldest school in the city.

Guess what? I still sing with the girls. I don't think my voice will ever change.

How is your paper route? Do you have more subscribers?

I miss you a lot.

Love, Your best friend.
JESSE
P.S. Happy Columbus Day

Chapter Twenty-Five
More Kenny Treatments

It took a few days for Henry Skillman to furnish our new apartment. Beds were first, then a small trundle bed that became a couch for the living room. Then there was a chair. The Skillmans got some furniture from members of the church and some from the neighbors.

I would sometimes have a meal ready for Mom when she got home, like macaroni and cheese with peanut butter sandwiches. Once, I peeled and cut potatoes and made French fries. I could boil hot dogs and even make grilled cheese.

We were back on familiar ground - an upstairs apartment, sewing, furniture that belonged to someone else. But there was no Lynn, no Joyce, no Arlene. They were replaced by the Skillmans, who were very friendly and generous, but Mom was not as close to them - maybe because they were the landlords.

Henry paid me twenty-five cents for raking the yard. It took a while with the crutches, but it was a small yard. It felt good getting paid again.

Sunday morning Mom said, "Jesse. Get your good pants on. You're going to church." She was already dressing Christina. "Take Christina with you."

I had forgotten about church. I missed it, especially the singing with Gloria Armey in Sabina.

"Did you really meet Dad at the Methodist Church?"

"Yes. It was just after Paula Jean's mother died."

"Did you know he drank and gambled then?"

"He didn't then. Your father was in charge of his company. He was always going to Chamber of Commerce meetings." She put Christina's dress on her.

"What's that?"

"Where important business men meet and make decisions. He got his picture in the paper a couple times." She pinned her hair back.

"Really? I never knew that."

"When you were two years old, he was very important in the Transportation industry."

"Do you have the article?"

"I might. I'll look later." She started putting Christina's shoes on her.

"Did you know he was in a bowling league? I'd go watch him bowl, hold you, and cheer his team." She put the second shoe on her.

Dad never told me any of this. Whenever we talked, it was me telling him something. I don't remember him telling me anything.

"The rest were bad memories," she said.

"What happened?"

"I've thought about that. It wasn't one thing. First, his bowling friends would come to our apartment to play cards. He loved his cards. Then, he'd invite the big shots from the chamber. He never earned the pay those guys got, but he liked to spend money like them and buy them liquor and food while he was losing money playing cards. That's when we started having problems with landlords. So, we'd move. Then, we'd move again. He lost one job, then he wasn't on the chamber committee anymore, but that didn't keep them big shots from showing up to play cards." She stared at Christina's coat, like she was talking to it. "He'd spend money on liquor and cards before he'd pay rent or buy food."

Her words reminded me of those nights when I'd wake up in the middle of the night to cards shuffling, men laughing, or Mom yelling at them to "Get the hell out of our house!"

Now that I knew Dad was once a man in charge of stuff, I hoped he'd be the one to tell me more about it. Maybe he could figure out how to be in charge again. Mom put Christina's coat on her.

Trinity Methodist Church was three blocks away, an easy walk by now with the stroller. When we arrived, I approached a group of ladies standing outside.

"Where is Sunday school?" I asked.

"What grade are you?" one of the women asked.

"I'm in the sixth grade. My sister is two," I said, holding tight onto Christina.

"Where are your parents?" she asked.

"It's just us. Mom stayed at home."

"Frank!" The lady yelled over to a tall man standing on the steps of the building next door to the church. "Here's a sixth grader." He and a lady walked over to us.

"My name is Frank Wells. This is my wife Wendy," he said. "What's your name?"

"Jesse Hall. That's Christina." I said.

"Jesse Hall. Are you related to Virgil?" Frank asked.

"Yes, sir. He's my uncle," I replied proudly.

"Let me get you two settled."

Before Frank could finish, I interrupted. "Where can we put the stroller?" I pulled out my crutches.

"I'll take them both, Wendy." The three of us went to the building next to the church. He put the stroller on the porch.

"Which Hall is your father, Jesse?" Frank asked.

"Marshall, sir. He lives in Dayton." I replied.

"Okay, here we are. Frances!" Frank called to an elderly lady with a blue dress on. "Frances, this is Jesse Hall and his sister Christina."

Before he could finish, she said, "You're Marshall's son.

How old is Christina?"

"She's two, ma'am," I replied.

"She looks just like Paula Jean," she said to my surprise. "My name is Frances Randall, and you will find out later we are kind of related. I'm Paula Jean's aunt. Come with me, and we'll get Christina to the nursery. I'll bring him back to your class in a few minutes, Frank."

My Sunday school class was all boys. Frank and his brother, Lane, taught our class. They passed out pamphlets, and we took turns reading, asking, and answering questions. The lesson was the Sermon on the Mount. I remember Joyce had told us about this story on my ninth birthday. Frank read from Matthew. After class, Mrs. Randall asked me to stay for church while the nursery staff watched Christina and the other kids. I knew Mom wouldn't mind. I knew that she would appreciate the time she could be alone. Sunday school and church would give her three hours, and Christina was having fun with all the toys in the nursery.

I loved the music. This church had a pipe organ and a good organist.

I propped my crutches beside me, and glad I did because of the standing we would do to sing hymns. That way I could use my crutches to prop me up and I could still hold the hymnal in both my hands. I loved the hymns, especially this day because you could sing loud. The first hymn was "O For A Thousand Tongues to Sing." Today, we sang all seven verses. "Hear him, ye deaf; his praise, you dumb, your loosened tongues employ; ye blind, behold your Savior comes, and leap, ye lame for joy." Like a promise to me. We never sang that verse in Sabina. It was comforting, but worrisome, too, because, what if this lame boy couldn't be healed. The sermon was about the blind guy and Jesus rubbing the mud on his eyes. When would he rub it on me, or my dad? Then I remembered this was the story Georgia told us about at Barney when Sam thought he got polio because he sinned.

Then we stood back up to sing the closing hymn. I liked the words, "No Matter what may be the test, God will take care of you." I believed the verses. When you sing the hymns, the words can get stuck in your head, especially if there's a good tune with it.

After the service, a man touched my shoulder. "I think I know you," he said. "I'm Dr. Thompson."

I knew him right away. I'd never forget him. "You did my spinal, sir. I'm Jesse Hall."

After I told him about my treatment in Dayton, he seemed concerned that we still weren't doing Kenny treatments. He asked for my address and said he'd drop by to see me.

When I got home, the clipping Mom talked about was laying on my bed. It was a photo of four men in suits standing together. This tall guy had his arm on my dad's shoulder. Dad was the shortest man in the photo. They were smiling, and I was sure that these were the big shots Mom was talking about. In just a short time, I had already developed a dislike for the men, but, for the first time, I was proud that my dad was there, in this picture. I wondered if he ever remembered it. The date was February 28, 1948. I wasn't even two years old. The clipping was coming apart.

On Monday, my teacher put tape on it to protect it for me.

After I got home from school, Monday, Dr. Thompson knocked on our door.

"Is your mother home, Jesse?"

"No, sir. She gets off work at 7."

"Who's downstairs?"

"Mrs. Skillman. They own the house."

In a few minutes he had ushered Kathy Skillman upstairs and started asking me a lot of questions about my hospital stays and if anyone was giving me any physical therapy.

It was like a miracle. By the time he left, he had arranged for the March of Dimes to pay Ellen Skillman to give me Kenny treatments twice a day, just like at the hospital. I didn't know who was happier, me or Ellen. I knew twice-a-day Kenny treatments were going to hurt, but if they worked for Scott, they should work for me. I was getting closer to a bike and a paper route. One step at a time.

Tuesday morning, at 6 a.m., I filled the washer with hot water. When Ellen arrived, she dropped two small towels in and then used a large wooden spoon to pull them out and ran them through the wringer. Mr. Skillman provided us with two wide boards that we laid lengthwise across the old claw foot bath tub and I climbed up and laid there while Ellen covered my leg muscles with the hot towels. These weren't those wool towels that stunk, but they were still as hot. Fifteen minutes later, she started stretching my muscles, forcing my toes toward my knees until it hurt, like at Barney, except we didn't have the board. Then, she said, "Time for physical therapy. Get dressed and go to school." We both laughed.

That evening, we repeated the process, the washer was drained, the boards stowed behind the tub, and I was whipped by the time Mom got home.

"How did you do?" she asked.

"It's like at the hospital, Mom. Ellen had more fun than I did. It's like having Bertha all over again."

"Dr. Thompson called me at work. He said you left Barney a little too soon. He said if this doesn't work out, we have to consider putting you back there."

"This will work, Mom. Ellen and I can do it. I don't think Barney has room anyway."

Ellen and Henry came upstairs and asked me to describe the board Barney used to bend the ankles.

The next morning, Ellen showed up with a small board,

just like I described the night before.

"Look what Daddy made for us," she said.

"That's it. That's what they used," I said. Day by day, my muscles were learning and finally on a Friday, I walked around the block on my own. Ellen followed me holding my crutches. Saturday, we walked to the park, with her pushing Christina in the stroller. It was tiring and exhilarating all at once. When I tried to run, I would stumble, so we took it slow. Sunday, we walked and did a little jogging around the block.

Sometimes a person would stop and offer me a lift in their car. As much as I wanted the ride, I would refuse the offer and let them know that this was therapy. My right leg seemed to get better faster, so Ellen increased the time we put hot towels on the left leg. The next Sunday I walked Christina to church but left the crutches at home. I walked to Sunday School and then church. Dr. Thompson made me sit with his family. That day, I met a lot of church members as he told them the story of diagnosing my polio and then curing me of it. I hoped he was right about the curing.

The next week Ellen continued my Kenny treatments and then told me that March of Dimes had two other patients in town for her to do in-home Kenny treatments. "We'll have a good report for Dr. Thompson this week, Jesse."

At school I was making more friends. Neil was the guy who loaned me his glove when I tried out for Little League. He sat by me at lunch one day and pulled out his billfold which immediately impressed me. I didn't have one. I kept my money in my pocket or in my chest. He lifted out a folded-up newspaper clipping. It was an announcement about his dad, who had died. I could tell, without reading, that he was important, a surgeon. Neil pulled out another clipping.

"Pop gave this to me the day before he died. He was fine one day and then the next day he was gone." It was sad to hear. I didn't know what to say. "He'd want you to have it. I know.

I thought about it all night. Here." He unfolded it and handed it to me.

It was a poem. I read it and fell in love with it.

"He gave this to you. You should keep it."

"It's okay. I have it memorized. I'll never forget it. Pop said we need a creed. I guess this was his."

"Wow." I reread the poem.

"My favorite line is this one, 'be glad in the choice which has fallen to you, to battle with something not easy to do.' He told me that it meant that you don't give up on doing something just because it's hard."

I figured that Proverbs probably had a verse like it. I folded it up and put it in my *Bible*.

That night, after my Kenny treatment I pulled out the poem. There was a big heading "Just Folks by Edgar Guest." The poem was called "Difficulties."

> *Stick to it, Boy, when the battle is hard.*
>   *Stick to it, Lad, when the going is rough;*
> *The proof of the Fighter is how he is scarred,*
>   *To vanquish a Coward one blow is enough.*
> *Just keep this in mind as you see the task through,*
> *It's the commonplace things that are easy to do.*
>
> *The thousands can follow the pathway of one.*
>   *The millions flock in when the fight has been won;*
> *There are many to go where another has gone*
>   *And many to do what another has*

done.
But to blaze a new trail there are only a few;
It's the commonplace things that are easy to do.

Don't ask for the easy and commonplace tasks;
*   It's the difficult problems which bring men to fame.*
Rejoice in the courage the day's trial asks.
*   For if you succeed men shall honor your name.*
Be glad in the choice which has fallen to you
To battle with something not easy to do.
Copyright, 1921, by Edgar A Guest

I remember Annie used to say, "one step at a time." I tried to skip a step by leaving Barney early, I guess, and it didn't work out. I was happy that Dr. Thompson made me redo the Kenny treatment.

November 1st, I carried my crutches to school and did so well that the next day, I forgot and left them in the corner of my room at school. The next day, I stopped at the bike shop, crutchless. Snuffy started to dance a little jig when he saw me walk around the bike lot.

"I don't believe it! You're cured, Jesse." He immediately surveyed all his bikes. Then, and there, Snuffy taught me to ride a bike.

November 2, 1956

Dear Mr. Davis,

*   How are you? I am fine now. I can walk and can even ride a bike. Thank you for the news articles. I have given most of them*

away.

I hope you can find me a route in Xenia. It's just me, my mom, and sister, so I need to help out. Here is my new address: 197 1/2 E Third Street, Xenia, Ohio. Our neighbor downstairs has a phone. Henry Skillman 555-2077. If you find me a route, I can buy a bike. I have one picked out.

Yours truly,
JESSE

Mondays, Wednesdays, and Fridays, just before lunch, the sixth and fifth grades would leave the classrooms and go to the auditorium, which also served as the music classroom. I knew I was still a soprano. I was a boy, I didn't want to be a soprano, but there was nothing I could do about it. I loved the class, even as a soprano. No one made fun of my high voice here.

The school had fees. There was insurance, physical education fees, and then my school lunches. It did not take long for my money to be gone and, now, it was up to Mom.

At school I met kids with common interests like music. Neil and I were closest. Wally Charles, the boy who helped me carry my books, was in the Boy Scouts. At age eleven, you could be a Boy Scout.

"Troop 18 meets on Monday nights at seven," he said.

"Where at?" I asked. "Here?" I hoped not because of the long walk.

"No. At First Methodist Church. In the basement." That was just a few blocks from my house.

Wally had a low voice, and our music teacher liked to choose songs that had little bass solos, so Wally's voice could be showcased. His brother Jake had a good voice, too, just not a bass.

"Does everyone do music in your family?" I asked.

"Mom plays the organ for our church, but she also gives piano lessons. My dad has a barbershop quartet that he sings in, and he even arranges the music. I play the trombone and Jake plays the French horn. We live in a small house, but it's always full of music." Wally was smiling as he described the musical prowess of his family. He was thin but had a smile that filled his entire face.

Tuesday, when I picked up Christina, Kathy handed me a note with a telephone number.

"The man with the newspaper called and left this number. He said you could call him collect." I asked if I could use their phone.

"Mr. Evans? It's Jesse Hall." I spoke loudly because I thought I needed to. "I just got your note. Yes sir. I am, but I can't start delivery until 7:30 every night. I baby sit my sister. Yes sir. No sir. I couldn't do it earlier. I understand, I'm sorry. Goodbye Mr. Evans."

I took my sister upstairs, wondering if there was any way I could take Christina on the paper route after school. This wasn't Sabina.

When Mom got home, I was frying bologna for sandwiches. Mom came in, set her purse on the table, and took over at the stove.

"Kathy said you called Mr. Davis."

"Yeah, the paper route idea won't work."

"Will you pour us some milk?" she asked

I set glasses on the counter.

"How was school?"

"It was fun. We had music today. Mom, did I tell you they still have me singing soprano?" It was still a shameful admission as far as I was concerned.

"You have a beautiful voice, Jesse. I hear you singing

from the *Hit Parade*."

I smiled. We ate our sandwiches with ketchup and pickles. Mom pulled out a bag of Oreo cookies. The milk never tasted so good as it did with Oreo cookies.

"Mom, they have Scouts at the First Methodist church on Monday nights. I'd like to go," I said.

"Will you be able to do the Scouts and a paper route?" she asked.

"I can't do the paper route during school. Not unless I take Christina with me," I said. "I thought about it. It won't work."

"I've been talking to Kathy. She agreed to watch Christina, so I can work a full day at Doug's. I will get home earlier. Do you want the paper route?"

Things were falling into place for me. A good school, a good neighbor family, a Mom who trusted me and a brown-haired, blue-eyed sister who clung to me. I could even walk. I called Mr. Davis back the next day.

I started the paper route and Boy Scouts on the same Monday that next week. Mr. Evans had to take me around again Tuesday and Wednesday. Thirty-two papers for this route. I had Southwest Xenia. I would net $6.40 a week. I picked up my papers at Pat's Market on Detroit Street at 3:30, and it took two hours to do my route. This was his fifth paperboy in six months and now Mr. Evans told me he was happy this route was finally taken care of. By the time I finished the route each day, if Mom hadn't made it home, I would pick up Christina from downstairs and take her upstairs. She would play but not before she told me all she did at Kathy's. Words flew out of her mouth. I replied in baby talk and could not leave her side without reading from one of her Golden Books. "Little Indian," she said. Mom walked in as I was reading.

"Rebecca Hall came in the drug store today," she said.

"Is something wrong?" I asked.

"No. She said your grandpa would like to come and pick you up for church this Sunday."

"Why, Mom? Which Church?"

"She said the United Brethren. I told her you were going to the Methodist Church."

"What do you think, Mom?" I asked.

"I think he wants to get to know you," she said. "I told her you would go. I hope that's okay."

"Sure, should Christina go too?" I asked.

"No," she said quickly. "But maybe we can let her go to the farm with you and your dad this Thanksgiving."

"Yeah, she would like that," I said.

"Paula Jean is pregnant. She and Charlie are going to have a baby, Rebecca told me."

"That was fast," I said. Mom looked at me funny.

"Here. You need to take one of these every day." She set down a bottle of Chock's fruit flavored vitamins. "Let me know if you start feeling weak while you're delivering your papers."

Saturday, I picked up my papers at Pat's Market. They had an awning I could sit under while folding my papers and stuffing them in the bag. Two other paperboys covering other sections of town got their papers there, too. I had the southwest portion and the fewest papers. Mr. Davis encouraged me to add more subscribers. The other two had a lot more papers, so I stayed and helped them fold before I started off.

My first stop was the house of Helen Santmyer who was a teacher or author or something. Her secretary lived with her and was polite when I delivered to them. She seemed to be always waiting for the paper. Then, I walked all the way down Third Street to Cincinnati Avenue.

When I got to the next house, I knocked on the door and Wally, from school, answered it. A piano was playing in one room. Wally introduced his dad, who appeared in a full regalia Indian costume, headdress and all.

"Are you an Indian?" I asked.

"Dad's barbershop quartet is called the Cheer O Keys, so they all have Indian costumes." Wally explained

"Hi Jesse," Jake, Wally's younger brother said.

"HOW, Jesse," Mr. Charles said holding his right hand up like the movie Indians. I knew I would like the Charles family.

"Uhh, How. $1.60 sir." I got back to business.

"Ugh, paper boy need wampum, squaw," he yelled, and Mrs. Charles appeared with her purse.

Then I went to Center Street, Short Street and South Miami Street where I had four customers. I had two more customers on High Street, one on Lynn Street, one on New Street, and two on Chestnut Street. One of those was Gary and Danny's aunt. She had no idea who I was, so I never said anything about Albert being my ex-step-father. I had six more houses before I ended up on South Detroit Street, standing in front of the train depot. When I took the paper inside, the manager told me the paper was for Cookie and pointed to a railroad car sitting on the track with smoke billowing out of a smoke stack. Getting to the train car, I had to walk around puddles, through sharp pieces of large gravel, and across two sets of tracks before I came to this dirty, once silver train car. I used the paper to pound on the door, and this guy, with two days growth of beard, and covered with flour opened the door and said, "What!"

My eyes got big and I stepped back.

"I'm your paperboy, sir."

"What's your name?" he said.

"Jesse. Here's your paper."

"Come up here." I was more than halfway on my route, tired and facing a step that was waist high to me.

"Give me that paper." I handed it up and then he reached

down to me. "Give me your hand." I instinctively obeyed and was lifted effortlessly into the train car that had been transformed into the best smelling bakery I had ever seen.

"Where's the other boy?"

"I don't know. I just started."

"He wasn't worth a crap. Couldn't get my paper here on time." He gave me instructions on where to leave the paper when he wasn't there. He was making chocolate covered creme fills and the smell was so good. I was so hungry.

"Here!" He handed me two dollars. "Two weeks. Keep the change." Each utterance from him was a warning not to cross him. He pulled out a brown paper sack, stuck four creme fills in it, and said, "Don't eat 'em all or you'll be fat like me." Then this broad smile filled his ruddy face changing every opinion I had.

"Thanks, Mr. uhh."

"Cookie. Just call me Cookie. Just get the paper here on time. Here, let me lift you down." Satchel and all, he gently moved me from the train to the gravel.

Once I cleared the step, he went back to his business. I thought I heard him singing.

I started eating the creme fill and was sure I got some icing on the next subscriber's paper.

My next stop was two houses on Hill Street, and then two more up on South Monroe Street where another classmate lived.

There was this big bridge going over the railroad tracks. I walked on it, careful to stay on the narrow walkway. Now I only had three more houses before I was back home. The last customer being just a block from my house.

I was grateful to Ellen for doing Kenny treatments on me. She insisted we get a treatment in after every paper route and was waiting for me when I got home. She and Mom had to eat the creme fills first, while I described my encounter with

Cookie.

The key to a paper boy succeeding was that he needed to collect at least the amount of money to cover what the *Cincinnati Press* was going to collect from him. It was a hard couple hours, because, rain, sleet, snow, whatever, the paper had to be delivered. Xenia had hills. Sabina didn't. This Saturday, I collected enough to have four dollars left over. I could buy my bike in just one more week.

Chapter Twenty-Six
Church with Grandpa Hall

I did not know exactly when Grandpa was going to pick me up for church. My newspapers were at Pat's Market at 6:30 a.m. and I was there to get them delivered. It took two hours.

I cleaned up and Grandpa Hall picked me up at 10:30 in the 1956 Hudson to take us to the United Brethren Church on West Third Street.

"Hi Grandpa," I said. I noticed it was the same car Paula Jean used to take me to Frisch's. It had new floor mats.

"How are you today, Jesse?" Grandpa Hall said. "Are you ready for church?"

"Yes sir, are we going to Sunday school, too?" I asked.

"Not today, just church. Do you go to church?" he asked.

"Yes sir. I go to Trinity Methodist Church," I replied knowing Grandpa Hall would be happy with that answer.

"Your father used to go there. Are you baptized?" Grandpa asked.

"Not yet. This year I go to confirmation class after Christmas and then I get baptized." I had learned all this in the last few Sunday school classes and was glad I did. "I go to Sunday school, too. I take Christina with me."

"How old is Christina?" he asked.

"She's two, Grandpa." Thomas Hall had not met his granddaughter yet. "Mom wants me to bring her to Thanksgiving this year," I said.

"Yes, Ruby would like that," he said.

"Where's Grandma?" I asked.

"She's not feeling well, Jesse. She's fighting cancer," he said, as if he was talking to another farmer.

"I didn't know," I said. "I met Mrs. Randall at church. She said she is Paula Jean's aunt."

"That's where your dad met his first wife Louise." That was a surprise. He met Mom and his first wife at the same church.

I tried to picture Dad attending church. He sure didn't want to go with me.

"How's school?" Grandpa Hall asked.

"It's okay."

"Where do you go?"

"McKinley. I go to Central next year."

"We're going to the Brethren Church today. It's like the Methodist Church in some ways."

"I go past it every day on my paper route." I opened my vent window.

"You do? What paper do you deliver?"

"*The Cincinnati Press*, Grandpa."

"We just read the *Gazette*." He rolled his window down about six inches.

I pulled the news clipping about Dad out of my *Bible* and studied it.

"What's that, Jesse?"

"It's an article about Dad." We were in the church parking lot. He slowly pulled into a parking space under a buckeye tree. I handed it to him.

"Oh my," he said.

"Did you ever see this?" I asked.

"No. I can't say that I have. When was this?"

"1948." I said.

"Those were better times for your mom and dad." He handed it back to me. "While you have that *Bible* open look up this. Proverbs 10:17."

Soon I read, " 'He who heeds instruction is on the path to life, but he who rejects reproof goes astray.' What's reproof, Grandpa?"

"It could be correction, or even punishment, but it's no good unless it makes you remember to do right. That's why we have rules."

"I remember that other verse, Grandpa." I put the article back in my *Bible*.

"What verse?"

"You remember. 'The way of a fool.'"

"Oh yes. It seems to have done good by you. You'll be just fine. Here we are. Let's go to church." He opened his car door.

We said no more as we walked into church.

It was a brick building, but as large as it was, it was plain inside. We were there just in time. Thomas Hall introduced me to a couple of his friends. I felt important as I was being introduced. We stood together, singing. I knew the hymns and sang loudly like a Methodist. After the service, Grandpa drove me home.

"I learned the third rule, Grandpa."

"And what would that be?"

"Do all you can to be close to God," I said. I looked over at him.

"Yes, that rule. Well, this has been good," he said as he slowed the car in front of our apartment.

"Do you want to come upstairs and see Christina?"

"Not today, but we'll do this again," Grandpa said. He reached over and gave me a dollar.

"Yes, sir. Thank you. Goodbye," I said. I watched the green Hudson Hornet pull away, wondering why, now, Grandpa made the short drive to visit and if, really, we would do this again. I was happy though, because with that dollar he gave me, I'd be getting my bike tomorrow.

I wish I'd shown him my article about Barney Hospital and the other one about Lynn, me, and March of Dimes. I wondered why Dad never showed him his article.

Chapter Twenty-Seven
The Green Schwinn Corvette

When I got home from Grandpa's church, Albert's blue Plymouth Belvedere was parked in front of our house. I hesitated, afraid Albert was going to talk Mom into going back with him.

The upstairs door opened, and Gary yelled down the stairs to me.

"Hey, little brother! You want lunch?"

When I reached the top, I followed him into the kitchen. "Is Albert here?"

"No. I'm driving now. We just stopped by to get something edible to eat! I brought Mom a chicken," Gary said.

As soon as he said it, Mom put the first piece in a skillet of hot Crisco, and the kitchen instantly filled with the smell of happiness, Mom's fried chicken.

I told him about Scouts and my paper route.

"How can you work with polio?" Danny asked.

"I'm healed. I've been off crutches most of the week. I'll be getting a bike tomorrow."

"He's getting stronger," Mom said. "Jesse, open a can of corn."

"What about Scouts? I mean, the hiking," Gary asked.

"I'll let you know. I have my first campout next weekend."

After lunch, Gary and Danny went home, but within an hour, Gary returned to our house with an old canvas backpack that was full of stuff.

"There's a shirt, a belt, a cooking kit, and a neckerchief

in there. My old manual's in there, and a bunch of jeans, too." Gary walked downstairs with me. "There's a lot to learn."

After he left, I started studying the Scout manual. At the time, I noticed unique smells from his stuff: a collection of smoke, dirt, streams, rain, mosquito repellent and food all rolled up in the backpack. I bet Gary had some stories to tell.

I memorized the oath, "On my honor, I will do my best, to do my duty to God and my Country, and to obey the Scout law; to help other people at all times; to keep myself physically strong, mentally awake, and morally straight."

Then I learned the Scout Law: "A Scout is trustworthy, loyal, helpful, friendly, courteous, kind, obedient, cheerful, thrifty, brave, clean and reverent."

Finally, the motto: "Be Prepared."

I was ready for Monday's meeting.

From an early age, I wanted a bicycle. I remember once having a tricycle and riding it in our upstairs apartment and making a wrong turn and bouncing down the stairs and, though in pain, insisted to Mom that I was all right. When she was convinced I was not seriously hurt, she paddled my butt, ensuring I would never go down the stairs on my tricycle. Then I got caught throwing mud patties at car windows and never remember seeing that tricycle again. I was four years old then.

At seven, I was ready for a real bicycle. Bicycle ads were all over the newspapers. I begged my parents and finally, for my birthday, Dad brought home a large red oversize tricycle. You could ride it, and someone could stand on the back platform between the back two wheels. But a tricycle was not as fast as a bicycle and owning a tricycle at age seven held you back in neighborhood esteem. The next day, I painted that tricycle an aqua blue color from paint leftover from Mom painting the bathroom. I painted that whole tricycle, because it was more fun painting it than riding it. Anyway, it caused a big fight between Mom and Dad, and that was the first time I ever saw him hurt someone.

Now, at eleven, I was ready to make the down payment on my new bicycle. At least it would be new to me.

On my way to pick up my papers at Pat's Market, I stopped at the bike shop. I visited the shop often, and Snuffy would show me new bikes he got in and tell me what he had done to each bike to make sure it was "safe and reliable." He told me about chains, and how they had to be tight, but not too tight, or they'd break. He showed me how each spoke needed to be carefully adjusted, so the wheel turned without a wobble. He described hand brakes and how much trouble they were compared to the Bendix pedal brake. Today was different, though, because I now had the five dollars for my down payment.

"Jesse, look at this baby." He wheeled out a green Schwinn Corvette, with the front bracket and rear bracket. It had hand brakes.

"It was in an accident, but the frame was perfect. I touched up the paint, readjusted the fenders and put new wheels on it." One hand was on the handle grip and the other pointed and stroked each part of the bike he described. You would have to study it close to see that it had any work done on it. He lifted up the back by the seat and spun the wheel. It spun perfectly, no wobble, no sound. He repeated the process on the front with the same result. The tires were new and had that new bike smell to them.

"It's a twenty-four-inch bike, which is perfect for you. We'll trade up when you get a little taller. Here, give me that bag." He reached over as I enthusiastically handed him the canvas newspaper bag. He expertly wove the shoulder strap around the handlebars.

"Look. Perfect." He stepped back and we both admired the green bike. After a moment, he said, "Twenty-five dollars. You'll have it paid off in twenty weeks." I reached in my pocket for the five one-dollar bills and after a few minutes of paper work, he told me to drive it around his store a few times to be sure I had the hang of it. I had already visited the store so many times before, and tried out so many of his used bikes, that this was easy. It was also the best bike I had tried. I was free.

"Stop by the police station and get a bike license," he yelled. "You need it."

I glanced back at Snuffy. I'm not sure who was happiest, his smile was that big. In less than a minute, I rode the two blocks from the Bike Shop to Pat's Market to load up my papers.

I got home a full hour early because my new bike was that fast. I started thinking about how I could get more subscribers. The next day, I got my bike license. I peeled the backing off and attached the license on the center post of my bike. I was official.

Troop 18's Scoutmaster was Mr. Combs. When he saw me in Gary's old Scout shirt he asked where I got it and after I explained that my brother gave me equipment to start Scouts, he gave me instructions, as he pinned new numbers on my shoulder.

"Get your mom to sew these where I pinned them. Your shirt tells everyone what troop you belong to."

"Yes, sir."

"Can your dad help us at camp outs or meetings, Jesse?"

"I don't think so. They're divorced. I don't see much of him because he lives in Dayton."

"That's too bad," he said.

"My mom can sew the numbers on shirts if you want. I'll ask."

"That could help. Let's get you started on your Tenderfoot rank and a merit badge." He handed me a pamphlet. "Start reading this."

It was a merit badge guide and said *Pathfinding* on the

front. There was an image of an Indian head with a full headdress of feathers. I always had Indian tendencies, and this was a great way to get my interest, studying an Indian skill.

"You return the book once you earn your badge. I'll give you a test to be sure you learn all the skills you need. We'll do that at the campout, if you're ready by then."

"Yes, sir." Our campout was this weekend.

One of the requirements to earn your Pathfinder badge was to draw an accurate map. By Tuesday after school, I decided to draw a map of my paper route. Using the compass Gary gave me, I figured out where north was and then counted paces, from house to house, marking each house where I had a customer. I even marked where other Scouts lived. I had to redraw the map a couple times, because I ran out of room and my next house would fall over the edge of the paper, but I finished it on Thursday, Thanksgiving Day, and couldn't wait to show Mr. Combs at the campout that weekend.

Victor Hess

Chapter Twenty-Eight
Thanksgiving on the Hall Farm

This year, Thanksgiving at the Hall Farm included Christina. She was two years old and consumed my time at the farm. While my cousins were in the barn, I stayed in the house with her. I took her outside to see the chickens, cows, and pigs, which she had only seen in picture books. She knew what they were right away. Grandpa Hall even held her. Paula Jean was gone because she had already moved to Boston. Finally, Uncle George Horn's daughter, Darla, rescued me by taking charge of her.

"You go play with your cousins, Jesse. I'll take care of Christina."

When I found them, they were playing hide-and-seek in the barn. We explored in special "caves" created by bales stacked haphazardly and used them as hiding places. The rules were modified. There was no base. If you found someone, you just said "I see Kelly" or whoever you saw. It was an honor system everyone observed. I found a tunnel and crawled through it to a point where I barely had enough room to turn around. I waited, sure I would not be found. There was a movement to my left and what I saw there was an orange cat with seven kittens suckling her teats. I took in the sight of the tiny kittens, the nursing sounds, and the mother cat trusting me.

"I found some kittens!" I yelled out, no longer focused on the game. Kelly was "it" and was first to the scene. She crawled to the spot and looked.

"It's Gretchen; Jesse found Gretchen. 1-2-3 on Jesse."

She crawled back out so that, one by one, Sharon, Karl, Jeffrey and Valerie could see Gretchen's kittens. We vacated

Gretchen's new home and decided to try some other activity.

"Jeffrey, does the pulley still work?" Karl asked.

"Yeah, I think." Jeffrey replied.

The barn had a pulley used to hoist heavy stuff, like multiple bales of hay or straw. There was a track that ran the length of the barn where you could pull the load from one end of the barn to the other. One person could do the work of two with the contraption.

We piled up bales on the left far side of the barn high enough to reach the rope of the pulley. One held onto the rope with both hands and started a motion that would systematically move us to the edge of the third level where we would get off. It was a workout. Someone else then used the pulley to maneuver back to the far side.

I sat on the edge of a hay bale on the third floor waiting for Sharon to swing the pulley from the end of the barn where we had piled the bales. She made it across in just a few thrusts of her body, and I helped her land up on the ledge.

She showed me how to hold the rope and then gave me a shove that put me one third of the way back to the other side. I tried to thrust my body like Sharon did but was only able to get a couple more feet. I did it again, but now I went backward a couple feet. Meanwhile, I had five cousins yelling advice. No matter what I did, I could not make progress in either direction. I was hanging onto a rope with my hands fourteen feet above the wooden floor. I knew that I couldn't hang there forever. Karl, Jeffrey and Kelly piled bales directly under me. One, two, five, seven, ten bales positioned under me. I was feeling weaker. Then Karl yelled, "Drop! Drop! You'll be okay."

I was afraid to drop. I was silently crying. All I needed now in my life would be broken legs.

"I'll break a leg!"

They added a couple more bales.

"Drop!" Sharon encouraged me. "Drop. I know you can

do it."

Just then, Uncle Russ walked in the barn.

"What's going on in here?" he said. My hand was in pain, I looked down. Everyone was looking at Uncle Russ. "What's this?" He was staring at the pile of hay bales.

"We're building a fort," Karl said. None of them looked up at me. I stayed still. I prayed for strength.

"You have a lot of work to do if you want a fort." His hands were on his hips. He had moved directly under me. My heartbeat was loud.

"Supper will be ready in ten minutes. Best start clearing this up." Then he turned and walked toward the door at the same moment my strength died.

I dropped and immediately landed on the pile of bales. They broke my fall without breaking my bones. My fear turned to laughter and they all joined in.

Uncle Russ turned around. "Don't be late," he said.

"That was close," said Karl.

"Let me try again," I blurted as he left the barn.

"I'll show you," said Jeffrey. "Watch."

Karl and I watched Jeffrey swing back across.

"Watch, Jesse." Sharon got back on the pulley, and Jeffrey gave her a heave, sending her a third of the way across. Then she stopped. Back and forth. The pulley wouldn't budge.

"Drop! Drop!" We all said. The bales were still positioned under Sharon, and she dropped, just as the farm bell rang out six times. Supper was ready.

We reset the bales like Uncle Russ told us, went back to the farmhouse, and announced to everyone we found Gretchen, the cat.

Dad was holding Christina and called me over immediately to change her. There was a wet spot on his pants. She reached for me.

Family together on Thanksgiving was always memorable and special. It never really went beyond the one day. Thanksgiving Day and Christmas Day. That was it. It was enough for me though. I cherished it.

As Dad brought us home from Thanksgiving on the Hall farm, Christmas was already on its way to Xenia. Half of Main Street was festooned with illuminated candy canes and garlands.

"Dad, come on up. Mom wants you to come up," I said as Dad pulled up to the apartment.

"I have to get back to Dayton, Jesse."

"She's wondering about the child support, Dad."

"Tell her I sent it last week. She should have it by tomorrow."

I picked up Christina, and as soon as I got out, the door to the Buick shut and Dad pulled away. In the same moment, Mom came out the front door, out to the sidewalk, and watched him drive away.

"He's gone, Mom," I said. "He said he sent it last week." We stood there watching Dad and his lie drive away.

"I collect on Saturday," I said. My sleeping bag would have to wait. I regretted, just a little, getting the bike. Money was that tight.

Chapter Twenty-Nine
Skunk Attack

Saturday morning, I was at the First Methodist Church by 9:00 with my gear for a one-night campout at Camp Birch. Instead of a sleeping bag, Mom rolled up two blankets and a sheet into a tight bedroll, which I tied to the backpack Gary had given me. A sleeping bag was essential for campouts, especially during the fall and winter when it could quickly drop into the teens without warning. The pack strapped on my back, I walked the five blocks to the church. The Scoutmaster noticed my bedroll.

"Jesse, don't you have a sleeping bag?" Mr. Combs asked.

"No, sir. I have to wait 'til next week. I saw one for nine dollars at the surplus store. I'm saving up." The list of things I needed was growing, but my money was always needed for other things.

"Be sure you sleep close to the stove. It's going to get into the twenties, but we're staying in a cabin this trip. You go in Mr. Lewis' car."

I was relieved we were staying in a cabin. I had a knife in a sheath and a cooking kit that Gary gave me. I had a flashlight and a canteen. I even had an ax. But I was the only one without a sleeping bag, and that embarrassed me.

Mr. Lewis' car took the Lewis brothers and me down roads I had never traveled before. I watched out the window as white fences and barns went by like a movie.

Mr. Lewis turned up a hillside with two severe hairpin turns, and the rolling meadows suddenly became a forest of all kinds of leafless trees clinging to steep hillsides. The car pulled onto an unpaved lane through a tunnel of overhanging branches that were whipping against the car, punishing it for its recent encroachment. Over the rise, there was the cabin, small, made of logs, looking natural in its surroundings.

When the car stopped, we sprang out, looking at the cabin and taking in the surroundings. The smell of burning wood, the heavy layer of leaves underfoot, awakened a spirit within my heart. We grabbed our packs and sleeping gear and went into the cabin where five other khaki clad adventurers welcomed us with "What took you guys so long?" and "We're going for wood; you wanna help?" and, "You guys sleep over there."

Packs, boots, canteens, knives, axes, flashlights, and web belts transfigured us into adventurers, pioneers, explorers. It all happened between the time we stepped out of the car to when we walked into the rustic cabin, all of thirty seconds.

I handed my map to Mr. Combs. He studied it for a few minutes. He checked with Wally to be sure I had his house marked correctly.

"Your legend is good; the scale seems right. Not bad for a green horn," and then he patted me on the back.

"Jesse just passed the first half of his Pathfinding requirement," he announced to the rest of the cabin. There were cheers, my back got slapped, a lot, and even whistles from the other Scouts.

"Jesse, you and Wally come outside." Wally was tall. It was like we were Mutt and Jeff in the comics. "Do you have a compass?"

We both pulled out a compass.

"You'll need your canteen." We patted our canteens already full and attached to our web belts. He handed us a paper with directions on it. It wasn't a map, it was just directions.

"If you follow these directions, you will find a piece of cut firewood with a blue piece of paper tacked on it, like this." He showed us a square of blue paper. "You have thirty minutes, but it really shouldn't take that long. Any questions?"

We stared at the directions. Each instruction had a direction, a distance, and some kind of landmark to watch out for.

"No, sir. We can do it." Wally said.

"Okay. Go over to that post. You start from there." He turned back and went into the cabin. Wally had a watch, so we checked the time.

"It says go NW 305 feet to the pin oak by a fence. This will be easy," said Wally.

"How long is your stride?" I asked.

"Uhh, I think thirty inches."

"Okay, that's two and a half feet. That's 122 of your paces."

We each stood with our compass lined up to the northwest and picked out a single point. Once we agreed, we started, counting out Wally's steps, one, two. It was easy because when we got to 110, we saw the pin oak close in front of us.

The next direction led us to a footbridge that we crossed. By now, the cabin was out of site. The last direction was four hundred fifty feet to the old scotch pine with a boulder by its trunk. We leaned against the boulder and saw the mouth of a shallow cave carved into the limestone cliff by years of rain and flooding.

We found the log with the blue paper resting on another log in the cave.

"We did it. Now let's get this back to Mr. Combs," said Wally.

We reversed the directions, which meant turning east into west, and northwest into southeast to get back.

"What if that Indian treasure is in that cave we found?" I asked.

"It's supposed to be by the drive-in."

"My sister said she and her friends looked all night once and couldn't find it. She says it's out here somewhere."

"Let's keep the directions," he said. I stuffed them in my pants pocket.

Once, we had to retrace our steps because we lost count, but finally we made it back to the cabin. We still had ten minutes to spare.

"Congratulations to Wally and Jesse for completing their Pathfinding merit badge," Mr. Combs announced when we handed him the log.

"Okay, boys. We need to scrounge for firewood. Each log needs to be no bigger than ten inches long, so it will fit in the stove," The Scoutmaster said.

I volunteered for that group and checked my ax. The other group took a can to get water from the well by the showers.

"We'll have lunch when you get back."

While the others gathered wood limbs, I sat on the ground by a stump and used the ax to cut them into short pieces. My arm strength and sharp ax let me keep up with the limbs brought to me by the others.

Back in the cabin, lunch consisted of bologna sandwiches, ketchup, mustard, and a cup of chicken noodle soup. Chocolate milk topped it off. My group had to clean up after lunch. I was experienced with that. The cabin was warm now that a fire was going. I was not worried about the sleeping bag. My blankets would work so long as we had wood. I felt so blessed that I could be doing this with other boys.

"Okay, you each passed the Pathfinding project. A couple of you have earned your merit badge. The rest of the campout we are going to work on the Signaling Merit badge. How many of you already know Morse code?" Two hands went up. Wally and Jake Charles.

"Good. We'll have you divide into pairs, so you can help each other learn the code. Each of you need to memorize it for the night exercise. You can do this inside or outside, but you need to know your letters and numbers by supper time. When you pass the written test, you can eat." Then he started his lecture, and we took notes and studied the papers he handed out.

"Morse code is a signaling scheme that can use light, sound, or electricity to transport a message over a distance. It was the initial code used when the telegraph was invented. It was adopted when they discovered radio frequencies could travel a long distance over the air. It was invented by Samuel Morse in 1838." Mr. Combs laid his notes on the table.

Wally and I were the last two to pair up. We went outside and sat by one of the walnut trees scattered around the boy Scout camp.

"A." I started.

"Dit Dah." Dit was a dot and dah was a dash.

"B."

"Dah dit dit dit." Wally went through them quickly. I could see why he was a straight A student at McKinley.

"J." Wally was saying the letters now.

"Uh, dah dit dah dah."

"No. That's Y."

I had problems with the letters that had four dots or dashes, so Wally focused on them.

"X."

"Dah dit dit dah." I got it correct.

After an hour, we took a break.

"I wonder how Dale and Jake are doing." Wally said, looking around to see where they were.

"I think they stayed inside," I said.

"Dad wants to see if we can put a barbershop quartet together," Wally said.

"Do you have to wear an outfit? That would be cool," I said.

"No. But we would if we sang good enough. I sing bass and Jake sings baritone. We need a lead and a tenor."

From music class I kind of knew what those parts were, except for lead.

"I'm a soprano." I said reluctantly.

"That's a tenor for us. We think Dale can sing lead." I liked the word tenor instead of soprano. He told me we could all meet Tuesday night at his house. That worked well for me, since they were one of the houses on my route.

Mr. Lewis pulled his car close to the cabin. "Jesse, let's get those papers delivered." He took me home and drove me around my entire route delivering papers in my Scout uniform. We got back just in time to eat.

Supper was spaghetti. Jake and Dale were working on their Cooking Merit Badge and prepared the spaghetti from scratch, including parboiling the tomatoes and cooking up Italian sausage. We were all hungry.

"Dale, Wally, we're going to need some wood to get us through the night," Mr. Combs said as everyone was getting ready to sleep.

"Yes, sir," they said. They went outside to where the wood was stacked up but came back to report that the pile was no longer there.

"Okay. Everyone, get your clothes back on and help find firewood. I bet Troop twenty-two raided our stack of wood."

"No. Not fair," said one Scout, already in his sleeping bag.

"C'mon. Everyone helps. You are Scouts."

It took a few minutes for us to assemble outside.

"Go out in pairs. If each team brings back three logs, we'll be fine. If you find a branch that needs cutting, bring it back here, and we'll cut it here."

Wally and I teamed up again. I carried the flashlight, and we ventured off one of the paths to what appeared to be a stack of perfectly cut logs that were hidden from view by a bush but had been there for a long time. It was like finding treasure.

I started handing logs to Wally.

"I can carry more," Wally said. I handed more logs to him. As he left, I heard a rustling sound, a hissing sound, and then an odor that was disabling to me.

"Ewww. Yuck. Eww!" I said loudly. I couldn't hold my nose and my logs, so I held my breath.

"Skunk!" Wally yelled as he retreated back up the path.

The only time I had smelled a skunk was along the road when Dad was driving and when we encountered the odor, he'd say 'skunk'. Multiply that by a thousand, and that was exactly what I was experiencing.

Wally got close to the cabin, still holding his logs. I followed, looking behind me expecting to see the skunk.

"Jesse, Wally. Stop there. NOW!" It was our Scoutmaster.

Wally distanced himself from me. I had been outrunning the odor, and now that I stopped, the magnitude of the stench made me gag.

"Wally, did you get sprayed?" Mr. Combs asked.

"No, sir. I don't think so. It got Jesse good."

The assistant Scoutmaster checked out both of us, holding his hat over his nose.

"Wally's okay," he reported. "Jesse's clothes got it bad. He can't go in the cabin."

"Whoa, Jesse, follow me," Mr. Combs commanded, marching me to the showers which were downwind of the cabin. "Get the tomato juice. And a blanket." Mr. Combs told the assistant.

At the showers, I listened to Mr. Combs instructions.

"Take your clothes off and put them on the floor of the shower."

"Do I have to?"

"Jesse, yes. You can't go into the warm cabin unless we get that smell off you," Mr. Combs explained as I started removing my clothes.

"Okay, stand on your clothes."

Naked, I was shivering, standing on my stinky clothes. This was worse than cleaning the barn or that time Grandpa made me retrieve dead chicks from the outhouse.

Mr. Combs poured tomato juice all over me.

"Rub the tomato juice all over your body," he instructed as he dribbled the tomato juice on my stomach and back and then on my head.

"Rub it in good, Jesse. Stomp all over your clothes and work the juice in."

"It stings. It hurts," I said, holding back tears. I was freezing.

The tomato juice got in my eyes and a couple cuts I had from cutting the limbs.

"Now, turn the water on and rinse off. Here is a bar of soap. Rinse out your eyes first."

The process took thirty minutes before Mr. Combs was satisfied that I had rinsed away most of the skunk. I wrung out my clothes and rinsed them and wrung them out again for what seemed like a hundred times. By now, whatever smell was left was not as noticeable to me.

When we returned to the cabin, the assistant was stoking the fire. I wrapped myself in a dark green army blanket. Near the stove, a clothesline was strung across the room and my clothes hung to dry. I crawled into my makeshift bedroll.

"What took you so long?" Wally asked.

"He soaked me with tomato juice."

"That's weird."

"I know. It worked. I think it worked."

I was shivering and was still four sleeping bags away from the stove.

The assistant started telling us the story of the one-armed frozen prospector, and we were soon sleeping deeply.

Even asleep, I was shivering.

"Jesse, wake up." It was Mr. Combs.

"Is it time to get up?"

"No. Here, put these on."

The underwear was first. I stayed under the covers and slipped on my warm shorts and undershirt. The sensation was amazing. The warmth provided an immediate impact on my shivering.

"Here's your pants."

The Scout trousers were khaki and held the warmth they had been collecting for the past few hours. It was as if I had never been cold. My entire body rejoiced with the relaxing, warming, sensation.

"Here's your shirt."

The shirt was hot to my back. I buttoned it and was now completely cradled by warm clothing. The shivering faded away.

"It's midnight Jesse. Get some sleep."

The clothes still smelled a little like the skunk, but their warmth was welcome.

After we got home, I delivered my papers, then Mom sent me to the tub to soak in Cashmere Bouquet soap. I told her how I got my Pathfinding and Signaling Merit badge, joined a barbershop quartet, and survived a direct skunk attack. I couldn't wait to include this in my next letter to Lynn.

Victor Hess

Chapter Thirty
Barbershop Quartet

McKinley School had a Christmas program every year. We were going to sing in two-part harmony, which we were practicing all year. The kids who sang high notes were mostly girls, and kids who sang lower notes were all boys. I was still in the high note group. My teacher agreed to call me a tenor.

This year, our part of the program was "Good King Wenceslas" and "Lo How a Rose ere Blooming." The other grades also had music to sing, and then we all would sing "Silent Night" at the end. As we practiced "Lo How a Rose ere Blooming," Mrs. Fawcett walked around us like she was searching for something.

"I want you all to keep singing this song. As I point to you, I want you to stop singing." One by one she pointed to this girl, that girl, and as each one stopped, she still was listening. All the girls were silent now and all that was left was me singing in the back row.

"You. Jesse. You'll do the solo!"

After class, I went up to her. "I don't think I should do the solo, Mrs. Fawcett. I'm a boy, and it's a girl's part."

"Jesse, you have a beautiful voice. Come over here. This will only take a couple minutes."

She played a recording of "Lo How a Rose ere Blooming" on the record player and then said, "That was a thirteen-year old boy singing the solo. He could do it because his voice had not changed yet. When his voice changes, he will be a tenor or a bass."

"His voice is beautiful," I admitted.

"So is yours. You were meant to sing this. I have always

loved this carol, and this is the first time I have ever had a sixth grader who could sing the solo. Help make my dream come true, would you?"

I agreed.

Wally and I decided our new barbershop quartet could practice on Tuesday nights. I would deliver my entire route first, and then back track to Wally and Jake's. Mrs. Charles kept fresh baked cookies on the dining table which held me over until I got home. While we waited for Dale, Mrs. Charles helped me learn my part. In our quartet, I wouldn't sing the melody. That was Dale's part. Wally, Jake, and I sang harmony. Mine was the high harmony. The first song we learned was called, "Tell Me Why the Stars Do Shine," and the words were easy to learn because there were only two verses to it. I think Mrs. Charles was surprised I could reach the high notes because she just stopped playing and said, "Mr. Charles is going to be really happy, Jesse."

"Mom, Jesse's singing the solo for the Christmas program. We're singing "Lo How a Rose."

"I love that carol. Yes, I could see how you'd be picked for that." I felt good about that.

We practiced until Mr. Charles got home, and then lined up shoulder to shoulder and sang the song to him.

He looked a little puzzled "Let's hear this part again." He pointed to the second line, "the ivy twines." We sang it again. "Jesse, that's a sharp there." He reached around Mrs. Charles and pressed on a black piano key.

I didn't know what a sharp was. I just listened to the piano and sang the notes that were played.

"I missed that, Dan," Mrs. Charles said.

"It's the key. Try it again boys." Mrs. Charles played it first. We sang it again, and I sang my notes correctly. This time it sounded so much better. Our voices were amazing as far as I was concerned.

"Okay, next week, work on diction. Each of you need to say the words exactly the same way. Anyway, I think we have a quartet here. You boys sound good, for half pints. I better hunt up some more songs. You need to work on a name."

Wally said, "How about Half Pints, Dad?"

"Or, Half Notes," Jake said.

"Yeah, Half Notes," Wally said and we all repeated the name.

"That's the quickest a barbershop quartet ever came up with a name," said Mr. Charles.

I hummed the song all the way home and then sang it to Christina to sleep that night.

> *Tell me why, the stars do shine.*
> *Tell me why, the ivy twines.*
> *Tell me why, the sky's so blue.*
> *And I will tell you, why I love you.*

Victor Hess

Chapter Thirty-One
Where is the Indian Treasure

Ever since Jim read us Tecumseh stories at Barney Hospital, I daydreamed about finding the treasure the Shawnee Indians hid. I believed Paula Jean when she said that it wasn't by the drive-in theater. She said it had to be at John Bryan State Park. That's where Camp Birch was, where we did our Scout campouts. I thought about the cave Wally and I found, and hoped we'd go back out there on another campout.

I told Frank Wells, my Sunday school teacher, about camping out, and I wished I had a map of John Bryan State Park. That's when I learned about the map room at the Greene County courthouse. It was on the way from school where I picked up my papers at Pat's Market. All I had to do was to get there before they closed at 4 p.m.

So, Monday, I raced on my bike from school and got to the courthouse at 3:15. There were a lot of doors that went into the huge building. It filled a city block. The ceilings were high, the floors were hard stone with designs, and paintings were hung on the walls. They were mostly of men in dark suits and most of them had mustaches or beards. Wooden doors led to places called recorder's office, auditor's office, and then I saw the words stenciled on one of those windows made of glass you couldn't see through, Map Room.

The clock struck 3:30, and I looked around for someone in charge. Men were seated around the table, using special black pens to draw lines on large maps. They had rulers and protractors and were very careful. These were so much better than the map I drew for our Scoutmaster when I got my Pathfinding Merit Badge.

"What do you need, son?" one of the men said.

"Do you have a map of John Bryan State Park?"

"Well, that depends on what kind of map you need. Do you want one that shows the roads and paths, or one that shows the hills and valleys?"

The other men looked over to me and the youngest one gave me a wink.

"He wants a map that shows where those Indians buried that treasure."

"There ain't no treasure up there. It'd be found by now. That's just a story," said the older man with a mustache.

"Do you have one that shows the rivers, hills and valleys?" I guessed that would help me find the treasure.

"That would be a topographic map," the young map drawer said.

"Do you even know where to begin looking?"

"No, sir."

"I'll tell you where to start. Go to the historical society on Monroe Street. I think they'll help you. What's your name?"

"Jesse Hall."

"Are you related to Thomas Hall?"

"Yes, sir. He's my grandpa."

"Well, look here." He turned a couple pages in the huge book of maps in front of him. I edged close to him. "Right here. This is Thomas Hall's farm. He pointed at an empty space bordered by four straight lines. "Eighty of the finest acres in the county." I felt proud and smiled.

"My dad is Marshall," I said.

"I know him," said another. "I used to play cards with him." The clock struck 3:45.

"Thanks," I said, and then there was a chorus of "See ya later, Jesse." And "Bye, Jesse."

When I got to Pat's market, mine were the only papers

there, but they were already neatly folded by the other paper boys.

Tuesday, I rode my bike to the historical society, which used to be someone's two story home. I was surprised when I was greeted by Paula Jean's aunt. Mrs. Randall handed me pamphlets about dead authors, judges, and senators who were from Greene County.

"What about the Indian treasure?" I asked.

"Come with me." She led me from room to room, then downstairs into the basement.

"They found two crates up in the clock tower of the courthouse and brought them here for me to sort out. It's supposed to have Indian artifacts found when they put the pump station in down by the drive-in."

"Paula Jean said the treasure wasn't there. She looked."

"Well, could be."

Each crate had a tag stapled to it. "Pump Station Relics #1" was printed on one and "Pump Station Relics #3" on the other. Before I could ask about Pump Station #2, Mrs. Randall started sneezing, so loud and long it startled me.

"Are you okay?" I asked.

"Let's go back upstairs," she said between sneezes. "Jesse, I've had those crates for two weeks, but each time I got near them, I get this allergy fit." She sneezed two more loud ones. "Does it bother you?"

"No ma'am." The clock on the wall said 3:50, and I needed to get my paper route started.

"How would you like to help me sort through all those relics? I can't pay you, but it might give us clues to where that treasure is."

"I finish my paper route after 5:30 every night. I could help then."

"How about the weekend? Can you work on Saturday?"

"I watch Christina while Mom works."

So, it was arranged that I was to meet her at the historical society after church and sort through the crates for anything that might be worthy of display at the museum.

The crates were the same size, about three feet wide, two feet across and eighteen inches high. There were four rusty screws holding the lids in place. I unscrewed the first and carefully lifted the lid. Then I dragged the box across the basement floor, so it set under the bare light bulb, hanging from the joist.

I wasn't sure what to expect. Maybe silver, gold, or jewels. Maybe arrowheads, arrows, knives, feathers, tomahawks, or moccasins. The first one had a bunch of straw on top. I put that in a brown sack after sneezing a few times. On a second layer of straw was a tattered leather wrapping, so I carefully unwrapped it, revealing a long straight handled tomahawk with a rusty blade, but the handle had colorful designs. I carried it upstairs to Mrs. Randall, whose eyes immediately expressed surprise followed by a huge smile.

"There's more, but I thought you'd want to see this," I said.

"This alone is worth the trouble," she said. No sneezing yet.

"It was wrapped in this." I handed her the leather piece and went back downstairs.

I removed the second layer of straw, that revealed two large stone bowls and two stone mallets. I set them on a table and removed a third layer of straw. There were dozens of different sized arrowheads and other things made of flint. This crate was now empty. It seemed to have more straw than relics in it.

The next box had more arrowheads and stone bowls but no more tomahawks. Some of the arrowheads were metal. Some of the flint pieces were too large to be arrowheads but still very sharp. Mrs. Randall said they were used to prepare deer and buffalo skins for clothes and tepees.

Once I took the bags of straw out to the burn barrel and swept up the basement, Mrs. Randall came back downstairs and only sneezed once.

"It was that straw," she said.

"Where's crate number two?" I asked.

"That's a good question. We'll look into that."

"Maybe it has the treasure in it."

"I doubt it. Let's leave the boxes here. Your sister might be right."

We went upstairs, and she told me the tomahawk was a peace pipe used by the Indians at council meetings and with white men. The Indians used the big bowls and mallets to grind wheat into flour and corn into meal, and also to make medicines. Some of the stones had once been attached to wooden handles and used as axes to hollow out canoes and cut pine poles for tepees.

Monday, at Scouts, I told my Scoutmaster about the two crates and how Mrs. Randall and I sorted out all arrowheads and stone tools. He asked me to write a report on it to describe at the next meeting, so I could work on my Archeology Merit Badge.

Tuesday, Wally asked about each thing I found. He seemed to know about the flat stone with holes in it and said his dad had a fake one he wore with his Indian costume.

We practiced singing two arrangements his dad wrote for Christmas songs.

"You already know the words, so maybe you can sing these for the nursing home next week." He was already booking gigs for us. One of the songs was "Lo How a Rose ere Blooming."

Chapter Thirty-Two
The Clock Tower Clues

During our last music class before Christmas vacation, Mrs. Fawcett announced, "I want all of you to get your coats and boots. Report back here. Bundle up good. We're going for a long walk."

We marched double file, six blocks through the snow to the Greene County courthouse. My bike stayed in the school bike rack along with the others.

When we reached the courthouse door, a man opened it and told us to follow him. He unlocked another door and led us up a narrow staircase. At the top, the man stopped us all and we waited on the steps. He glanced at his watch, smiled and then the clock rang out the first quarter hour Westminster chime, ding dong, ding dong. Then he led us into a cold room with a wooden floor and a collection of huge gears.

Everyone within earshot of the clock tower would pause, look at their wrist watch, pocket watch, mantel clock, or grandfather clock and either nod that they agreed with the old clock tower or adjust their time-piece, so they can continue their life to the right time.

"Kids, the city asked us to do part of our Christmas program up here. We will do "Lo How a Rose ere Blooming" and "Silent Night." There is no piano, so we are going to get our notes in our head first." Mrs. Fawcett blew on a pitch pipe and made us keep humming our starting note.

She positioned everyone around the microphone and put me right in front of it. Before any nervousness could set in, I was singing into the chrome plated microphone.

"Lo how a rose ere blooming," I sang while the choir

hummed in the background.

We could not hear how our voices were floating out to the downtown, but I felt calmness and warmth standing there in a jacket too small like when I had put those warm clothes on at the camp out.

"...from tender stem hath sprung."

The Friday shoppers stopped and turned their eyes up to the clock tower. Merchants opened the doors to allow the message into their stores.

"Of Jesse's lineage coming, as those of old have sung."

By now I knew that the 'Jesse's lineage' in the song was King David and Jesus' lineage. I was proud to share the name. I sang the phrases exactly like Mrs. Fawcett told me during our rehearsals.

"It came, a floweret bright, amid the cold of winter, when half spent was the night."

Store clerks turned off the music in the stores, the sound from the tower was so compelling. It was children's pure voices. It was Xenia's children's voices, lifting spirits of those in earshot of the clock tower. It drew a ring of people close around the courthouse. When we finished our music, the man who had led us up the tower staircase went to the microphone and announced they had just heard the McKinley School sixth grade choir.

"The soloist was Jesse Hall."

The announcement was a surprise. I hadn't hit a home run at a baseball game, but now I knew how it might feel.

Wally grabbed my elbow. "Jesse, look." He pointed to the amplifier.

"It's an amplifier."

"No. Look what it's on."

My eyes focused on a familiar shape with a tag on it – "Pump Station Relics #2." Kids passed us as we stared at the lone box setting on another box. The man moved in front of us and flipped the power switch.

"What's that?" I asked.

"That makes the sound loud. It's an amplifier."

Wally pushed me over toward the box. While the man described the power and reliability of the PBK 150, I saw the second crate had a label like the first, except it was labeled, "Pump Station Relics #4." There were two missing crates.

By now one of the kids came back in the room and told us to hurry up. Mrs. Fawcett was mad.

We marched back down the clock tower stairs talking about Christmas.

As we walked to the corner to cross the street, a group of people applauded us.

"Way to go, Jesse," Frank Wells, my Sunday school teacher, said.

"That was beautiful, Jesse!" Mom yelled from the drugstore door. Then I saw people shake her hand.

We walked back to the school, knowing this was the last day of school until 1957. We were not thinking about our performance anymore, or how many residents had heard it. We were hoping school was going to let out early.

I couldn't wait to tell Mrs. Randall about the two crates.

Victor Hess

Chapter Thirty-Three
The Sinking Stroller

School let out early enough that I had time to ride my bike to the historical society before I needed to pick up my papers.

Once I told Mrs. Randall about the other two crates, she got on the phone and repeated my story to someone, then hung up.

"Wait a few minutes, Jesse."

Then the phone rang.

"It is? They are? You will? Perfect. I'll be here."

"Jesse, can you be here next Sunday? We'll get those two crates you found next week."

"Can I get a friend to help? He's in Scouts with me. I told my Scoutmaster what we found, and he said I could do a report and get the Archeology Merit Badge."

"Can we trust this friend?"

"Yes, ma'am. We'll be here Sunday."

When I picked up my papers, I had a very unusual request from the guy at Pat's Market.

Pat's Market was a store that was stuck in the past. It had oiled wood floors, salt fish in a wooden barrel, fresh cracklins, fresh chickens, and when you checked out, your items were added up by hand and then the total punched into the huge cash register machine. Sale signs were made by tearing off a section of butcher paper and writing the message, Cracklins – 29 cents. Their clerk, Becky always wore a long dress since she was a local Mennonite. They all wore white full bib aprons.

As I was folding papers, Mr. Patterson peeked out the door. "Can you drop a couple things off for Miss Santmyer?"

"If it's not too big."

He handed me a small sack that fit snug in my bag. "She's expecting you," he said.

The Santmyer house was just around the corner from Pat's market and my first newspaper stop. I pressed the door bell and immediately the door was opened by her assistant.

"Jesse, here's a dime. Thank you. Oh, Helen has a gift for you. Merry Christmas." She handed me a present, wrapped in plain brown paper, tied with brown twine. I knew it was a book.

"She thinks you will like this."

"Thank you," I said and then handed her their newspaper.

"How's Miss Santmyer?"

"Today's a good day," she said.

"Tell her I'm helping Mrs. Randall sort through Indian relics."

Miss Santmyer was a local author. Sometimes, when I handed her a newspaper, she would ask if I knew about Simon Kenton or Tecumseh. More than once I had to excuse myself and leave or I'd be late delivering papers. She knew so much and loved to talk. I would tell her next week what we found in the crates.

Wally was waiting for me at his house.

"What did Mrs. Randall say?"

"Okay. We can go through them next Sunday."

"Is it okay for me to help?"

"Yeah. I told her it was for Scouts."

Dale and Jake were by the piano waiting for me.

"Dad got us a gig at the nursing home by the hospital. He wants us to learn one more song, so we have four songs."

We learned "Down by the Old Mill Stream."

"When do we sing?"

"The day after Christmas. Wednesday at noon."

I cleared around six dollars each week delivering papers. Then, Saturday, I got another twenty-three dollars and fifty cents in Christmas tips, almost thirty dollars altogether. I wondered if Lynn did that good with her route. I made my Christmas list. Mom, Christina, Lynn, Dad, Karl, because I drew his name at the Hall farm. I added Gary and Danny. That would probably take half my tips.

Monday, Christmas eve, I babysat Christina and took her with me to buy Christmas gifts. I was able to find something at the Kresge store for each person on my list. Then, I took Christina to the park. We shared a little box of animal crackers with the ducks. They swam around one little corner of the pond so much that it created a tiny pool surrounded by ice.

I was holding Christina's hand when this big dog raced by us. It must have gotten away from someone, because it had a leash dangling behind it. My instinct was to chase after it, but just then its leash caught hold of one of the stroller wheels and the stroller started dragging behind it only slightly slowing the big dog down. In a wink, the dog and stroller were sliding in all directions on the frozen pond. Sometimes the dog pulled the stroller and another the stroller yanked at the dog. Both were getting closer and closer to the part of the pond that was still thawed by the ducks.

More than once, I looked down to be sure I had Christina in my hand, but as the stroller got closer to the water, I realized all my Christmas gifts were in it and watched helplessly as the stroller, dog, and gifts slid in the water. The stroller disappeared quickly. I picked up Christina and ran to the edge of the pond, barely stopping on solid ground. The black dog dragged the stroller through the few feet of open water and then clamored up the bank of the pond just as the dog's owner reached him. Maybe some of the gifts could be saved, I thought, as the owner's arm reached down and cut the leash. The stroller slid backwards into the pond, completely submerging the handle, and everything that was in the stroller. The man scolded the dog, and left, never saying a word to me or Christina.

"All gone," said Christina.

Someone else said, "Tough luck kid."

No sleeping bag this winter.

Kresge's was still open. I just had enough money to buy each person something. It just wasn't as nice as the first gift I bought. It was hard carrying the bags of gifts and holding Christina's hand. Mom was going to be angry about me losing the stroller.

Ellen was waiting for me, bundled up, sitting on the glider on the front porch.

"What happened to your shoes?" she asked.

At the pond I got my shoes muddy and wet and so did Christina.

"We better clean these up before your mom gets home."

"How come you're out here. It's cold," I said.

"Here, I'll help."

She grabbed Christina while I carried the packages upstairs.

"Take your shoes off," she said.

When we got inside our apartment, Christina exclaimed, "Look. Look, Jesse. A twee."

In the corner of the living room was a white plastic Christmas tree with lights, balls, tinsel, and garland. Except for last year, my Christmas tree experience was always at Grandpa Hall's farm. This year neither Mom nor I talked about getting a tree. Trees cost money. But today, Christmas was in our living room.

"Does Mom know?"

"Not yet. It's a surprise. Daddy got a new tree this year. Mother just remembered this was in the garage, so we put it up here."

Christina ran to it, touching everything until she burnt her finger on one of the colored light bulbs.

"Keep the bulbs off the plastic or they'll melt the limbs."

Christina was crying. We put butter on her finger and blew on it. Her crying turned to sobs and, in a few minutes, she was back exploring under the tree.

"What's in the bags?" Ellen asked.

She helped me pull my second batch of gifts while I told her the story of the pond.

"Oh no. We need to find a stroller."

"Mom's gonna kill me."

"Let's get these wrapped." She went downstairs and after a few minutes came back with wrapping paper rolls and scotch tape.

Chapter Thirty-Four
Dad, the Big Shot

I still had papers to deliver. When I got to Pat's Market, Mr. Patterson came outside with another package for Miss Santmyer.

"Be careful with this. It's eggnog." It was a milk bottle double bagged.

Miss Santmyer led me into a large room with lots of chairs.

"Tell me about your polio," she said as I handed her the eggnog and newspaper. She handed the bottle to her assistant who shook it and poured it into three cups. I wondered how long this was going to take and glad I got an early start. As I told my story, she seemed more interested in the nurses, and when I told her about Ellen, she reached for my hand.

"Please tell that girl to come visit me. She sounds like a remarkable young woman. Now, drink the rest of your eggnog."

"Yes, ma'am. Oh, we open two more Indian crates next Sunday. They found them in the clock tower," I said as I walked out the door.

I raced to get the papers delivered, watching for icy patches, and hoping for a few more Christmas tips. I lucked out with one five-dollar bill in a card on Chestnut Street and one with two two-dollar bills on Center Street. I was slowly replacing what Christina and I lost in the pond. I was getting closer to a sleeping bag.

When I got home, there on the porch was a stroller, much better than the one dumped in the pond. I know Ellen had worked a miracle, like she did with my polio. I ran upstairs and Mom opened the door.

"You have some serious explaining to do, young man."

Ellen was in the living room holding Christina, and they both started laughing. I repeated the pond story to Mom, who finally sat down. "You get it, you lose it, you get it again, but you don't give up," she said. She slipped off her heels.

"One of my customers would like you to visit her, Ellen."

"Who would want me to visit?"

"Miss Santmyer on West Third Street."

"Really? Helen Santmyer? Why would she want to see me?"

"I told her about you giving me the Kenny treatments, and she was suddenly more interested in you than me, especially when I told her where we lived."

"Will you take me?"

"Sure, how about when I deliver her paper on Wednesday. She's my first stop."

"Okay. I'll help you fold them." I thought about Lynn. She'd be folding her papers at the same time I would.

After Ellen left, we stayed up, listening to the Bing Crosby Christmas show full of Christmas music from all over the world. He even had sailors singing Christmas carols from a Navy ship and soldiers singing "It Came Upon a Midnight Clear," all the way from Korea.

Tuesday was Christmas. Like other Christmases there would be new jeans, at least one size too big, shirts, and underwear. This year, I got a ball point pen and a wrist watch. I wondered how Mom could pay the rent, buy us food, and get us gifts when Dad was always behind on child support.

I got the Christmas edition delivered early. The holiday papers were always early. Wally was waiting for me to remind me about our quartet singing at the nursing home the next day at noon. I was glad Mom got me a watch. On the way home, the clock in the clock tower struck ten. I looked at my watch, and adjusted it, like other people in the city were doing.

When I got home, Ellen told me to get Christina and come downstairs for a treat. They had a present for each of us. Christina got this tray with squares, triangles, stars, and circles that you match up to holes of that same shape. They gave me a sweater with colorful zigzags. That wasn't all. Henry took me out to the garage where I stored my bike and helped me attach a battery powered bicycle light with a push button switch that lit the flash light or caused a loud buzzer sound, like a horn. We set it up, so the newspaper bag wouldn't mess up the aim of the light. It was a great gift, the days being so short now.

Dad showed up to take Christina and me to Grandpa's house. I put our gifts in the back seat and gave Dad the Zippo lighter I got him at Kresge's. With Christina and my *Bible* on my lap, we left for the Hall farm.

When we got to the farm, the TV was showing the movie, *Heidi*, and the cousins were playing Tripoley on the floor. I tried to play and hold Christina at the same time, but that was impossible, so I bailed from the game and carried Christina around while the aunts and Grandma pinched her cheek and held her for less than a minute each, in between rolling out pie crust, preparing dressing, and boiling potatoes. When Grandma snatched her out of my arms, she asked about my polio and seemed pleased when I told her I hadn't used crutches for two whole months.

"Praise God," she said.

"Thomas told me about your newspaper article." She set down the rolling pin and Aunt Rebecca started lining pie plates with the dough.

"I brought some with me, Grandma."

I found my *Bible* under where we laid our coats in the downstairs bedroom.

One by one, I laid out the three articles on the end of the dining room table that was not already occupied by Pinochle players. First, Dad's article from 1948 about him and the chamber of commerce. The second was about Lynn and me raising money for the March of Dimes in Sabina, and finally the two-page article about Barney Hospital with me in a wheelchair.

"Let me see that," Uncle Russ said. "Marshall, is that you?"

"What?" Dad said. Uncle Russ handed him the article. "Oh, that. Where'd you find that, Jesse?"

"Mom kept it in her purse."

Then, there was the moment when Grandma locked her eyes on Dad so hard, he couldn't look away. They both looked hurt.

"I didn't know you were famous," Uncle Virgil said, while he leaned over Dad's shoulder to get a closer look.

"Jesse, is this you in the wheel chair?" Grandma asked.

Later, Aunt Rebecca brought four large blank pages out of a photo album and helped me put the articles under the plastic to protect them. "These need safekeeping."

During Christmas dinner, my cousins asked me questions about polio, just like the Skillmans did that night I first met them. Dad's brothers asked him about the men in the pictures with him. It was the most I ever saw them talk with my dad during our holiday meals.

"Jesse got a paper route," Grandpa said from his recliner. Grandpa's voice was magic. No matter what was going on, how many people were talking, if Grandpa said something, all eyes and ears were on him.

"Pretty soon he'll have his picture with some big shot businessmen. Mark my words."

Dad looked at me and smiled. I smiled back. Grandma had taken charge of feeding Christina while Aunt Rebecca kept food on the table.

"Who's Santa Claus this year?" Uncle Russ asked as we ate our pie and cake.

Each year, one of us kids was to pass out the gifts. Aunt Rebecca kept tabs on who got gifts.

"Jesse, it's your turn," Grandma said.

She handed me a fist full of money envelopes that everyone looked forward to. This year was different. Instead of a single twenty-dollar bill, each aunt or uncle got a twenty and a ten. Instead of a couple two-dollar bills, each cousin got a five-dollar bill. I passed out the envelopes based on their names. There was one for Mom, too.

Kelly jumped to the tree. "I'll help."

She handed me a package and read the names while I made the delivery to someone on the couch, or chair, or still sitting at the table. Aunt Rebecca made a check mark on the list as I handed out the packages.

"Paula Jean," Kelly yelled. Paula Jean was still in Massachusetts.

"Bring that one here. We'll send that to her," said Aunt Rebecca. We passed out twenty-one packages, including one to me.

"Here's one more. It's from Paula Jean."

Grandma handed me a large package, that was soft, like clothes, and when I opened it, I smiled at a new blue jacket, just like the one Paula Jean gave me three years ago, except this one fit. I had already outgrown my other one.

Then, I learned Santa Claus was also responsible for cleaning up the mess.

"Jesse, be sure no one put their money envelope in with the trash."

Kelly helped me gather everything up and we took the

wrapping paper out along with discarded boxes to the burn barrel. My new jacket was warm. Aunt Rebecca came out and stood by the fire with us.

"Jesse, Mom wants to know if you'd sing something Christmas for her. We heard you sang something from the clock tower. Uncle Virgil said he heard it."

"I guess," I said. We went back inside once the fire died down.

On the way home, Dad wanted to know about the article Mom gave me, and he was sorry I had to go through so much with polio. By the time we got home, he decided to park the car and join us upstairs even though he was still behind on child support. There we had Christmas all over again, because Gary and Danny were there waiting for Christina and me.

This time, Dad gave Mom the extra ten from his envelope.

Chapter Thirty-Five
The Nursing Home Gig

The day after Christmas, I rode my bike to Wally's house, so Mr. Charles could get us ready for our first gig. We didn't have matching outfits, but Mrs. Charles had vest sweaters that kind of matched. They were definitely Christmas colors with bells and zigzags. We had long sleeve shirts, so once the sweater vests were on, we looked like a quartet.

The nursing home had a room that was crowded with wheelchair patients and others with walkers. It reminded me of Barney Hospital, except Barney never smelled this bad. It was worse than Christina's diapers. Mr. Charles positioned us in the corner of this room, made eye contact with us, motioned us to smile, and blew a note on the pitch pipe. We were finally set as we sang "Tell Me Why." Some of the patients listened and smiled, and, maybe, remembered something pleasant. A few stared at the floor, lost, maybe hearing us. I couldn't say. One lady in the back was singing the words with us. We finished our concert with "Silent Night." When we walked out of the nursing home, my watch showed it to be 12:20. We were back to Wally's house by 12:45.

That afternoon at three o'clock, Ellen knocked at our door, ready to help me fold papers and then visit Miss Santmyer. We walked my bike up to Pat's Market and after a couple attempts, Ellen ended up watching me fold the rest of the papers. Mr. Patterson came out of his store with another package. "I hope she tips you when you deliver these packages," he said.

"Yes, sir. Sometimes a nickel, sometimes a dime."

Ellen carried the package from Pat's Market while I pedaled slow.

"Why does she want to see me?" she asked.

"I don't know. She's been sick."

Miss Santmyer opened the door as soon as I pressed the doorbell.

"Good afternoon Jesse. Is this your nurse? I'm Helen Hooven Santmyer." She reached for Ellen's hand. Then she turned to me.

"Jesse, you go deliver your papers while we girls talk."

Ellen did not hesitate, and the next thing I knew, I was alone on the small porch, facing a closed door.

Chapter Thirty-Six
The Old Lady and Indian Spears

Saturday morning five young men met in their Scout uniforms at the Methodist Church for a three-mile hike to the pump station site where four crates of Indian relics were found. It took one hour through a mist that turned into snow flurries and when we arrived at the field adjacent to the drive-in theater, Mr. Combs had us erect a canvas cabin tent at the edge of Old Town Creek, one of the small streams that fed into the Little Miami River. We learned from him we were standing on what used to be a large Shawnee Indian village called Old Chillicothe.

"Recently, Indian artifacts were found on this site and, we have permission to search from the bridge to the pump station, to the creek, and then down to the railroad trestle. Jesse can tell you what has been discovered here while they were building the pump house."

"They found four crates of stuff. In two of the crates were flint arrowheads and a tomahawk that was also a peace pipe."

"Where'd they find that?" one of the kids yelled out.

"I don't know. I just know it was from down here."

I pointed toward the pump house and swung my arm around toward the bridge, when I saw a small figure in a long coat walk down the gravel lane that met the bridge. My eyes were locked on her and finally, six set of eyes had seen the character. Once she crossed the bridge, we could tell her destination was our tent. Mr. Combs moved toward her.

"Now, see here. What's going on here?" she asked.

"Ma'am, I'm Mr. Combs. This is Boy Scout Troop 18 on a hike."

"Does a hike require a tent?"

"This one does. Our boys are looking for Indian artifacts. They have county permission."

"Well, your permission doesn't go past that bridge or that stream."

She motioned her arm toward the wooded hillside beyond the Oldtown Creek. Through the leafless trees, I could see a large brick farmhouse at the top of the hill.

"What are you looking for?" she asked.

"Artifacts, Indian relics. Arrowheads."

"Hmmf. Whatever was here has been found a long time ago. There's nothing left here. This was my property before the commissioners stole it from me."

There were moans from the Scouts. Her words were disappointing to our merit badge hopes. She walked on to her mailbox and just stood there watching us.

Scouts found items along the creek bed and gave them to Mr. Combs. If anything was interesting, he'd hand it to me. Later, the old lady came by the tent.

"Have you found anything yet?"

"Just some arrowheads, ma'am," I said. I was responsible for cataloging what was found and where it was found, like Mrs. Randall told me. I was supposed to measure it and put it in a little brown sack, each one numbered. Other Scouts were paired up searching for items.

"Mr. Combs. Bring those boys up to the house in ten minutes, and I'll show them my collection."

Her dining room had shallow drawers laid out with Indian relics. There were musket hand guns, long rifles and spears, some tipped with steel points and others with flint. It took the old lady thirty minutes to describe how she found the tomahawks, knives, arrowheads, and stone tools.

"Did all this come from your property?" I asked.

"Yes, but it started with my great grandfather. He used

to trade with the Indians. He used to fight the Indians."

"Wow," more than one of us said.

"Did he know about the treasure?" I asked.

"Treasure! What treasure? That's just a made-up story. It's made a mess of my property. People trespass back here looking for that make-believe treasure. At least once a month, I walk around my farm and find holes dug. They do it at night. Some of my hillside washed away because of these raiders. There's no treasure here, or I'd have found it."

Wally looked hurt. I knew how he felt.

"There's a box over in the corner there with items I don't need to keep. If you'll haul it out, you can have anything in it."

Mr. Combs took a quick look inside and agreed to carry the box and all it contained out of the woman's house. We moved it to our tent and while three of us cataloged it, two other Scouts heated up a pot of pork and beans with cut up hot dogs.

With each item I cataloged, I imagined someone, years ago, chipping away at a piece of flint rock, lining up sharp edges into the shape of an arrow point, small for the rabbit, larger for the deer, and even larger for the buffalo.

"I wonder how long it takes to make one of these?" I asked.

"When I was younger, I tried my hand at it," said Mr. Combs. "It took an hour, but it never looked as good as these points. You have to practice and get good at it. You have to be taught by someone who knows what they're doing."

"Where'd all this flint come from?"

"Mostly south and east of here. It's Ohio's gem stone."

"You mean like a diamond?" Wally asked.

"Yep. It just doesn't fit on a ring very well. What's that, Jesse?"

I was laying out various size seashells, each with two holes where shells might hinge together.

"I think you have a necklace there," he said.

I repositioned the shells, larger in the center, smaller off to the sides. I wondered who might wear such jewelry, a woman? A girl? Was it a gift? Eleven shells.

"Okay boys, let's break camp. Clean up your gear and get ready for the hike back.

That afternoon, while I delivered papers, I imagined firing a flint tipped arrow into a deer, and then using a flint knife to separate the hide from the meat and making soft leather moccasins and wearing the leather breech cloth. However, it was now below freezing, and my imagination had to add leather pants and a deer skin shirt before I'd freeze. Maybe a buffalo skin blanket, too. Then I thought about what we would find in those two crates Wally and I discovered in the clock tower.

Those Indians used to live on that old lady's farm. I wondered if her great-grandfather bought it from them.

Chapter Thirty-Seven
Inside the Clock Tower Crates

The Sunday after our hike was cold and cloudy. When I got to the historical society, Wally was already there. He was holding paper sacks Mrs. Randall used to organize relics. Mrs. Randall handed me the notebook and pencil to document what we found. I was to number the sack, put the date on it, and then record a description of the item on however many lines it took on the notebook.

Crate #2 was the first one we opened. It had the familiar layer of straw which we bagged and set aside. Like the other two crates, this one had two stone bowls used to grind grain and herbs. As the next layer of straw was stuffed in a bag, we saw layers of sea shells, all white, with purple designs on them. There were hundreds of them.

"How do I do this? I don't have enough sacks," Wally said.

We both took a handful of shells upstairs to show Mrs. Randall.

"We have hundreds of these," I said. "Do we have to do each one?"

"Let me see." She sat at her desk, reached for one of the shells and took her time studying it. "These are clam shells."

I picked up one and remembered seeing shells like it at Grandpa Smith's creek. His were a darker color. She pulled out a box of pamphlets and removed the pamphlets about Benjamin Whiteman. "Will they fit in this?" She handed us the box.

"They should," Wally said. We carefully transferred the shells to the cardboard box. All that was left was another layer of straw.

Crate #4 only had two screws holding the lid in place. Instead of the layer of straw, we saw a large leather pouch or sack. Inside it were five smaller pouches. The first small pouch had hundreds of purple beads, like we used in Scouts, only larger. Three other pouches had beads, too, only different colors. Below these pouches was a layer of straw and, then, there was the collection of bones. They were small animal bones, some large animal teeth, and another leather pouch with metal awes in wood handles, like corks from a bottle. We took a pouch of beads and the tools to Mrs. Randall, careful that the leather pouch not fall apart, it was so tattered.

She studied the purple beads. "Those two crates are what's left of a wampum factory," she said as she rose from the chair.

"Wampum. That's money," Wally said.

"It's not just that. It's treaties, it's breaking treaties, it's friendship, it's marriage, it's everything. Whenever Indians had something important to say, they first said it with wampum. The way they'd arrange the beads on a string was a message all on its own."

"Like a letter."

"Exactly. Is that all there was?"

"No. We have another layer or two," I said. We went back downstairs.

Wally held the sack while I stuffed the last layer of straw in it.

"What's that?" Wally asked.

I lifted out a roll of leather. "That's it. There's nothing else in there. Let's take it upstairs."

"We chose a good day for this, boys. It's so cold out there, no one's gonna visit the museum today. No interruptions. What do we have here?"

She laid the roll of leather on a round table. It was eight inches thick and fourteen inches long. It was tied with leather strips, thicker than what they used to make baseball gloves. We stared at it quietly, except for a "Hmm," or "What to do," from Mrs. Randall. Wally and I glanced at each other. I reached in my pocket, pulled out my pen knife, opened it, and handed it to Mrs. Randall. Without hesitation, she cut each strap. Slowly, she started unrolling the ancient find. The leather wanted to hold the shape it had held for a century or more, probably. She was patient with it, like she had done this before. Unrolled, the package lay there, three or more layers of leather.

"Come close and look."

On top, was a short, beaded belt with designs. "Look, there are eight rows of beads." It must have been two feet long.

"What do they mean?" Wally asked before I could.

"What do you see?" she asked.

"One's a triangle," Wally said.

"Look closer."

"A tepee?" I asked.

"Okay, what's the next one?"

"Crossed arrows," Wally said.

"That's right. What's the next one?"

"It looks like a family," I said.

"Okay, so the first is home. The second is friendship. The third is family."

Home, friendship, family. I knew those symbols. I yearned for them.

She did not take the bead work off the leather piece. She just lifted the entire leather layer with both hands and moved it to another area of the table.

The next leather piece had the single imprint of a hand, completely open, like it was dipped in black ink and slapped on the deer hide.

"Success," Mrs. Randall said softly.

"The treasure?" Wally asked.

"No, the sign of success. The hand print is the sign of

success. If a squaw saw this on her husband's horse, it meant he was successful on the hunt and was proud of his accomplishment."

I imagined Dad's handprint was like his newspaper article.

Mrs. Randall then moved the deer hide to another part of the table leaving one more piece of bead work laying on its own leather piece. It was simple, just one symbol, two arrows, pointing at each other. "War, black beads on white. The university will spend a lot of time with these. This is a treasure." She lifted up the piece to confirm this was the last deer hide. "When they come to pick up these items, I'll make sure you are here to observe how they handle them. Right now, we need pictures." She pulled out a camera. "Be sure you hold it still," she said, handing it to Wally. I was already busy copying the symbols in the notebook.

"Boys, that box over there has things we aren't going to keep. Choose what you want and take it with you."

The next night, the Skillmans invited our family downstairs to watch the New Year's Eve celebration at Times Square on their TV. All of us together reminded me of Sabina.

Ellen told me what Miss Santmyer wanted with her.

"Her assistant is going to spend some time with relatives, and she wants someone to stay with her for a while."

"What'd you say?"

"I had to say yes. I'll stay there, except for the time I'm in class. It's perfect. I love writing. I'll learn so much. If it wasn't for you and your polio, I wouldn't have had this chance."

I told her about opening the two crates and showed her my drawings.

We watched TV as they reviewed 1956. Elvis Presley, then the Suez Crisis, Eisenhower defeating Stevenson, *The Ten Commandments* movie, Rocky Marciano retiring, IBM's new computer that took up sixteen square feet, Grace Kelly marrying that prince, Castro leading that revolt in Cuba, and Sabin's oral polio vaccine. For other reasons, 1956 was a year I would never forget.

Chapter Thirty-Eight
Treasure Map

Tuesday was New Year's Day, and I spent the morning studying my Indian artifacts. One of the things Mrs. Randall gave me was a round flat piece of slate called a gorget. It had two holes in it, so I found a leather shoe lace I used on one of my Scout projects and fit it over my head. It was heavy and a small piece of slate chipped off it. When I picked up the piece from the floor, it crumbled in my hand, more like clay than slate. As I got up, the slate hit the door knob, and another piece broke off, another piece of clay. It was time to deliver papers, so I wore the gorget over my new jacket.

Miss Santmyer noticed it right away. "What is that?" she asked. "Is it one of your Indian relics?"

"Yes ma'am."

"That's an odd design." When I looked down, I could see what she was seeing. That wasn't there when I put it on earlier. The rain had washed away some more of the clay. I couldn't make it out, but waited until I got to Wally's to study it better, and that was my next stop.

We both studied it under the piano light and could make out two half circles, one inside the other and three pointed symbols underneath. I had to deliver my papers, so we decided to study it further the next day.

"Can you come to my house tomorrow? I have to watch Christina while Mom works. You can help me with my papers later if you want."

"I'll try. What time?"

"Ten? Ellen has to do a Kenny treatment on me."

I finished my route in drizzling rain and by the time I

got home, there was this brown stain down the front of my new jacket. There was still mud on that slate gorget. I laid the slate in the sink and showed Mom the stain. She took it to the bathroom to wash it out. I rinsed off the slate. The muddy residue came off slowly, so I took a brush to it. The image became much clearer.

"It was just mud, honey," Mom said. Your jacket's drying in the bathroom.

"Look, Mom. What's this?"

"Maybe it's an igloo, you know, like the Eskimos?"

"Wally's coming over tomorrow. We're going to figure it out."

"Give me a pencil and paper," Mom said. "And a dark crayon."

She dried off the slate, covered it with the paper and then started coloring the entire piece of paper, nearly using all of the crayon point. When she was finished, an image appeared I still could not understand. I studied the colored paper while I was in bed and woke up with it in the morning.

We studied it before Mom went to work.

"I think the thing pointing down is an arrow. It still looks like an igloo. Stay here with Christina until you deliver your papers. Don't leave."

"Wally's coming over. We'll figure it out."

Wally arrived at ten and we laid the paper and the slate on the coffee table. We studied it. We were sure about the upside-down arrow.

"It's like X marks the spot," Wally said.

"Is the other thing an igloo?"

"Maybe a turtle."

We debated its meaning.

"Jesse, you up?" It was Ellen's voice from the door. "You ready for your last treatment?"

"Maybe Ellen can help. Come on in." She came in and

picked up Christina right away.

"Who's your friend?"

"Wally, this is Ellen, my nurse," I said with an air of importance.

"Look at this, Ellen. What do you think it is?"

She bent over, Christina still hugging her neck.

"Twee," Christina blurted. "Twee," she said again with her smile.

Ellen pointed at the three arrowhead looking symbols.

"Those do look like Christmas trees in a field." Then Christina pointed at our Christmas tree, that was still up.

"Twee!"

"Trees in a field. That could be anywhere," Wally said.

"What's the circle?" Ellen asked. "Wally, I'm going to work on Jesse a while. You can watch if you want."

But he stayed in the living room and studied the paper, while Ellen put the hot compresses on my legs and then bent them. The pain of Kenny therapy was less intense. This was the third time the treatment was not as painful.

"We've licked it, Jesse," she said, giving me a big hug. "Let's look at your map."

"Map," I repeated.

"It's a place with trees." I ran into the living room.

"This is either a pond or a big rock." Wally was pointing at the round circle next to one of the three trees, if Christina was right.

"My sister said the treasure is at John Bryan."

"What is?" Ellen asked.

"The treasure. The Shawnees hid treasure."

"Wasn't that what we found in the clock tower?" Wally asked.

"I guess. But this was in one of those boxes." I held up the slate. "Look, trees, rock, a big rock with a hole in it?"

"A cave?" Ellen asked.

"We saw a cave at Camp Birch. See this boulder? It was at the cave we found. See this?" I pointed at the two semi-circles. "That's the cave in the rocks. See these?" I pointed to the pine trees. "This one's the big scotch pine in our directions."

I could see in Wally's smile that he agreed.

"How do you know it has treasure?" she asked.

"It has to. Why would they put that arrow there?"

"When do you guys go back there?" Ellen asked.

"Not for a while. I'm not sure."

"Tell me again about your cave." Ellen was holding the slate now. She had already seen my other artifacts from that farm and what Mrs. Randall gave us.

"Maybe we could ride out there," Wally said. "It's only ten miles."

"How long does that take?" I asked.

"One hour," Ellen said. "Each way."

"I can't. I'm watching Christina."

"Aren't you finished yet Ellen?" Cathy yelled from downstairs.

"Well, I've got to go," she said, and slowly put the slate back on the table. "Bye, boys."

"We have to wait. Maybe Mr. Combs can take us on a campout soon. Nobody's going to find that spot. How long can you stay?"

"I told Mom I'll help you with your route until we get to my house," Wally said.

"Swell, do you like Crazy Eights?" I reached for the deck of cards on the table.

Then I heard someone running up the stairs, the door opened, and Ellen ran in and sat on the couch.

"If I get you to Camp Birch, can you find the cave?"

"I guess so." I looked over at Wally.

"Sure," he said. "We have the directions."

"Okay. Mom's gonna watch Christina. I bike ride a lot.

We can make it there in an hour. We need to find the cave in half an hour and then we come back here in time to get your papers. It's going to be a tough ride. You have to keep up with me."

I couldn't believe it.

"It's mostly level 'til we get to the old mill," she said.

"We can share my canteen," I said.

"Mom's making us sandwiches. Peanut butter, okay?"

"Sure," Wally said.

"Get your jackets on. You need muffs and gloves. I'll take Christina downstairs. Get your route book and changer, Jesse. We may not have time to come straight home."

Ellen was in charge and was about to lead two eleven-year-olds on the search of a lifetime. A search for Indian treasure.

Chapter Thirty-Nine
The Race to the Indian Cave

Ellen came upstairs with a sack full of sandwiches, a thermos of water, and a canvas bag with tire patching material and tools to pull a bike wheel.

"Have you ever ridden out there?" I asked.

"Yes. Penny and I went there a couple times. We went to the John Bryan pool. We'll be fine. You'll see."

I trusted her. She healed my polio. She had already got our bikes out of her dad's garage and inspected each one before we started riding, leading us around the block once and then inspected the bikes again. Our journey began up Monroe Street across Main Street, and when we got to Columbus Avenue, I was on a highway I had never seen. I looked at my watch. It was noon.

As we rode on Columbus Avenue, houses there reminded me of Sabina. The road became a highway with a lot of traffic. When Ellen would yell "Get behind!" we followed her in single file. She kept looking back and a couple times we'd pull into a driveway and wait for a string of cars to pass us. The traffic made the experience exhilarating. After three miles, we turned left onto Wilberforce Clifton Road and the traffic died down. It was 12:25. At 12:30, we stopped at a farm lane and ate half a sandwich and drank water.

"Wally, did you bring a scarf?" Ellen asked.

"It's in my pocket." She wrapped it around his neck and pulled it up over his mouth and nose. My jacket collar went all the way up past my mouth when you rolled it up.

"Get ready for a ride."

We waited for a pick-up truck to pass and pulled out on

the road. We spent part of this stretch coasting through twists and turns in the road, and then slowed and pedaled through a slight hill and then, at the top, stopped pedaling and coasted behind Ellen, past Jones Road, past Clark Run, past Bradfute and then left onto Grinnel Road. There was no traffic as we pedaled up the hill, and it was a good thing, because the road was narrow with deep ruts on either side. We crossed Clifton Road and Bryan Park Road, and then stopped at Grinnel Mill.

It's all uphill from here," she said. "We'll eat when we get to Camp Birch."

We drank more water. It was colder because the trees hid the warm sun.

Simon Kenton Road was a narrow gravel lane that, once we got past the trees came to a set of cabins. We were looking for the one cabin with the brown post where Wally and I did our Pathfinding Merit badge exercise. We led now, walking our bikes around until he and I were sure we were at our starting point. We propped the bikes against trees, pulled out the directions and that's when Wally and I stared at each other. In our haste, we left my compass at home. We needed a compass to know where north and east were. It was 1:15. We were already over one hour in our journey but weren't prepared.

"Be prepared," I said. Wally looked around.

"Look. Remember, moss grows on the south side of trees and rocks. It didn't take long for us to figure out the general directions, and let our memory take over from there.

"That's northeast. Remember that tree with the nest?" he said.

"You guys are good."

We made it to the pin oak tree. Then we crossed the foot bridge. When we got to the scotch pine, and the boulder, I pulled out the drawing. Ellen stood behind me, and we stared at the cliff that swallowed the cave.

"Is that it?" she asked.

"Yes," we both said.

"It doesn't look very deep," she said.

"Good, because I didn't bring a flash light," I said.

"Be prepared," Wally said. "We should have stopped and planned."

"Let's eat," I said. I was hungry and cold. The cliff started hiding the sun. It was 1:30.

Wally wandered the area until he found a sturdy stick. "We might need this in case something lives in there."

"Like skunks?" We both laughed.

"I'll stay back here," said Ellen. "We don't have much time. What now?"

Wally took the stick and we both approached the cave. He made sounds with the stick with every step. We heard nothing from the cave.

"What are we looking for?" he asked.

"Silver. There was supposed to be silver," I said.

"Indian jewelry?" he asked.

"Maybe. Maybe things they stole from the English or French."

He hit the outside of the cave opening with the stick. He poked it inside and scraped across the floor. Leaves rustled as he swept the stick through them. He did it again.

"There's nothing in there. I'll go in," I said.

"Here." He handed me the stick.

I stooped down and entered the cave, tapping on each side, and on the ceiling and scraping the stick across the ground.

"This is where we found that log on our campout. Can you see the end?" Wally asked.

"Not yet. It's dark. We should have brought a light."

"What about the light on your bike," Wally said.

"I'll get it." Ellen ran back toward the footbridge.

"I hope she doesn't get lost."

"I'll go with her," Wally said.

I went into the cave another yard and studied the log, embedded in the ground. It wasn't more than a foot in diameter and by the time Ellen and Wally returned, I had a six-inch trough dug out on each side of it.

Ellen shined the light on my digging project, and Wally and I got on one side of the log. With the stick and our hands we slowly moved the log from its position. We shoved the log to the side and inspected the long trench it left in the cave floor. I scraped it with the stick and nothing but dirt was there.

Ellen shined the light on the back of the cave. It had stopped at the end of the log, about three feet. I pressed the stick against the wall and hit solid stone.

"Do you think we're missing something?" Wally asked.

I dug the stick in the dirt that was under the log.

"It's getting late, boys. I've got to get you back home before Daddy gets back."

"I'll move the log back," I said.

Our trip only confirmed this might be the cave in the drawing. If it was really a cave in the first place. Ellen shined the light onto the log, partially stained by the years of being embedded in the dry soil.

"We can always come back," Wally said.

"What's that?" she asked.

The light was fixed on a dark narrow rectangular spot on the log. I crawled closer, she brought the light closer. There was a hollowed-out place in the log, stuffed with leather or something.

"Make sure it's not a snake," said Wally.

I pulled back.

"Just poke it," Ellen said.

It was leather, but it felt like something solid was inside. I took my gloves off and carefully slid the package out of the crevice.

"What is it?" Wally asked.

Someone had purposely hollowed out the log just large enough to hide a leather package.

"It's wrapped in leather."

"What time is it?" Ellen asked.

I backed out of the cave with the package. "Two-thirty."

"How did that happen. We have to leave now."

I rolled the log back into its hole and handed the package to Wally.

"We'll open it at the house."

"We only have an hour." Ellen said.

We walked to our bikes, put the package in my newspaper bag, drank more water, and ate an oatmeal cookie.

"What do you think it is?" Wally asked.

"I don't know. It doesn't feel like something we had seen in those crates."

"When will you open it?" Ellen asked.

"I think I'll give it to Mrs. Randall. What if we break something trying to open it?" Opening the crates with the artifacts and sorting them taught me to be careful.

We were already on Bryan Park Road, passing the entrance to John Bryan State Park.

"They have a swimming pool there, Jesse. We'll take you there this summer."

"Neat."

"Let's take it when she can open it in front of us," Wally said.

Even though it was downhill, there were turns so sharp you didn't know what was on the other side until you came face to face with a car or truck and their loud horn.

"Are you guys okay?" Ellen yelled.

"Okay," we said.

"Keep up. Let me know if I need to slow down," she yelled.

Once on Wilberforce Clifton Road, she stopped us at the

farm driveway again. It seemed like it had been days instead of hours that we were there before.

"We could drop it off to Mrs. Randall on the way back. We go right by the historical society," Wally said.

We just got onto Columbus Pike.

"Did you know that there is an Indian mound right down that road?" Ellen yelled.

"We learned about those in school," Wally said.

It was 3:30 when we got to the city limits. I sped up by Ellen.

"Let's stop at the historical society," I said.

"Okay, but we have to be quick. Mama's going to be worried."

"I'll explain it to Mrs. Randall. Give me the package. You deliver your papers," Wally said.

And so, we split up. Ellen went home. I headed directly down Main Street toward Pat's Market. For the second time, my other carriers were gone already, but this time I had to fold my own papers.

"Jesse." Mr. Patterson opened the front door. "Miss Santmyer needs this. It was a small pack of sausage in a cloth bag. You're late today."

I was already worried about being late, grabbed the package, loaded my papers and sped to Miss Santmyer's home.

Wally caught up with me just as I was taking the paper to his house.

"Mrs. Randall couldn't believe what we did. Don't tell my folks. We might be in trouble."

"Was she mad?"

"No. She said we can open it on Sunday."

"How was your bike ride?" Mom asked.

"We did twenty miles, Mom. Ellen said I have it licked. No more Kenny treatments."

"We'll see what Dr. Thompson says."

I didn't say anything about the cave. Later I asked Ellen if she wanted to meet Wally and me at the historical society Sunday, and it was arranged. We'd bike up once I got home from church.

I put the slate gorget around my neck like an Indian would and rode with Ellen to meet Wally and Mrs. Randall.

"Now, first, you need to know there are rules about removing things from Bryan State Park."

"We were at Camp Birch, Mrs. Randall."

"We'll see. Anyway. This is cloth, not leather, and I don't see how it ever survived from the time Indian's were here. It's as dry as a bone and there's no sign of insects or mold. What kind of log was it in?"

"I don't know," I said.

"It smelled like my hope chest," Ellen said.

"It makes sense if it was cedar."

She walked us over to the table where the cloth wrapped treasure was.

"The cloth is coated with some kind of wax. It softened when I warmed it by the heater."

She peeled open the cloth wrapping. "Maybe a feed sack, we'll see." She said.

It had another wrapping underneath that looked like the same material. We hovered over the treasure as Mrs. Randall unwrapped the second layer of cloth revealing a brown leather-bound book.

"This isn't the treasure you expected, but it's a treasure."

She carefully opened the cover to a page, hand written.

> To Tecumtha
> Msi ugimv
> Msi-pasi

> Ni usgemv
> Wahi mosvtuwi uwasi lwi drku
> Rebecca Galloway
> 1807

"Take a picture of this, Wally." She handed him the camera.

It was a *Holy Bible*, King James Version, printed in 1791 by Clarendon Press, Oxford.

"It was printed in England." She turned the pages. "Get this page Wally," she held it open to the Old Testament Table of Contents.

"It has the Apocrypha," she said.

"What's that?"

"Hidden books. They aren't in a regular *Bible*. Most *Bibles* don't include the Apocrypha," Ellen said.

"They are from Old Testament times," Mrs. Randall said.

"I know my Bible doesn't have anything like that in it."

"Where did you find this?"

"In a cave and it was hidden in a log. A space was carved out so this can fit," I said.

"We need that log. I'll talk to the John Bryan people. I hope this doesn't get messy," she said. She turned back to the front inscription.

"I have some Rebecca Galloway letters here, so we'll see if we can match up the handwriting. The book's authentic, I'm sure and that date fits in when Tecumseh was calling on the Galloways. There's a book on my desk called *Old Chillicothe*. Would you get it, Jesse?"

It was a green hard cover book with Galloway engraved with the title on the spine.

"Maybe we'll get lucky here." She turned to the back of the book. "Okay, *msi ugimv*, look here, it means Great Chief."

She pointed to the words in the back of the book. "*Msi-pasi*, or Panther. You know, Tecumseh was called the Panther in the sky, or something like that. *Ni Usyemv*, or My Brother. Look, she calls him brother. Legend says, he wanted to marry Rebecca, but he wouldn't leave his Indian ways. Hmmm." She was talking to the two books in front of her.

"*Wahi mosvtuwi usasi lwi drku*, means Let us always do good. It's like a pact. He always protected the Galloways. They made a pact that Tecumseh's family and Galloway family renewed just thirty years ago.

"We really need that log, Jesse. I think you found Tecumseh's retreat. See this?"

She turned the page and pointed at a smudge on the page.

"I bet it's where his perspiration fell on the page and he wiped it away. I've seen this in old letters. There will be a lot of people interested in this. It is a treasure alright. We may want your slate as part of this little collection, Jesse."

I held the slate and lifted it off my neck. I laid it by the book.

"Arrowheads, beads and *Bibles*," I said, summing up the extent of our treasure hunt.

"You did good boys. This is all very special."

Wally and I gave each other half smiles. Ellen put her hand on my shoulder.

"The romance between Tecumseh and Becky Galloway was never proved was it?" Ellen asked.

"No, but at least this shows Becky must have had some good feelings for Tecumseh."

"Did he really give her a canoe?" Ellen asked.

"He made it for her. They would go for canoe rides on the Miami River. She taught him how to read. He loved her books."

"How romantic. The *Bible* would be a special gift for

him," Ellen said.

"She wanted him to convert to the white man's ways, then she would agree to marry him, according to legend."

She thumbed through more pages. "I can't believe this is in such good condition. Look here." She pointed to a verse that was marked with an arrow. "Proverbs 20:1."

"Wine is a mocker, strong drink is raging; and whosoever is deceived, thereby is not wise," I blurted. There was a silence around the room. "Grandpa Hall taught me that verse."

"Tecumseh and Blue Jacket both saw the evil of liquor to the Indians. They hated the murders and kidnapping and torture some of the Indians did. Don't get me wrong, some white men weren't much better. They wanted peace, but it was different with all the tribes and pioneers, the French, and the English." Mrs. Randall had our attention. She had this way of using her eyes to capture your attention and a slow speech giving you enough time to drink in every word. She turned the pages carefully.

"It ruins families," I said. She grabbed my hand.

"Here's another arrow." Our eyes went to the book. "Romans 12:10."

"Love one another," I said.

"Be kindly affectioned one to another with brotherly love; in honor preferring one another," she read.

"You're an odd one, Jesse. Tecumseh was an orphan. He lost his father when he was just six years old and was raised by his sister and brother.

"Tecumseh died in 1813. Becky gave this to him in 1807. This has survived 150 years. It's an amazing find." Mrs. Randall turned more pages.

"Do you think the silver is still out there somewhere?" Wally asked.

"If that legend is true I believe the Shawnees would have retrieved it. What you three discovered is far more valuable.

Jesse, you tell Paula Jean that you found Tecumseh's treasure."

"Can I look through the *Bible* to see if there are other marks?" I asked.

"Hmm. That's a good idea. I think it might tell us a lot about Tecumseh. I'll help you. Write them down, each and every one. Here, take this and read it, so you will know more about Tecumseh and Becky." She handed me the green book, *Old Chillicothe*.

"Come with me," Mrs. Randall said and led us outside.

Next door was an old log cabin. She unlocked the padlock and swung the door open. We followed her inside and once our eyes adjusted to the darkness, we could see hand-made furniture, two huge stone fireplaces, stairs leading to a second level and a shelf with books. An old flintlock rifle was mounted on the wall above the door.

"This is the Galloway cabin. Imagine having just this fireplace to keep you warm on days like today." We were all shivering. "Tecumseh visited the Galloways and learned to read here. They became very close friends. Can you imagine Becky giving Tecumseh that *Bible* in this very room? He probably sat in that chair." She was pointing to a plain ladder-back chair.

"It is so romantic," said Ellen. "How sad it didn't work out."

"That cave was Tecumseh's room, I guess," I said.

"We'll need you to show us where that cave is. There might be more there. I'm freezing. Let's go back in."

Ellen and I took the *Old Chillicothe* book home and studied it.

On Sundays, I went to the historical society and wrote down each verse Tecumseh had marked, and as I read each one, I became closer to his spirit. We led people from the university back to the cave but found nothing else. The log that hid the *Bible* for over a century was studied, and it was confirmed that only the *Bible* was to be found in that cave.

Tecumseh marked a lot of verses I had already studied. He marked the story about healing the blind man and the raising of Lazarus. He marked verses in Exodus. Mrs. Randall thought it was because the Shawnees had twelve tribes, just like the Israelites. He marked verses about the evils of drinking. She said he hated what liquor did to good people. I read more about that in the book, *Old Chillicothe*. I bought a larger spiral notebook to write out Tecumseh's verses.

Discussion Questions

Who were the prominent characters of the book? Were they easy to visualize? Did they remind you of people you know?

Did you develop a good appreciation for the setting, especially, place and time? Did it enhance or take away from the story?

How does Jesse change or grow throughout the story? What events or characters are responsible?

What conflicts stand out most?

What specific theme(s) did you perceive throughout the book?

Were Jesse and Lynn hoping for the same thing from a new father in Chapters Five and Six?

Is a book like the Bible able to change a person? Did Pastor Armey do a good job explaining how it could to Jesse in Chapter Seven?

Polio frightened America during the 40's and 50's. How did Jesse deal with his experience? How did other characters respond (Karen, Lynn, Mr. Davis, Viola, for example?)

Did any part of the book make you feel uncomfortable? Did you change any viewpoints you may have had?

Did you think that Grandpa Hall could have done more for Jesse and Viola?

A creed is a set of fundamental beliefs or a guiding principle. Where did Jesse find his Creed(s)?

Acknowledgements

The Clock Tower Treasure is the second book in a three book series following Jesse Hall from Elementary School age to Young Adult. Though this is a work of fiction it refers to historical figures and legends associated with them. The following are resources I used to provide credibility to this fictional tale:

Victor Hess, Jesse Sings, Self-Published, 2017 (The First Book in this series)

Shelley Mickle, The Polio Hole, Wild Onion Press, 2013

Peg Kehret, Small steps: The Year I Got Polio, Albert Whitman & Company, 1996

Timothy James Bazzett, Love, War & Polio: The Life and Times of Young Bill Porteous, Rathole Books, 2008

David M. Oshinsky, Polio An American Story, Oxford University Press, 2005

Boy Scouts of America, Handbook for Boys, Fifth Edition, 1950

J Leitch Wright, Jr., The Only Land They Knew, The Free Press, 1985

John Sugden, Tecumseh, Henry Holt and Company, 2013

William Albert Galloway, Old Chillicothe, The Buckeye Press, 1990

Bible verses are from The Revised Standard Version Presentation Bible, William Collins Sons & Co., Ltd. 1952

The Edgar Guest Poem, "Difficulties," appeared in the "Just Folks" column, The Indianapolis Star, September 2, 1921 (Public Domain)

"Tell Me Why" lyrics (Public Domain)

"Panis Angelicus" lyrics (Public Domain)

Greene County Ohio Historical Society, Xenia, Ohio, for its insight into the Tecumseh and Rebecca Galloway legend and a first hand view of the Galloway cabin.

Dayton Metro Library, Dayton, Ohio for research on the Barney Convalescent Hospital

Johnnie Bernhard, author of *A Good Girl* and *How We Came to Be*, for her editing skills and awesome encouragement.

Victor Hess' first novel, *Jesse Sings* was acknowledged as a finalist in the William Faulkner – William Wisdom Creative Writing competition in 2015. It was also recognized as an Award-Winning Finalist in the Fiction: Inspirational category of the 2018 Best Book Awards sponsored by American Book Fest. His short stories have received Honorable Mention in a recent Glimmer Train competition and one made the short list for the 2017 Faulkner competition. He is currently working on a third novel centered around Jesse Hall, the main character of his first two novels. Besides being a successful businessman he has been an Army Bomb Disposal Instructor, and, for decades, has taught Bible study for both children and adults. He lives in Slidell, Louisiana with his wife and dog.

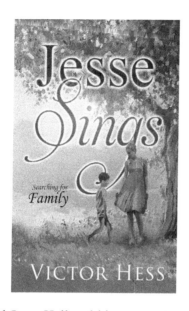

Eight-year old Jesse Hall and his pregnant mother move to a small rural town in Ohio, to escape an abusive father addicted to gambling and alcohol. There, Jesse is bullied by the most popular school kid, denied a church experience by a self-righteous preacher, and threatened with foster care by a well-meaning social worker. Can Jesse fulfill his dream of a normal family with his own parents and brothers and sisters? See what he does with the help of a fatherless eight-year old girl, the lovely Five and Dime clerk, and a mummified corpse.

Jesse Sings is available at Amazon, Barnes & Noble, and other book stores.

CPSIA information can be obtained
at www.ICGtesting.com
Printed in the USA
FSHW022236200619
59220FS

9 781732 215580